DOUBLE-
DECKER

By the same author

Thirteen (Bachman & Turner, 1976)
Published in the U.S.A. as *Evalore* by J B Lippincott
Just a Woman, poetry (Magpie Press, 1969)

DOUBLE-DECKER

DECKER

Eva Jones

Bachman & Turner

London

Bachman & Turner
5 Plough Place
Fetter Lane
London EC4A 1LD

First published 1978

Typeset by Inforum Ltd., Portsmouth
Printed and bound in England by
Chapel River Press, Andover

For
R

Rock
and
Refuge

This is a work of fiction. None of the persons portrayed in the book is related to any actual person living or dead. Some of the events depicted are based on the author's life.

Those not busy being born
are busy dying

Bob Dylan

Never trust the teller
Trust the tale

D.H. Lawrence

PART ONE

Lower Deck

All our best rows took place in the basement kitchen. There is something about the domesticated atmosphere of that room which stimulates my baser instincts: a large clean scrubbed wooden table, saucepans and crockery, dried rose leaves, strings of French onions and black tiles. It's just a bit too cosy. Alan sat on the table, long legs on a chair, long bony (read *sensitive*) fingers curling round a spoon.

'You ought to be more grateful,' he said, regretting it instantly.

'Grateful? For what?' Those three words rattled like the horny rings of a snake's tail. My head was swelling as I spat out some of the poison which never stopped reproducing itself. 'What should I be grateful for? Your passport? That you fed and clothed my sweet little bastard?'

'Don't, Julia, Don't!'

'But I must, I must. You — you just happened to come along at the crucial moment' — the venom spurting out freely now — 'when somebody else would have done just as well. No need to look like a martyr. For you've had your money's worth at night — I'm as well trained as any tart. Only you get better value, my sweet. *I* put my heart into it.' The fight was under way.

We had developed a particular highly efficient method for those occasions. Tone of voice, my own: dead serious, loud and sharp, harsh, almost strident, altogether nicely out of control, echoing back from the walls, welling up from the depth, the *undermind* exploding its time bombs. His voice: also dead serious, not very loud, a rather superior sneer, a vile showing off of deadly accurate vocabulary. Unfair of course. Alan tried to pacify me without much conviction.

11

The danger flag was hoisted. He could have saved himself the trouble.

'What's wrong with you, darling? What's come over you lately?'

'Everything's wrong. *I'm* wrong. Stale and stagnating. No pep, no drive, no initiative.'

'It's that fellow back in Berlin, isn't it?'

I laughed. Uneasily. 'I'm a happy woman, you ought to know that.' Appropriate leer. 'But please, try to understand the situation. I have not outlived several kinds of hell to cook a stew!' Sweeping gesture to take in the pots, pans, rose leaves and onion strings.

'Survived is not the word — you've come out armour-plated.'

'You see,' I said meekly, 'there you go with your splendid native words. Armour-plated. I'm at such a disadvantage. I so wish I could talk in my own language. These foreign words positively stifle me.'

'Rubbish!' Alan's deep blue eyes were blazing. He looked good, even through my haze of fury: a cross between a fifteenth century ascetic and a modern explorer. I could — almost — love him for the little tuft of fair hair standing up like the comb of a fighting cock.

'If you got it clear in your mind, dear Julia, you could talk Hindustani. I've never known you at a loss for words.'

'But I'm at a loss altogether. Life's stale, boring, unproductive.' (He winced.) 'Damn it, there must be more to it than this idiotic daily round of stuffing the goose.'

'I know many people who would envy you this kitchen.' (Designed by him down to the last detail — it's his *job*.)

'I can't spread out.' Deep sigh. 'Yes, yes, I know. I'm home and dry. I've done it. I've saved that precious little body, stood up against the monster. Wrong. I've not stood up. I've run away, managed to come out of trouble with a few bruises. But what for? Can you tell me that? And what now? — where do I go from here? It's all too flat, too unrewarding, too unadventurous.' I put my head on his shoulder, murmuring apologetically: 'You know I never mean the two of us. But I can't help myself, I'm all tied up in knots.'

'Nice knots,' Alan said and started kissing me.

There I was, melting into my husband's arms, just like on the first night. With just as much joy and pleasure as then. And look who's complaining. They say when the body is fed the soul gets hungry. Mine was starving. After the quarrel with Alan things were running smoothly for a while. Too smoothly, I thought. There must be something wrong if I'm not moaning. But look what you've got, look! Ease. Freedom and liberty (they're not the same). So what was squatting at the back of my head, what was hammering away, turning over big clumps of earth, what was digging and excavating, working night and day as in a deep, deep mine? What went *on*?

Don't look, don't go down into the shadows. If you look you'll turn into a pillar of salt. But I feel *compelled* to look. I've got to see what I'm made of. Or the hectic work down below will never stop and give me peace. For nothing is ever past. . . .

*　　*　　*

I see myself in a queue on the fifth floor of the Prefecture in Paris. Why just there? Why couldn't my private performance have started somewhere else more dramatic? You don't have to shout and scream; you can be just as unhappy between dirty badly-lit walls, downcast with misery, sweating with fear, without any outward signs of violence. There we are, refugees everyone, either Jewish or 'political' or both, fresh from Germany. We want a permit to stay in this beautiful hostile city. We look very bad and feel worse. Because the man behind the counter might not give us a permit, or not extend it if we have one. Most of us have fled the German fatherland when Hitler came to power in nineteen-thirty-three. Now that's a single sentence, fifteen words and one full stop. But squeezed into it is such misery, such torment and pain that it could not be contained in a hundred volumes.

I *know* we're not the only ones. A fat lot of good that would do to us! It makes it worse, worse! Not the only ones to have left the warm ebb and tide of our daily life and out into the icy blast of a foreign country. And their arms weren't exactly wide open to receive us.

My self-esteem melted rapidly the nearer I got to the counter. Look at that moron with his rubberstamp at the ready. . . . Come, come, the man's doing his duty. Badly paid and afraid of all those foreigners coming to take away his job. Put yourself in his place. I can't. I came to France because it's always been a shelter for the *Misérables* of this earth, the haven of all fugitives and persecuted — for three *months? Dass ich nicht lache!* What then? Where do we go from here? Don't be unfair — the French *did* take us in, they did not send us back at the frontier, back into the jaws of the crocodile. But they took us *de mauvaise grâce*, with a very bad will indeed.

We'll take you in, but we'll make you feel damned uncomfortable, so much so, that you might prefer to take refuge somewhere else and the sooner the better. You still insist on your human rights? Fine, here are another lousy three months in which you can stay in our lovely city. That's not enough? You can't settle down under those conditions? Who wants you to? Why not try your luck somewhere else? You wouldn't know who else would let you in? That's too bad, my friend. You now see how generous *we* are.

The implication was: why did you have to pick Jewish parents? Or alternatively: who asked you to fight the Nazis? A government knows what it's doing and if you say they'll fight *us* one day you have another think coming — you are deluded.

Standing in the queue I see four people I know. They are always here on the same day as myself and we usually adjourn together to the Committee — more of this later. Karl, Bettina and Heinz I only meet on those occasions; Benjamin and I have become friends, talk-and-coffee friends, that is. But *what* talks! A man who says to me, tidy your own backyard before you put the world to rights, has my rapt attention.

Karl, who's standing behind me in the queue seems to be in full possession of his faculties. He was a brilliant student physicist at Berlin University. He was barred from entering University one day, stopped at the entrance door. Because he was Jewish.

'There I was with my books under my arm and that large beast put his paw on my shoulder. *"Keine Juden,"* he said and pushed me back. I could have murdered him. I knew words could not reach him. No brains, grinning from ear to ear, his small dull gorilla's eyes looked into mine. I felt the world was coming to an end.'

'It did,' Bettina says, right in front of me. 'Haven't you grasped that yet?' A lovely girl with blond hair and very red lips. 'And look at those officious asses here,' she fumed, 'making us stand and wait like criminals before judgment. But they'll see.' She started to raise her voice but was hushed immediately by the rest of us. 'Our fellow countrymen' — an audible sneer — 'will all blow you to smithereens soon enough.'

'There will be no war,' Heinz Blaufeld says firmly. An elderly lawyer, bespectacled and whitehaired. 'They'll have the whole world against them.' Karl says that lawyers are the most naive people on earth and that the Nazis can't wait to send their armies all over the globe.

Finally we get our extensions and are on our way to the 'Committee' (charitable organisation).

What a farce! Charitable — no such thought ever entered their minds or if it had it's long since vanished. Their present behaviour is a cross between Prussian correctness and Teutonic force. Another queue for heaven's sake! They are doling out a few miserable francs — the bare, the absolute *minimum* — to their clients who'd mostly left Germany with nothing more than the clothes they stood in. The Committee officials bark like wolfhounds — otherwise Alsatians — not unlike the repulsive sounds emitted from the Führer's fuming lips. Still, you don't need to listen, just open your hand and receive. Good — another week's bread and cheese and, if you're careful, a bit of the local variety of plonk. Quite pleasant really.

Karl says he hates everybody and hasn't ever done so much hating in his life. He hates the petty minded French, the barking Committee members and most of all he hates himself for hating *them*. It spoils his character. He is smiling sadly and says that his better nature is dead. No more tolerance. Shoot everybody.

'I always knew you were a brute,' Bettina says tenderly. 'But then who isn't? Given half a chance. . . .' She lowers her head and takes Karl's hand. My heart gives a violent jump — she is not alone. Like me.

Anyway, what are we complaining about? We got away. You can't really blame the French for checking up on us. *Métèques* (foreigners), as everybody knows, are always up to no good. Especially — so our hosts reasoned — if refused a working permit. A decent foreigner does not come here to work, stealing our citizens' jobs; a decent foreigner spends his money in the Moulin Rouge or chasing the girls in Cannes and Nice. That was the general idea. . . . if you can look at it in that way. But you can't. You are lonely, frustrated, bored and hungry. You feel like an outcast and start to behave like one. Suppose — suppose the man behind the counter decides not to extend your permit. Then what? Go into hiding? Nobody in his right mind would take you in. Steal away on a boat to England? They'll send you back by return. Why in heaven's name does nobody want us? Karl has a nasty mind for he says, Julia dear, if we were street cleaners or professional farmworkers they would.

Maybe I should have waited until my parents left and not struck out on my own. But then I had reasons — one reason. Personal. But the personal has a tendency to flow over into current events and to lose its boundaries — at least in Europe, at that particular time. . . .

You have to go back just one step further. One step, no more. My hands are cold, my head is swimming.

* * *

I was eighteen, sitting for my finals at school. Small, slim, spoiled and sheltered. Hair dark brown. Eyes light grey. Shoulders sloping unfashionably. Family, friends, school, the occasional dance. Novels but few newspapers. Delighting in classical music as every Jewish girl should. No religious upbringing. (Let her choose when she is old enough to know her own mind — no indoctrination.) Concern: getting through my finals at school. Not on to university but to study singing. I felt the world would be a poorer place without the sound of my voice ringing from an opera stage.

I came home from school one day and heard somebody practising the piano in the flat upstairs. My parents said, new people have moved in and their boy is an exceptionally gifted pianist. He has to practise several hours a day. He might be another Rubinstein, but how am I going to do my homework with that beastly hammering going on upstairs? Up and down the scales for hours on end. It sounds perfect to me but obviously not to him. He keeps repeating and repeating the same tunes until I can stand it no longer. I'm racing upstairs and bang furiously on the flat door.

'Stop it! Stop this horrible noise at once!' I'm beating with both my fists on the door with such strength that I nearly fall on the boy who opens the door.

'And who are you?' he says calmly, pushing a strand of

16

dark hair from his forehead. He looks like Gustav Mahler, my mother's favourite composer. He's much taller than myself and older, well over twenty.

'I live downstairs, right under you. Your bloody scales are driving me crazy. I'm sitting for my finals. . . . if you go on like that I'll fail. I can't concentrate. Why don't you play something different for a change or is that the only thing you know? If I fail. . . .' My words became slower and slower; I hardly knew what I was saying for I kept thinking that's it, that's what I want, and feeling faint from the impact of the boy's golden brown eyes, like a golden pond. Don't be so *kitschig*, so corny, that's women's magazine stuff. No it isn't, oh God, what's his name? It's too soon, I'm not ready, I'm too young. All of it in one second flat while I got tied up and pushed helplessly into the current.

'What's your name?' he said.

'*I* wanted to know. . . .'

'Sebastian,' he said very slowly. The bell had tolled. We stood quite still, now and then dropping a single word. His hair was as fine as mine, only mine was lighter and straight and his was black and it curled all over.

We exchanged some sort of information, what I did, what he did before he came to this house, his parents, my family, my school — all the while not moving from the spot where we had been struck afraid to break the spell. He was leaning against the frame of the door, one arm above his head, stretched like a slim arrow.

'Tomorrow,' he said after a long time.

'Yes, tomorrow,' I answered. We did not smile at all as strangers do when they separate. We did not shake hands. I turned away and went dreamily down the stairs. The boy stood in the same position, still, unsmiling, with that stricken look on his face which people have after a big shock. Perhaps I looked the same. I had 'recognised' him as if I'd seen him before, as if I knew what was lying in wait for me.

I thought the impact might wear off once I was back in my flat. But it was only transformed into a permanent current like a second bloodstream. I sat in front of my writing desk, pushed the books aside and put my arms round my body for fear of losing the fullness of the feeling. The piano was silent. His image stayed in my mind, the dark lock of hair on his forehead, the thick brows and the golden brown

17

eyes. I said his name over and over to myself like a prayer.

We met every day. Sometimes we talked, sometimes we made love, it did not matter which. One was the preface to the other. They always say wait till you know each other better, you might not feel the same. We never knew each other 'better' for we had assessed each other at first glance. And yet he seemed different each time we met. I never saw his parents. They were both musicians too and were frequently on tour.

'Julia, you are changing,' my mother said one day. 'Is it that serious?' I nodded. 'Would you like him to come to the flat?' No, I did not feel that would be right. My mother looked at me more closely. It struck me, perhaps for the first time fully, how very beautiful she was. Her large dark eyes were full of sorrow and concern. I must have looked awfully pale, strained, secretive and excited, constantly living at such high voltage.

'You are not.— feeling ill?'

I had to smile. Mothers — 'No mummy, I'm not. . . . ill or anything.' She stroked my hair. 'I would tell you — I promise you.' She kissed me and left the room. I loved her very much at that moment and would have liked to talk, but couldn't. Perhaps just because I loved her. I spent all my free moments with Sebastian as if we knew that every moment counted. The Nazis were everywhere, marching, singing their beastly, murderous songs, stirring up trouble. Why — why this insane hatred against the Jews? Maybe it was easiest to let all hell loose against people so dumbfounded and defenceless. Maybe it was because they kept quiet, afraid to stir up trouble even now.

For the first time in my life I was conscious of being 'different'. Previously, being Jewish did not seem unlike being Catholic or Protestant; it was not important in any way. My upbringing was the same as that of the other girls at school, I dressed the same, spoke the same, behaved the same. I could not begin to understand why that tremendous wave of malice and loathing suddenly rose from the people, my people. Something sinister, perverse and vicious was crawling out of the dark: evil I would say, had I been religious.

I said as much to Sebastian who listened carefully but made no comment. Strange — especially as he was mostly on his own, without support of the family. I knew he was Jewish. Why didn't he react in any way? I felt with absolute

18

certainty that some catastrophe would befall us, some horror which was so immense, of such outsize proportion, that I could not even name it. Even now my thoughts are frantically chasing round for some apt description of the cataclysm which shook the whole country and eventually the world. A sickness. Incurable, inhuman and incomprehensible. Flight seemed the only possibility.

One day I was sitting with Sebastian under some dark pinetrees by a lake. He had been very quiet on the way out and I had talked a lot, willing him to break the silence. He still had not said anything about the present situation, although people were hardly talking about anything else. We were watching some brilliantly white swans sailing by on the blue lake. I was feeding them bits of bread. Sebastian touched my arm, then put my head on his shoulder covering my face with his hands, as if he did not want me to look at him.

'Julia — I shall leave tomorrow, I must.' I pushed his hands away and looked at his white face. Now, I thought, it's coming now. He spoke quickly, with a new rough voice I didn't know. He belonged to an anti-Nazi organisation, had been very active those last months and was now in acute danger. A collegue at the Conservatoire, his music school, had denounced him. Friends had warned him of impending arrest.

'I shall not return to the house but stay with friends for the night. They will collect my things.' His eyes were black with pain as he turned towards me: 'I shall not try to contact you until you too have left.'

'How will you know?'

'I shall find you wherever you are.'

A great wave of hatred swept over me. I began to hate the clear blue water, the swans drifting along so smoothly and unconcerned, the high, sweet-smelling pines, the clouds sailing above — as if nothing had changed. As if my own world had not been broken up. I hated the grass and the sun, the small ladybird sitting on my hand and the pebbles on the beach. I looked at my friend's face, pale and hard as a stone, and thought that he should cry. It did not matter that he was a boy, he should do the crying. But why did he not ask me to go with him?

'You have no passport,' he said at that moment. 'It would take too long to wait for it. I have to leave right away.' True.

19

'Where will you go?'

He looked away. 'I am not sure. The less you know about it the better. They might question you. . . .'

I wished the lake would rise and sweep over the shore swamping everything. I wished the sky would fall in. I still did not cry.

'I *will* find you — we shall be together again. You must believe me, Julia, please Julia. . . .' Then he broke down. The easy tears of a girl come almost as a pleasure, but when a boy sobs it breaks up the crust of the earth. Sebastian threw himself down on the sand and his back shook with harsh ugly sobbing. I watched him silently. Yes, *he* must cry for us, not me. He's the one who's leaving.

We took the train back to the town and separated outside the station. We did not kiss. Just looked at each other. Then turned away at the same instant. I will never see him again, I thought. Now I wish I had been right.

*   *   *

I went straight to my room and did not come out till next morning. I had breakfast and went to school. Some people's emotional life spreads over the years. Mine had been compressed into a few months and had the force and violence of an earthquake. I knew even then that it would remain unique, that it was impossible to reach that peak of intensity ever again.

The thought of him never left me. Thought is too feeble a word for the furiously passionate longing which stretched over me like a second skin. I dimly thought that all I ever read in books was true, at least true for me — that I would fall ill and waste away if I did not hear from him. There were moments when I was afraid to look people in the eye for fear they might discover how completely I was taken over by this monstrous yearning. But I did not fall ill. I went to school and passed my finals, went on seeing my friends. I told my mother that Sebastian had left. She asked me whether I could manage or whether I needed help. I said there was nothing anybody could do. But I would like to leave Germany. As long as I stayed here. . . . It's odd you never see your parents cry. It seems to be an unwritten law that children can, but parents can't. After a little while I said that there was something after all she could do: talk to my father. I

20

must leave, I said, I had no choice.

Sebastian would not get in touch with me as long as I stayed in Germany and quite a few of our friends had left already. My father was determined to stay. He had been an officer in the German army. Decorated with the Iron Cross. First Class. 'They' could not possibly touch him, a man who'd fought so bravely at the front. Germany was his country and he was not going to run away, even if it was momentarily under the rule of madmen. Justice must prevail in the end. He was a barrister at the High Court and justice always prevailed there. Anything else was unthinkable. Anyway the present regime was not going to last, everybody said so. Except uncle Leo. He said it was the greatest catastrophe that ever befell Germany, that sadistic lunatics were at the helm and that Sodom and Gomorrah were a kindergarten by comparison.

My family stayed, getting away at the last possible moment by the skin of their teeth. So many others did not —

I shall not intrude into the sacred area of those who suffered the ultimate horrors. I cannot, because I would be ashamed to do so. I was not there.

I left Germany without my family. As long as I stayed there Sebastian would never contact me. But apart from that: it was hard to breathe in that mental climate. The monstrous madness, the persecution of an integral part of the population was spreading through the whole country like the plague. Berlin, my lovely Berlin was changing in front of my eyes. I felt almost physically how the town, the entire country was engulfed by a poisonous cloud of hate and fear. It was when things began to happen in my immediate surroundings that I decided to leave definitely and for good: a close relative was arrested with his family. Friends disappeared overnight. None of them could be traced. The police kept a stony silence. The writing on the wall was clear and cruel: Get out or perish.

France, I thought, I must go to Paris. It's civilised. . . .

I arrived at the Gare du Nord in Paris. There I was, eighteen, straight from school, straight from *home*, turning my head in utter confusion from right to left and back again. I stood on the platform and literally did not know where to turn. Why didn't I do my French properly in class? Class? Light years away. I can't even boil an egg. What now?

What does one *do*? I didn't know a soul in the city. Where

21

does one go? A hotel? I'm sure I looked like an orphan in my grey coat, my little brown case next to me, clutching my handbag. All those travellers going through the barrier looking purposeful. *They* knew where they were going. If that sounds daft, remember it was the year nineteen-thirty-three. On the whole one wasn't exactly worldly wise and experienced at eighteen. I had made the decision to get away — that was all. I looked at the grimy roof of the station. Not really desperate, just helpless.

'Miss, you speak French?'

'Oh — yes, I do, just a little.'

'Are you by yourself? Do you know anybody here?' The man was wearing a blue uniform and a matching cap. So I thought (good Prussian reasoning) he would be neither after my passport nor my suitcase nor (white slave trafficker, brothel keeper) myself.

'Yes, I am alone and I don't know anybody here.'

'Where are you going to live?'

'Yes — eh, I mean I was just thinking of that. I really don't know.' A nice kid, the man must have thought, but a little feeble-minded. He had a kind face and it said *Armée du Salut* on his peaked cap. The Salvation Army. Brief vision of my Jewish family in Berlin, raising their well-bred arms to high heaven.

'I shall find you somewhere to sleep,' that kind man said, restoring my faith in the natural order of things where requests were immediately attended to and all needs fulfilled. 'Have you got a passport?'

'Yes, and a visa.' I was proud of that visa and there was a hint of a smile on the smooth pink face under the cap.

'Where do you come from?'

'Germany. I've just left school and I wanted to study singing, but they wouldn't admit me at the singing academy, because I'm Jewish, and anyway it's no use staying in a country where, where. ... My family is getting out too, but I couldn't wait, I. ... I —'

'All right, all right,' said the man patting my shoulder.

'It's the first time I've been by myself in a foreign country.' The last two words were whispered.

'You are no longer by yourself. We are going to look after you. Come along with me. 'He carried my case and we went in and out of the Metro, emerging in a grey tattered-looking district. Houses supported on large wooden beams to stop

22

them falling down, children running wild, cats slinking along the walls and not a car in sight. I had not grown feelers for that kind of place. Therefore the whole situation was relegated to the 'adventure' compartment. See all the interesting things that happen to me.

We entered a building, as grey and miserable as all the other houses in the street. My companion had a quick word with a stout woman behind a desk who said: first door on the right.

I slept for twelve hours fully clothed and woke to utter disgust with my fellow creatures : women sprawling on the floor, coughing, belching, swearing, quarrelling. They stank. They scratched themselves and spat on the floor. I was not ready for pity. Or else I could not afford it. I grabbed my suitcase and fled.

*   *   *

After bolting from the Salvation Army I made straight for Montparnasse. I sat down on the pavement outside a café and wondered whether I could afford a croissant with my coffee. Fool — fool! Why didn't I make proper enquiries before leaving home. Working conditions, for example, where to live, how to live. My parents should — but then I said I would arrange it all by myself. They trusted me. They shouldn't have.

I wouldn't wait, though they said I should. I could not. Not after Sebastian.

'Julia! What on earth? My dear *child*! Why are you all by yourself, where is Fritz, I mean your father? Are they all right? You look starved. I'll get you something to eat. What's in that suitcase?'

'Uncle Leo! What incredible luck. . . .'

'Not so incredible. I come here every day. So do we all.'

Good old uncle Winterhalter popping up in Montparnasse. The best thing that could happen to me : he cared, he really cared. He made other people's business his very own, he was his brother's keeper. Once he had cared too much, it appeared, helping some people to escape from Germany. He had been a colleague of my father's at the Court and had fought alongside him in the last war. It did not seem to have helped him much.

But his appearance worked an immediate transformation

on me. A slice of home. A father. The foreignness of my surroundings was no longer threatening. Things tipped back into the mould.

'Have some chocolates,' Uncle Leo said. At this moment the 'mild' period of the emigration began. I coped, or perhaps people helped me to cope. Things could be *managed* with a bit of goodwill and imagination. A certain amount of determination was required. But nothing that touched the inner being.

Uncle Leo opened a huge box tied with a blue ribbon. Those sweets! They sat in their nest of crinkly brown paper, covered in almond, nuts, filled with marzipan, coffee cream and liquor.

I sighed. 'That looks gorgeous. Where did you get them?'

'I didn't get them anywhere. I make them.'

'What? Why do you do that?'

'*Kindchen, Kindchen* — think!'

'I'm not a child and I can't think why you should make your own chocolates when you can buy them in a shop.'

'I make and sell them for a living, my stupid *Kindchen*.'

'Oh — I'm sorry, I always thought. . . . I mean you have such a big house and the Mercedes, couldn't you have taken some money with you? You were always so, so. . . .'

'Realistic?' I nodded. 'I did not have time to be. I had to run for it. And it's all gone, the house, the car, the money — they confiscated the whole lot. I count myself lucky to be still in one piece.' He shivered, closed his bulging blue eyes for a moment. 'If my friend at the police station hadn't given me a warning. . . .' He moved his head slowly from side to side, sorrowfully and somehow resigned, in a smooth pendulum movement: when will they ever learn, what can you do, how can the world look on and do nothing, they probably don't believe it anyway — the gesture meant all that.

'So now I'm making chocolates instead of preparing briefs.' He looked at me, taking in the crumpled grey coat, the brown suitcase, the general air of indecision and purposelessness.

'I hope you will help me to sell my chocolates,' he said pleadingly, as if he was asking me to do him a favour. 'Where do you live?'

'Not anywhere in particular yet. I haven't looked round.'

'So so,' uncle Leo said, wagging his head, 'and where were you going with this case of yours? And you live

24

nowhere.' He squinted at me. 'Perhaps you are meeting your boyfriend?'

'I haven't got one and I wasn't going anywhere. Oh, uncle Leo, I don't know what to do. I've hardly any money left and I'm not going back to the Salvation Army, I don't know a soul in this city — what *can* I do?' A soul in distress. I could not have offered him a greater gift. If you had dropped uncle Leo in the middle of the Sahara he would establish a one-man Red Cross in no time at all — a natural giver. He went into action at once, paid for my coffee and, happily chatting all the way, piloted me to his small hotel in the Latin Quarter, where he had set up a sweet factory on his dressing table.

He showed me various bags filled with sugar, cocoa, marzipan, coffee beans and almonds.

'Well,' he asked proudly, 'isn't that beautiful? Doesn't it smell heavenly? Do you think anybody could resist *that*? And look at those gorgeous boxes. They are all going to be filled with my homemade manna.'

I agreed that they looked great, that nobody would be able to resist the temptation.

'Right,' he said. 'I make them, you sell them and we'll both be happy. I hate running around and you are prettier than I am.' He patted his bald head.

'But I wouldn't know where to begin, I've never sold a thing in my life, what would I say, where would I go. . . .?' No use protesting. Uncle Leo had made up his mind. He spread out a map of Paris and organised the selling campaign as if he were preparing the most important court case. He overlooked nothing.

In the course of my selling trips I worked my way through every single Paris *arrondissement* and through some of the suburbs. I stayed in doorways, at cinema exits, near restaurants, I drifted through cafés, flowermarkets, dance halls. I knew where to shelter myself and the boxes (carried in a large leather briefcase once containing legal documents of staggering importance) from the cold and where to sit quietly and unobtrusively in the open, making sales without having to move around too much.

I soon sensed who was likely to buy and who would waste my time chatting. What was a girl like me doing in the streets selling stuff like that? was treated in the same efficient way as, did I feel like having dinner to-night in a nice quiet spot (like his apartment)? I opened my small grey eyes

25

very wide, pursed my lips regretfully, gazing sadly in front of me: 'As soon as my mother is better. . . .' I did not think anybody would fall for it, but uncle Leo had said they would, because they were up to no good and had a bad conscience and with a bad conscience you believe anything as he as a lawyer knew only too well. It worked perfectly.

'How about a nice warm dinner to-night?'

'My mother. . . .' Sad eyes, pursed lips. It never failed to provoke mumbled apologies. It became a reflex. I never had much trouble.

Factory girls were the best customers. They bought quickly without fuss, cracked dirty jokes of the 'is that the only thing you're selling, little girl' variety and asked me to return in a month's time, when they would buy more chocolates for their sweethearts, mothers and children.

I kept a wary eye on any policeman — street traders' licences were not easily granted to foreigners — but nobody seemed interested. Unpleasant thoughts were brushed aside quite quickly: the mail from home (the family still had not left), the headlines in the papers which became daily more alarming — war was imminent and unavoidable —, the gruesome tales of newly arrived refugees. It all hurt badly, but soon rolled off my mental oilskin. Every night I delivered the money from my sales to my uncle's hotel where, naturally, he had found me a room next to his. I always got more than the agreed percentage because, he said, I looked skinny and should spend the money on food.

'Do you cook?' he enquired one evening.

'I wouldn't know how, but I buy all those nice ready-made things in the rue de Buci and lots of fruit on the market. Really I'm perfectly all right.'

'You are not, you look terrible. You need a new coat.' I knew I looked shabby, downtrodden heels; no stockings, my hair held up in a pony tail with an elastic rubber band, my fringe cut with nail scissors.

'You've got to look presentable — you'll be picked up as a vagrant next. Here, buy yourself some decent clothes and go to the hairdresser. What would Sebastian say if he saw you like that? It might not have mattered in the Salvation Army but,' he called after me as I dashed out of the room, pocketing the money, 'don't go to the other extreme either.'

I did not enquire what that might be and threw myself headlong on the bed in my room. I wished he had not mentioned Sebastian. I wished he had not said his name aloud. It upset the precarious balance of my mind. It pulled me apart.

There had been times when I thought I could not possibly live another hour without my friend. The longing tore at me like great physical pain. After a while I had overcome that and finally persuaded myself that I would most likely never see him again. I can't say I loved him. That's a very pale, watery word compared with my feelings. I simply could not function properly without him. Until I met Sebastian again he remained *the* most perfect being in my thoughts, almost godlike. His remoteness allowed me to shape him completely to my wishes, to comply with my most outrageous demands on his understanding, his sensitivity. I began to build up his image like an idol. I had no country to cling to, my background had melted away, my ambitions did not go further than the next meal, so I built a shrine round his person.

In the last resort it was a very positive thing to do. It filled a void and gave me hope and purpose. Finally I managed to drive the thought of him underground where, no doubt, it played havoc in the basement. A dull ache persisted but nothing more. I had taken a painkiller of gigantic proportions: Paris. The inexhaustible beauty of this city, the avalanche of fresh encounters, the need to make a living — all that muffled Sebastian like a thick blanket.

I still went every day to the poste restante. In vain. But I knew now that I would not wilt away if I never saw my friend again and I existed, wisely, only on the surface. I couldn't look back or forward or listen to music or be alone too long. Most of the time I was a zombie. I lived with this permanent longing as with an incurable disease. Crippling but not deadly. A pain which is just bearable. I did not think of him any longer from morning to night, but when his name or face flashed through my mind it still felt intolerable.

After a few months in Paris I met Joachim. What a Teutonic name! I called him Joc. He had picked me up — literally — me and my boxes. It poured on the Jardin du Luxembourg, drenching me to the skin in a minute. The boxes looked a proper mess with their bedraggled blue ribbons. Me likewise — a drowning rat.

'A cup of coffee' he mumbled rather shamefacedly. And he would switch the fire on. I hesitated for just a fraction.

27

And why not? Who is going to stop me. Do as you please. Go on then, here's your chance. Forget. .... forget. Joc looked nice even under the pelting rain. Shy blue eyes, a jumper with a rolled neck. Slim and tall. Yes, I'll sit by his fire and get warm. I went with him without saying a word. We had coffee in his hotelroom and he *did* switch the fire on. Quite cosy. I stayed for good, but made Joc take the chocolate boxes back.

Uncle Leo came round to see me and disapproved of Joc on practical grounds. How was I going to live seeing that Joc was a student? What about babies? — did I know? Yes, I did. Not to worry. What would my father have said? Plenty I think. A boy I'd never seen before. Why couldn't I have picked somebody with money? I blushed. Uncle Leo said finally and illogically that he hoped I would be very happy. He raised his eyebrows waiting for an answer. I sighed, said Joc was a nice boy and did not play the piano. Oh, uncle Leo said, you're growing up — fast.

I was, I could almost feel it. Joc was a decent chap, with occasional flashes of nice dry humour. But not for a second could I forgive him for not being Sebastian. Or for never digging very hard into my past. He should be more curious about me. He should *know* what it was I never said.

Joc studied Economics at the Ecole des Sciences Politiques. A famous institution with now famous students. Only they did not take any notice of Joc at all. He was a foreigner. That's how it was at that time. They looked right through him; he might as well not have been there at all. But he did well. He was bright and better than most, even in a foreign language. At first we lived on his money sent from Germany for study purposes, by agreement with the German government. But they soon put a stop to it. As to the French : no working permit. That was final. We were obviously meant to live by the grace of God.

Some girls tried to walk the streets, but the French professionals would not stand for it. There was enough competition without those German sluts spoiling their business.

I became a dogwalker to make a living. Every morning for two hours I walked a real brute of a dog through the streets of Paris and down to the Seine. 'Garçon' was his name. 'Boy', indeed! I loathed the little beast, flea-ridden old bag. I called him 'Teufel' because that suited him to perfection; he

28

was a real devil. I should have taken out life insurance before venturing out with that creature, I should have been given a bodyguard instead of the miserable few francs his master saw fit to bestow on me.

I took him to the river every day for a swim. There was nothing playful about him. He was a fiend. Absolutely foul in the devilish cunning and malice he showed at every turn of the road. Can one feel hatred for an animal? I could as I held on to his leather leash, screaming abuse at him while he was dragging me down to the banks of the Seine just opposite the Chatelet on the Left Bank.

'I hope you'll drown!' I shouted above the noise of the steamers, 'you flea-ridden bastard, you brute, you *Unmensch*!' The steamers and barges were hooting like mad, making careful circles round the dog who was paddling unconcerned in the oily water and looking like a giant rat. Could his fleas stay alive in the water? Teufel always emerged covered in them. Or did he leave them at the shore like a pair of sandals? Maybe it was the fleas that made him so unmanageable and bad-tempered.

One day I watched him very closely as he came out of the water, dripping, tail between his legs. He scratched his nose furiously, but only his nose. I bent down and had a good look at him. Ah, that's one puzzle solved. The fleas had jumped on to the one dry spot on his coat — his muzzle — as he immersed himself in the water. They had gathered there as on a raft. The end of his nose looked like an antheap, crawling with insects. They were just waiting there for his coat to get dry to come and torment him again.

I quickly slipped the leash on and dragged him back into the water before he knew what happened to him. He had not the slightest wish to go back into the river. Strong as an ox. Still, I had a lot of strength too. I was mad at the fleas, the animal itself, at the whole sorry business of going dogwalking for a living. I dipped his head into the river nose first and held it there long enough to see hundreds of small black spots drifting away in the water. I gave Teufel one breather, saying, 'You fool! You'll feel all the better for it and I'm only doing it for your own good!' before immersing him again. He looked at me reproachfully as he came up for air and barked furiously.

Teufel did not scratch himself a single time on the way home. He followed me like a lamb. No tricks at the kerb, no delaying tactics at corners, no procrastination at lampposts. I believe his mean yellow eyes showed some measure of gratitude. There certainly was an understanding between us. No straining at the leash, no trench-warfare before crossing the road.

'You see, doggie, I'm looking after you, I won't let those beastly fleas eat you up. No, my darling, you are not really an *Unmensch*, a subhuman, you are a good and healthy animal with no worries at all.'

Joc was looking out of our hotelroom — the cheapest room in the cheapest street in Paris.

'Why were you so long?' he enquired amiably. 'I thought the dog had eaten you.'

'Teufel?' I patted his clean glossy coat. 'But he is a good dog, a lovely little dog — aren't you, my sweet?' He licked my hands. 'See? He likes me, I'm good to him.' The dog curled up at my feet.

'You must have doped him,' Joc said, looking puzzled. 'How did you manage to make him love you so suddenly?'

'I liberated him, I freed him from his tormentors.' I related the story to Joc.

'You could have drowned him with those repeated duckings, you know. Monsieur Ponceau would have murdered you.' Monsieur Ponceau, Teufel's owner was a human brute. Maybe he had fleas too.

The dog went to sleep and we had lunch: brown bread and cheese and a quickly emptied carafe of wine. Birds passed by the open window. A car hooted. Children played in the square opposite. A churchbell rang. I sat on Joc's lap, my head on his shoulder, so peaceful. Why couldn't we always be so peaceful and untroubled?

But outsize quarrels seemed an important part of our relationship. Blows, kicks, deadly accurate insults — we never ran out of fuel. I could have written a manual on our behaviour on the battlefield.

But the more outrageously Joc behaved the better I was pleased inside. It did not tarnish the memory of Sebastian: *he* would never have acted like that. I was quite aware that we both used our fights as lightning conductors. The worse the headlines, the more nervous we became and the more frequent our quarrels. Had we been older, outside events might have brought us closer together. As it was we had to hit out at each other regardless, perhaps even spurred on, by

30

the presence of friends, all refugees of one sort or another.

There was not much resentment afterwards on either side. Just when we were at each other's throat, Joc would say, 'small girls should know their place,' and carry me around the room like a child. He was fair, wide eyed and looked like a professional athlete. Good, good. He had never listened to music in his life and could not tell a military march from a Chopin nocturne. Good.

What did we quarrel about? Friends, books, food, politics, anything handy. Frequently my make-up. I used a lot on my eyelids by day and doubled the dose by night. My only luxury. I thought my narrow dark skinned face needed a focal point. Blue, green, black, silver — I loved to slap it on really thick.

'Take that muck off your face!' Joc yelled one day. Kurt was in our room, Kurt the faithful friend who never harmed anybody.

'I like it and so do others.' I winked at Kurt who was watching us uneasily from a corner in our room (one chair, one table, one large bed, a curtain for a wardrobe, a three-legged spirit cooker, flowers splashed wildly on faded pink wallpaper, bare wooden floors, a wash basin).

'Leave Kurt out of this,' Joc cried angrily. 'Why do you have to put all this filth on your eyes?'

'I like it. My face does not suit me without it.'

'Oh really? And you don't suit me, did you know *that*? Where did you get the money for all that rubbish? Did Kurt give it to you, did he? Did he? Answer me!'

Kurt looked at us like a member of the public strayed by accident into the boxing ring.

'I am still waiting for the first present *you* give me!' I shouted furiously. 'I think I'll go back to selling chocolates. Look at my dress! Look at my sandals!' I tore angrily at the halfbroken straps. 'Other men. . . .'

'Yes?' Joc advanced slowly towards me. I was sure he was going to hit me. But he walked past me to the window with suppressed fury and grabbed my little make-up pots spread out on the window sill. He flung them out into the street. I heard them crashing down hard on the pavement like little bullets. I went hot with rage and threw Joc's precious notebooks after them. The ultimate revenge — they contained the essence of his lectures. Professor Mandel's words of wisdom were scattered all over the cobblestones.

31

That was more than Kurt could bear. He went downstairs and collected the papers and my make-up pots. He coughed discreetly as he entered the room as he found us in a tight clinch.

'Ahem. Here are your papers. You'll need them for tomorrow.'

'What good will it do,' Joc said miserably. 'I won't ever be able to work here.'

'I know,' Kurt said, wagging his finger like uncle Leo. 'But we can't afford to waste these precious years. It can't last forever.'

'Things change, governments alter,' Joc said without much conviction. 'We'll come into our own one day.'

I put the kettle on. More friends came for endless discussions. Present and past history, the uncertainty of our future, the precariousness of our whole existence. How very sad. Words were all we had.

*   *   *

I often thought that we were like people living close to a volcano. They drink and eat and make love like everybody else. But the volcano is rumbling all the time and an extra dimension is added: tragedy. You don't complain too much, but you make strange arrangements and adjustments. I bet if you turned us inside out you would find the most peculiar fortifications, ball bearings and shock absorbers. You would find soundproof walls and thick layers of cotton wool. And besides that some small personal gadget, some trick, some survival device ticking away — a mechanical kit of great ingenuity.

Maybe we really would come into our own one day. But not just yet. Personally, I thought I had wasted enough time and I was going to train my voice, no matter what. I was going to demonstrate to everyone — including myself — that there is no such thing as an 'impossible' situation.

Five years training? Who would pay for that? Where would I practise? What about a teacher? (A singing teacher has to be more compatible than a husband, I was told.) Would they let me sing here in France without a proper permit? How would I live in the meantime? All this was brushed aside when a friend of a friend said she knew somebody 'superb'.

Madame Renault's reputation was tremendous. She was an ogre. She was the best teacher this side of the Atlantic. She asked for fees guaranteed to ruin anybody but a millionaire. She made you work till you dropped. And when you were ill she doubled the working time.

I went there all the same. Although Joc had said that singers have large chests and that they, the public, would need magnifying glasses to locate my presence on the stage.

Madame Renault lived in the depth of Montmartre in a lovely old house with lots of balconies. The studio was vast with yellow silk curtains, signed photographs all over the walls and a huge concert Pleyel. She was sitting behind it, her purple hair piled into an impressive topknot. A singer's flexible lips were painted the same purple as her hair.

'Julia?' Her deep resounding voice made my name sound like a chord. I nodded. Before I could say anything she commanded: 'Scales. Start with the lower C and open your mouth properly. Keep your tongue down flat, C C C — now!' I produced one note.

'No! No — not like *that*! Bring the sound forward.' I coughed madly and started again.

'Start with a C, I said. You must be tone deaf. And you screech like an owl at midnight. Carry the sound on your breath and not on your vocal chords. Haul it up, girl, up and out. You've got a lump of clay in your throat. I want a sound. Music, Julia, not a factory siren. You're going to choke if you don't let go.' She hammered on the keyboard like a blacksmith.

Owl indeed! I'll show her! When she stopped playing her infernal scales I flung a high C to the ceiling that made the windows tremble. She laughed her head off and asked me whether I had any money. Then she caught sight of my sandals and asked me what I lived on. Dogs, I said. I take them for walks. I could also do translations but nobody had asked me to.

'What about your private life?' she enquired without smiling.

'Yes, I've got one, I mean I have a friend. We are living in a little hotel, I like him —'

'Like? Aren't you happy with him? I can't have any emotional mess.'

'Oh no, it's great, it's really beautiful,' I said fervently.

'That's lucky for you. Can you type in French?'

'Easily,' I lied, 'I do it all the time.'

'Right. You'll do my correspondence and you can have lessons for free. Go and get yourself a small upright piano and I don't care *how* you get it. You must practise constantly. I won't have you if you don't work.'

'But our room is not big enough and the landlord. . . .'

'Move if it's not suitable. Do you want to sing or don't you?'

I said I wanted to sing and to hell with everything else.

'Can you play the piano?'

'A little,' I said modestly remembering ten years of butchered sonatas in the music room at home. (Red velvet music stools and a Bechstein grand. It seemed more remote than the ice age.)

'I'd like to hear you sing a complete song. Right through.' She put her fingers on the keyboard. 'Anything you like.'

'*Heidenroeslein,*' I proposed. That was safe enough. No German could go wrong on that. I remembered all the verses and I could not possibly forget the tune. They had flogged poor little rose to death at school, in the choirs, on the wireless, on records. Roeslein had been plucked, had stung, wept, and was broken by the boy lover a thousand times over. It had become a joke. It was a ridiculous choice.

But the first bars brought back all the things I did not want to know. I tried to keep my voice steady while tears were pouring down my face. I wept for my parents, my sisters, my house, my street, my school, my friends, the boy I had lost and the terror which gripped my country. I wept for everything broken and spoilt, for the whole gigantic *mess*.

At the last 'Roeslein rot' I started sobbing uncontrollably. '*Mutti — Mutti!*' I cried in despair. It was the first and last time I called for my mother. . . . I turned away from the piano and hid my face in my hands.

Madame Renault stood up. She did not try to console me or offer me her handkerchief. She stamped her foot and cursed loudly.

'*Merde* and *merde* again — politics! I wish one did not have to bother.'

I had to bother — permanently. I started with her the next day.

* * *

The rows with Joc increased right after the beginning of the lessons. He said he was playing second fiddle and I should give up those idiotic efforts as I would never get anywhere. And he would have a word with Madame Renault. That was it. There was a really nasty scene. I got an ugly black eye and my face was swollen. I decamped immediately and went to see Benjamin. The talk-and-coffee meetings had developed into that rare thing: true friendship.

He was the one bright spot amongst a sea of hostile faces on that day. They all looked particularly aggressive and unpleasant. Even the cafés looked forbidding. But Benjamin had become a good friend. He never let me down, he shared my worries and kept quiet about his own. It suited him; he wanted one-way traffic. He did translations, wrote books himself but, unlike other friends, never offered to read from them.

I found him writing in his room, ginger hair hanging over his forehead, his moustache forming two ginger crescents on his upper lip. His large body was full length on the floor, almost hugging the writing pad, pen poised, looking at me from steel-rimmed glasses.

'My goodness!' he exclaimed, catching sight of my maltreated face. 'You must be in love with the man.' I said nothing.

'What about Sebastian? No good going on punishing yourself. A broken nose hasn't helped anybody yet.' He made coffee, put a cold compress on my face and stroked my hands.

'It's not broken — yet.'

'Haven't you heard from your friend at all?'

'How can I? He doesn't know I'm in Paris.'

'Hm. . . .'

'What is that supposed to mean? He can't send letters to every town and village in Europe.' *I* would have done, I thought unhappily. 'I shall leave Joc,' I continued. 'But I hate to be on my own. Especially here. Especially now. I'm out of my depth — oh God, I feel awful.'

Benjamin waited for the dam to break, sitting quietly on the floor, hugging his knees.

The dam broke. (And has been breaking ever since, frequently and with great relish.) What a relief to say it all out loud and have a willing ear to receive it. I broke off abruptly and said that was all and I was truly grateful that he had listened. But when I opened the window the town down below looked so beautiful that I had to start again.

'Look at it, just look! What beauty! And what do we get? Worry, worry, worry. From morning to night. How will I eat? How will I live? Where *shall* I live? Will they let us stay? How long, how long? And that lousy hotel with that lousy boy. I loathe him, he has no feelings and he's bad for my voice.'

Benjamin giggled.

'There's nothing funny about that. Neither is there about the nightly screaming on the radio from Germany. Although the French think it's hilarious. I don't belong with that kind of Germans, thank God!'

'Not everybody makes that fine distinction.'

'How can I develop in this atmosphere? I can't grow.'

'On the contrary — you grow quicker this way.'

'You puzzle me. Why doesn't the whole situation upset you more?' I looked at the clock. 'I must go. We have a performance tonight with hundreds of guests. It's open house, I'm allowed two songs. I'll do Figaro and a folksong. Can I wash my face? Do you think the swelling will go? Won't you come along, Benjamin, you've never heard me sing. Please?' But he did not want to interrupt his work for too long and I made a dash for the Metro.

Madame said: 'You'll be an immediate hit tonight, if that's the right word to use. Put some powder on your face and start your exercises. Come on then, scales first. Now *voi che sapete* . . . my dear Julia, you look like a defeated heavyweight. Open your mouth properly,' she shouted above the noise of the piano. 'Keep your tongue flat, how often do I have to tell you? Come on then. You should know all the delights of young love. . . .'

It really hurt. How dare he bash me about like that. He could have injured me permanently, disfigured me for life. And I only said I must have been temporarily insane to come and live with him. I am sure people say that to each other all the time. When you live with somebody you've got to speak your mind. Or it is not worthwhile in the first place. It's bad to keep things back, it makes you ill.

I sang my two bits reasonably well, considering my handicap. I smiled a little lopsidedly when people clapped. Madame Renault explained I had a toothache and had made a brave effort. People clapped some more and I bowed like a professional. I felt they were clapping more for my brave effort than for the actual performance. But some of the students were first rate. I could not understand why I was not more envious of their accomplishments. Perhaps I did not take my studies seriously. Pity though, for there was a producer in the audience and a couple of film directors, a few people from agencies and even a man from the Opera. Nobody found my singing irresistible. I made a beeline for the cold buffet; stocking up. Should I slip a few little gateaux in my handbag for Joc? I decided against it. Women batterers could look after themselvers.

Kurt was with Joc when I returned home.

'What happened to your face?' he asked anxiously.

'I fell down the stairs,' I said, smiling like a martyr. I lay down on the bed with a sigh, resigned to my sad fate. The look Kurt gave to his friend is usually reserved for child murderers. It really made me feel good. Underneath I did not mind at all for I knew I was going to leave Joc in the morning. I would play it cool and inform him precisely one minute before I decamped.

I stuck to my decision and had the satisfaction of seeing Joc — abject and apologetic — making great efforts to keep me with him. I did not say anything, just shook my head gently and sadly and left. I stayed a week with uncle Leo while I was looking for work. . . . well, some means of earning money, however little. As I had no permit, no qualifications, no references and no connections my efforts were somewhat restricted. But I could not face lugging the chocolate-boxes around once more. So I decided to try the advertisements and forget about working permits.

I was lucky. It said in one of the dailies under 'Educational' 'Experienced German teacher wanted for language school immediately'. I went there right away and was received by Monsieur Orange, the headmaster. He was also the French, Italian, Spanish and Portugese master. I can't think why he missed out on German. He had a noticeable squint in the left eye, magnified by thick-lensed spectacles. He was a small man, just up to my height of five feet or so, but built like a boxer. His coarse brown hair was plastered down with greasy cream. He looked revolting. His chin was jutting out like Mussolini's: a human bulldozer.

'Speak to me in German — anything you like, but speak!' he commanded as I entered his basement flat in the Latin

Quarter.

'Excellent,' he interrupted me after two minutes. 'Ten francs per lesson. I take it you have a working permit.'

'I haven't. But if you give me a contract I can apply for one. There is a chance with foreign languages.'

'I will not give you a contract,' he bellowed. 'Indeed I won't even consider it. I shall now offer you five francs a lesson, deducting the other five as danger money for myself. I'm doing you a favour. Take it or leave it — no discussion.'

I took it. It would pay the rent.

Monsieur Orange showed me round the school : his flat. One big room for his classes and another as big as a towel for mine.

'You can start tomorrow; you get paid by the week. I take it you have your own schoolbooks, seeing that you are a trained teacher. . . .' He squinted at me to see whether I would flinch. I didn't and said I would use my own. I bought a second-hand grammar and managed to be just one lesson ahead of my pupils always. There were four little girls, pale and listless, nice but mentally somewhat underprivileged.

What a vile temper Monsieur Orange had and what a magnificent command of swearwords in all the languages. I believe be hated his pupils with unflagging fervour because he shouted at them for the best part of the day. It was hard to see how they could stand it and why their parents forked out considerable sums for them to be insulted non stop.

'Can't you read? Well *can* you?' The walls between our two rooms were paper thin. We could hear every word. My pupils and myself used to sit spellbound listening to him. He sounded like a sergeant major on parade.

'You are nothing but a bunch of idiots.' He was warming up. 'Morons, cretins. Why do you waste my time if you can't be bothered to listen? I said translate, not gibber. God has cursed you with the foulest brains in France. Have you ever heard the word *imparfait* — have you? What is it and when do you use it? What? What did you say, Lamotte? Speak up, boy, don't mumble. The boy's an imbecile! Im-par-fait, you blockhead, when is it used?' Lamotte answered but we could not hear what he said. Whatever it was, it was not what Monsieur Orange wanted to know, because we heard him roar:

'Is *that* what they taught you at school, is it? God give me patience or I'll beat the life out of you.' He never touched the pupils, but the constant threat of violence was almost worse. He frequently appealed to his Maker for patience which the latter never seemed to grant. 'Speak up, you little nitwit, why do you whisper into your handkerchief? Don't mumble like that — or do you want to keep it a secret?' Lamotte must have been in a state of complete hysterics by now. 'What the hell did you say? I told you to speak up! What — what? Where other people have a mind you have a rubbish dump. . . .' followed a series of *nom de noms*, progressively becoming more menacing.

We heard him knock on the desk with his ruler. He threw books about or maybe at his pupils. He was in full swing. Needless to say that my own work suffered. We were straining to hear every syllable from next door. He ranted and raved like a man possessed. Never mind the unfortunate students — he had worked out a most effective therapy for himself and his ungovernable rages. He wanted his money's worth or rather the students' whose parents were dishing out handsome fees for the privilege of having their children off their hands.

By now he had worked himself up to screaming pitch. You could feel the walls reverberating. '. . . You don't know what an adjective is? An adjective? You must be insane or else you have slept all through your schooldays. Gringoire, are you crying? A *boy* crying?' Then gleefully: 'He is insane, stop snivelling. Lamotte, you take over. You don't know either? Sit down, you clod, and leave that hanky alone. The boy's mentally deficient and shouldn't be allowed among decent people. Grandmontagne, you do it. Start from the very beginning. What gender is *padre*? Feminine did you say? I can well believe *your* father is! Maybe he is at that — that would explain. . . . No, no, no! A bunch of lunatics — that's what you are — demented. . . !'

It suddenly became quiet, the performance was finished for the time being. My girls and I started work again. They progressed very slowly. You could not really expect anything else in this outfit. They were probably doing some written work next door, as I heard Monsieur Orange pace up and down. Suddenly his voice boomed again.

'Illiterates! Why do you bother to come to my school if you don't even know your own language. How do you spell *travail*? With two ls and an e? *Le travail*? You bunch of feeble-minded nitwits — what makes you think you can learn a foreign language. . . . ' He was off again. Perhaps his blood pressure was too high and he found that shouting so madly was the best way to bring it down. He called his pupils pigs, dogs, morons, bastards, nuts, crackpots. He cursed them in Spanish (where you do unspeakable things to God the Father) in Italian (where your mother's profession has been well known for thousands of years) and in German (the only words he knew — where you are invited to do incredible things to your opponent).

When the bell went he calmed down immediately and said in his ordinary voice: 'Don't come here again without preparation.' The boys filed out pale and shaken, but nobody ever left the establishment while I was there. I think the parents bribed their children. He asked me now and then whether I was getting on well and I always said 'fine'. He did not really want to know. No records of the schoolwork were kept, no tests taken. The school was never inspected.

Monsieur Orange swept the classrooms with a large broom after the pupils had left. He then adjourned to his favourite bistro round the corner and spent the evening drinking and joking with his friends.

There must have been a genuine need for this kind of institution. If you were able to survive Monsieur Orange's furies you might become a brave man and do great things in the world. Or perhaps the outrageous contempt with which he treated his students held a sinister fascination for them. He was never short of applicants. I was his only employee. This sort of life went on and on in a comparatively pleasant way — as I was later to recognise.

*   *   *

'Do you ever eat properly?' Madame Renault asked me one morning.

'Of course, of course. Most of the time.'

'What's that supposed to mean and what are you doing to your hips?' Madame sighed loudly and I sighed inwardly. Regular meals were out of the question. I got liberal supplies from uncle Leo's boxes which had the curious effect of lodging themselves on my hips. The rest of my figure remained lean, but my hips unfolded like a Roman vase. Benjamin said: put handles on and stand on the mantelpiece. It did not worry me very much as I never bought clothes at all.

Once I caught my reflection in a shopwindow, going along the rue de Rivoli. It really shocked me. I was walking with a curious slow shuffle like a very old person. Bending forward, drifting along, never striding out properly, with the heavily ambling gait of someone not really sure where to go next.

But what can you expect? Of course you're bending forward, of course you're hunching up your shoulders when a hostile wind assails you month after month. You begin to drag your feet if you can't take part in the life around you. Not won't — can't. No French homes opened their doors to us. No helping hand was ever extended. All right then: I was proud of my status as an outcast, a complete outsider. A hostile fate will make me better, more sensitive and humane. I would soak up every scrap of experience and somehow *incorporate* it. That did not prevent me longing for shaded lights, white porcelain cups with golden rims, armchairs, soft curtains, the lost paradise of warm meals and of belonging — the last one most of all.

But there were the other refugees of course. They must have felt pretty much the same. We helped each other when necessary. Refugee doctors hardly ever took money from their fellow patients. If you had nowhere to sleep there was always a mattress handy in someone's room. But there is not very much you can do in a vacuum. Anyway, it did not matter all *that* much for we were going to return home one day in the near future.

War rumours circulated among us at least a year before the war actually started. France was going to win. There was no doubt of *that*. We would return to a new Germany and deploy our talents and gifts which were fabulous but had never been put to the test.

Suddenly I got my chance contrary to all expectation. A cabaret had been opened by one of the more enterprising refugees, thanks to the sale of a valuable ring which he had smuggled out of Germany.

'Madame,' I said to my teacher very proudly, 'I'm going to earn a lot of money and I can start repaying you for all my lessons. I'm sorry that you never asked me to type. . . .'

'I would not deprive you of your practising time,' said Madame and grinned. 'Just how will you earn the money?'

'I'm going to sing. . . .'

41

'At the Opera?'

'No, no. In a cabaret in the Latin Quarter.'

'It must be those hips of yours. Do you have to strip?'

'But Madame, it's serious, they are all professional.'

'Like you?'

Madame came to the opening night, sailing in with a fur-cape and a string of pupils in tow.

We played, we sang, we danced. We had a famous composer for our songs. A French actor did a turn. We rehearsed night and day. The pent-up enthusiasm of years of frustration and misery exploded into artistic performances. Or so we thought. We were going to 'show' them. Our sketches would be sharper, more ironical, more biting than anything done anywhere else. We would open people's eyes to the German plight and to their ruthlessness, to our own plight and outsize talents. The director was pleased. The producer was gratified. The first two performances were sold out. We were going on tour, when we would do less German numbers and more French. Approach agents. Get working permits. In fact, conquer Paris, France and everybody else who would have us.

I did three songs on my own and three sketches with the others. At first my knees were trembling but I soon gained confidence and flung my songs at the audience — recklessly. We can do anything anywhere. That was the general idea. For a fortnight. Unfortunately, unjustly and wholly to our surprise audiences began to dwindle. We changed our material. We acquired a backcloth. And a blonde.

The blonde began by being a damned nuisance. One of the actors had picked her from the file of an agency — or so he said.

'We know where you picked *her* up' said the director to Franz who had proudly presented her to us. 'In The Trèfle,' he sniggered, 'she looks cheap enough.'

'I thought she would fit into the second sketch,' Franz said, 'you know the one in the hotelroom with the rickety bed.'

'Can she speak at all?' The director walked over to Vera who grinned at him seductively. Two upper teeth were missing.

'Say something — anything. Come on, then.'

'Chéri,' she said, or rather croaked. 'Chéri.'

'Right,' The director was a man of action. 'We'll use her

in the hotel scene and she will say nothing but that one word 'chéri' — whatever happens. It'll be a scream. We haven't got a funny scene at all. We need one among all that heavy stuff. Here we've at last got a bit of local colour. You're on, Vera. If we earn a lot, you'll get a lot. If we take nothing you'll get nothing. Right?' Vera nodded.

'And don't go to the dentist. You look great as you are.' Vera gave another devastating smile. When she finally understood that neither the male nor the female members of the cabaret would want her services before, during or after rehearsals, she made up her mind to become a proper 'artiste'. She never missed a single performance.

But even Vera's unusual charm could not save the show. The cabaret closed down after two months.

I reported to Madame, saying that I could not understand why people did not flock to see it.

'Maybe they objected to your top notes! Put it down to experience. Now, I've got something else for you. You can't work up enough energy for your songs if you don't eat properly. I've got a friend, Monsieur Poulot. He's a film producer and lives near the Etoile. In a magnificent flat. Go and see him. Say I sent you.'

'But I have nothing to wear. I can't even have my hair done.'

'That's why I thought of you. You have that naturally scruffy look about you — no need to look offended, it's an asset. He's looking for somebody like you. Anybody can look smart. Do not arrange your hair and no make-up please. Try to look harrassed, a little forlorn — like that, yes. Let your arms hang limply by your side and turn your feet inward. Excellent. Don't overdo it though. You'd better go before I start weeping. See you in the morning for breakfast. No protests — I am expecting you.'

I did not have to act very much when I went to see Monsieur Poulot. It was a long time since I had set foot in a home like that. I just felt awful, out of place and thoroughly downcast, with a mixture of envy, self-pity and outrage. A maid opened the door, letting me in like a little stray dog. *She* pitied me!

I watched my feet in the torn sandals making their way across a gorgeous Chinese carpet of delicate blue and I went on to the balcony where the man was sunning himself in his bathing trunks, covered in suntan lotion, greasy all over. I

43

just stood there not saying a word. He did not even get up. He removed his sunglasses and said: 'You must be the girl Helena recommended.'

I nodded, not trusting myself to speak. I felt so furious and humiliated.

'Turn round' he said.

'What for?'

'Never mind. Just do as I say.'

'I get dizzy when I turn.' I felt unaccountably elated all of a sudden. I sat down on the nearest chair. What did I have to lose?

'Will you get me a coffee and something to eat. Two lumps and a dash of milk. I'm starving.' I managed to say this very politely like a well brought up girl at a party. It got him to his feet immediately. He crossed the room and pushed the bell frowning all the while.

'Bring some coffee for this — lady,' he said to the maid, 'and some croissants with butter.' He turned towards me: 'Why are you so hungry?' he asked curiously.

'Because I don't eat all that much,' I said in my best French adding 'monsieur' which made it sound preposterous.

'By choice?' That did it. I let him have the whole lot, a great big incoherent jumble of personal details, politics, hate, fear, apprehension and downright misery. It all gushed out madly. I forgot somebody was listening; I talked and talked getting it 'off my chest', hurling my words into the air like so many rocks. Finally I started accusing the man, his country, the whole world who stood by looking the other way. Our personal fate was his concern, I shouted, his fault! By now I was quite unaware of my listener who was shrinking into himself with a pained expression on his face.

After a while he coughed discreetly: 'I am glad you told me. I had no idea. I did not realise, I truly didn't.'

'You do now.' I turned to leave.

'But — but the film!' he called after me. I honestly had forgotten about it. He was more than a bit embarrassed when he said: 'I needed a girl for the part of a refugee, you would have been exactly right, but now I am not sure that you would. . . . I mean you may not feel like playing your own —' He looked away.

'How much?' I asked. 'And I have no working permit.' The money he offered would keep me for three months,

44

three meals a day. My more delicate feelings were buried, the little mouse became a king rat in an instant.

'It is not enough,' I said looking him straight in the eye. 'How shall I pay the rent?'

He was still staggering under the weight of calamities I had unloaded on him and doubled the sum. I accepted.

'I heard of your performance,' Madame said the day after. 'The man rang me the moment you left. You must have upset him deeply.'

'Good,' I said 'I've learnt a lot. Survival is everything.'

'I understand perfectly. But there is something else besides, isn't there?'

'I am living on the surface, I don't let myself think —'

'Of whom?' Madame asked, looking at me with moist eyes.

'My friend — I don't know where he is. It's all pretty pointless without him, I don't even know whether he managed to get out of the country. I — I can't. . . .' I stopped, clenching my fists.

Madame stroked my hair and kissed me, lifted my chin: 'My little girl, think of this when it gets too bad. Listen: *Les Juifs empêchent le monde de dormir.*'

The Jews prevent the world from going to sleep. Yes.

Letters from my parents were guarded and carefully worded. But I could read between the lines that matters were going from bad to worse for them.

War. I felt in my bones that a catastrophe was imminent. The past seemed almost cosy, because survival itself had never been questioned so far. The 'mild' period was over. We did not admit it at the time.

When finally war did break out we would probably have taken up arms if the French had let us, including the women. As it was, they clapped me and many thousands of other refugees into a camp in the South of France: we were German nationals. No explanations were accepted. Or perhaps we were being punished for our monumental stupidity.

Without a murmur I went with all the rest when we were told to assemble at the Velodrome d'Hiver. This was a large hall for cycle racing. Like the obedient, non-thinking citizens we were, we actually *queued* up at the doors of the internment camp, hoping the authorities in their wisdom would be discerning enough to let the right people out in the end.

45

Many were not admitted the first day because there was simply not enough space for all the lunatics who had rushed to the doors to be interned. They came back to report once more in the morning — everyone. People who had acted quite reasonably so far took leave of their senses. We stood waiting at the entrance doors with our rucksacks, blankets and sleeping bags as if ready for a mountaineering trip. It hardly seems credible now. There must have been a softening of the brain, a momentary lapse from common sense.

Perhaps we were more afraid of becoming 'illegal' in a foreign country than to be interned in a camp. More afraid of trying to find a hiding place than to be shut away. Or we might have thought that 'justice' must prevail in the end. For God's sake, we were on *their* side. They did not want to know.

I see myself sitting in the camp in Southern France, howling like a wolf with misery and frustration. I am not a German, I sobbed loudly. My identity papers said otherwise. I am hungry, thirsty, I am treated like a criminal, we have the same enemy — or words to that effect. Nobody took any notice.

The camp was at the foothills of a huge, snowcovered mountain range, the Pyrenees. It was surrounded by barbed wire and flanked by four watchtowers with soldiers equipped with machine guns permanently pointed at the camp. Forty women per hut. The earth inside covered with straw. Nothing else.

'The soldiers —' I gasped turning to the woman next to me. 'I don't understand.'

'Don't upset yourself. Look at the bright side.'

'What's bright about this?' I pointed at the women sitting on the straw in abject misery.

'The sun,' she said, 'the sun *is* bright. Come out of the hut and sit outside.' We sat against the wooden wall letting the sun shine on our faces.

'There,' the woman said, 'stock up the vitamins. You won't get many in here. I'm Ida. Where do you come from?'

'Berlin,' I said. She raised her eyebrows. 'Well — Paris really. I live there. And you?'

'Brussels. I'm a dancer and was on tour. Something was wrong with my passport. Stop snivelling, it isn't too bad, apart from the food. Nobody pushes us around. Lots of different women here, Dutch and Gypsies and a few vagrants.

Can't see much system in all this. But,' her eyes twinkled, 'look over there. That'll stop you crying.'

Not three yards from our own encampment was another one behind a different barbed wire. All men. Straggly beards and dark brown bodies. They were remnants of the International Brigade who had fought on the losing side in the Spanish Civil War.

'Hey, psst,' from across the barbed wire. 'We've got some spare bread. Do you want it?' A pretty wild looking fellow in rags held up a crusty loaf.

'Throw it!' Ida called. Her red hair glinted in the sun. Damn! the loaf fell right in the middle between the two camps.

'We've got to get it. You. . . .' she shook me, 'you fetch it. I'm sick of those potatoes. Come on then — you're the smallest.'

I slipped quickly underneath the barbed wire, wriggled out, flattening myself against the ground, grabbed the loaf and crawled back in before I had time to hesitate. Like most daring actions this one was committed before there was time for reflection.

That was the precise moment when I was finally tipped out of my mould. I was never the same again.

I slipped in and out almost daily, now more prudently under cover of darkness, to collect more and more food. How did the men obtain it? And why did they have enough to part with it? What did they expect in return? I never found out. I provided, I took the risk — it felt glorious. The guards did not catch me, my friends depended on me. What greater achievement? In the midst of disaster: personal contentment.

I began to think about other means for me to supplement the potato diet. All sorts of crazy schemes flitted through my mind, then suddenly I knew. I had long been fascinated by the weird pattern on the inside of my hands. There was more time to gaze at them now than ever before. I looked at my palm intensely. There were islands, crosses, stars, dots and a net of fine lines etched in all over. Did it mean anything? Could there be some sort of significance in the pattern?

I had nothing to do all day but lounge about on the dirty straw or sit outside and gossip. No books, no papers. My mind tried to fasten on anything, *anybody*. I started looking at the women's hands with great attention, their infinite variety of lines, shapes and textures. The thumbs seemed to give the show away: pointed thumbs for moody and changeable people, broad and forceful for determined ones.

Bilba, a girl from Amsterdam, had hands which mirrored her face to perfection: wild, untamed and permanently enraged at our present confined state. Her hands were like claws ready to pounce. The space between thumb and forefinger was remarkably wide. When she folded her hands, her right thumb came to rest over her left. Most people did the opposite. Later I knew that this was a strong sign of willpower, determination and individuality.

I looked at my own hands as avidly as a woman looks into her mirror. My thumbs were stiff, unbending and completely straight. Bound to the 'ego' it meant, relating all events to your person. Fine, fine. Years afterwards I absolved myself from all responsibility for my favourite occupation and no longer felt guilty searching into my own state of mind. How comforting. I was born like that.

I was hooked by the game. Fine, elongated thumbs with fine, sensitive people; flabby palms, flabby mentality. Too many lines, too many worries; too few, not enough or underdeveloped personality. All this fascinated me and my stimulus-starved mind fastened on the girls' hands more and more. People began to notice. I said vaguely I was gathering material for a book, but that was not what they wanted to hear.

Hundreds of women cooped up together, nothing to do all day but wait for the next round of potatoes, and with but one thought: 'When are we going to get *out*?' Families and friends lost, dispersed all over Europe. Grief, hope, despair. They all but forced me to look at their hands, to *tell* them — Were they ever going to see their families and friends again? But would I be justified in putting my 'feelings' into words? A twinge of conscience, a reluctance to pretend, to 'con' my co-prisoners, a desire to show off, to have something to 'do' at last, and the presence of the black market in the camp. I fought it out quietly. My moral scruples did not last very long.

Where there's misery there's money. The French cooks, who kept us barely above starvation level, thought that we would part with our last possessions in exchange for food. Logical. Watches, jewelry, clothes bought carrots, apples, butter and raw eggs — all very much in demand. There were

48

also sweets and chocolate, craved for by most women. It was a thriving business.

Inga, slim as a reed, with long fair hair and sad blue eyes thrust her palm under my nose one morning and said she just *had* to know. I heard myself say that she was pregnant and was shocked to learn that she was. How did I know? To this day I can't explain. I made several further wild guesses which proved uncannily correct.

Maybe my brain works better with a minimum of food. Or my nervous system was charged by events, or the sun beating down, or the wind from the mountains, the fear underneath gnawing away relentlessly. Who knows.

It spread through the camp like wildfire that there was a girl who could 'read' palms. I was in business. If you are in real trouble you want a witch to tell you what's going to happen next — or you can become one. Later I knew from books what the lines in the hand meant but I never achieved similar results. The tension was gone and my ESP with it.

Inga really was pregnant. What was going to become of her in the camp? I said blithely that she would be soon out of it. (She was!) I never took money, I only asked for food. The women were soon queueing outside our hut to have their palms done. Even the gypsies came. I was given cheese, eggs, sweets, ham. Even wine. I shared it with the girls in the hut and I must admit I had a very interesting time.

I scored more direct hits than just luck could account for. It became quite natural. A palm was spread out in front of me and life seemed to take visible shape within the mountains, valleys, the sharply drawn lines and squiggles. Every detail assumed significance. The muscles, the length of the fingers, the 'bracelets' round the wrists (three of them), the shape and colour of nails, the way a hand lay open (defenceless), the outer rim of the palm, the consistency of the skin.

Inga came back for a second reading. Was Paul, her French boyfriend, still thinking of her? Of course he was, he would contact her, he was even trying now — desperately. As this was the time when the German armies began to overrun France. You didn't have to be a clairvoyant to say that. But Inga was happy. Ida and I retired to the hut and got sloshed on the quiet. The hut was quite empty on that summer's day.

'Lovely stuff' said Ida, curling up on the straw next to me. 'I need a hairwash and a man.'

49

'Which first?'

'Both together.' She giggled, pulling at her lovely red hair, covered in straw and dust. 'You know, I think Max fancies me.' He was the bearded fellow who had thrown the first loaf across the wire. 'He would be terrific, absolutely terrific. Those boys from the International Brigade haven't had a girl for years. . . . just imagine what he would do to me, just ima. . . .' She was asleep, smiling.

The more I drank the surer I became I would soon be out of here. I ought to get going, I thought hazily, before my fellow countrymen come crashing through the camp gates, no good waiting till it's too late. The empty bottle rolled on the floor.

Two days later Inga's friend, a French soldier in uniform, stormed into the camp commandant's office and claimed her as his bride. She was freed on the spot. I still have the small silver ring she left me as a parting gift.

*   *   *

There was one luxury in the camp: showers. I loved to go in the same time the gypsies went. They stood there, fully clothed, water running down their hair, dresses, petticoats and all, dripping into their shoes and stockings. Did their religion forbid them to undress in public? Or was this a simple way of cleaning their belongings? They emerged from the showers soaking, their clothes clinging to their bodies, marching up and down in the sun till they were dry. I knew them quite well by now.

One day a dark, bright-eyed girl approached me: 'Julia'. She lowered her voice. 'The Germans will occupy the camp in the morning. I thought you ought to know.'

'How do *you* know?'

'My friend overheard a conversation in the Commandant's office.'

'*What* was she doing there?'

'She was ill. She is going to be transferred to a hospital tomorrow. You know they always fear epidemics, as we never have a doctor here.'

'Who let you out of our sector?'

'The guards of course.' There were always two guards patrolling the highway connecting the different camp sectors. I kissed the girl, felt my heart beating against my ribs

50

and raced over to Ida. That was it then. I *had* to get out. Ida could afford to stay; she was 'only' Belgian. Charlotte, another girl in our hut, could stay. She was Dutch. Martha and Pola would be liberated, as they were German, but not Jewish. I was both — an impossible combination.

'Sorry to lose you,' Ida said, 'but you've got to go — now!' I hesitated. 'Get your things together. Leave it to me. . . . hurry up then, what are you waiting for?' I stuffed my things in my rucksack and said that I was ready.

'Oh no, you're not. Do as I tell you.' Ida made me lie down on the ground, plastered me with sand all over and said: look miserable! She gleefully messed up my face and hair and made my left arm dangle between the barbs of the wire: a ghastly sight. Then she stood next to me, waiting for the guards to come by. I got kicked in the ribs by her: you don't look sick enough, go on then, cry. Another violent kick. 'They are coming.' I started to moan and groan.

'Guards, guards!' Ida called anxiously, 'come over here quick! Quick! My friend is ill. Oh do come! Please hurry.' She did it beautifully, a womanly appeal to the strong lads outside. Her looks helped of course, her red hair and lovely smile.

'What's the matter with her?'

'I don't know. She's so hot, so feverish. Maybe it's the water. She ought to be seen to right away.' Another smile, heart-breaking this time. 'Could you — could you carry her, or is she too heavy for you?' Two big strong fellows like you, her eyes said. I squinted through my tears and saw the gate open. One man picked me up easily, carrying the head, the other the feet. Ida handed over my rucksack, saying, you *are* nice, and blew them a kiss. They grinned back at her as the gate closed behind them.

'Where shall we put her?' This was in the office at the end of the camp. The Commandant looked down at me.

'Can she stand up?' The man was human. The guards shrugged. 'Can you?' He saw my dirty tearstained face. 'It can't be as bad as all that? Try to stand.'

'I will try.' I whispered this bravely as the soldiers put me on my feet and then collapsed in a heap on the floor. Might as well do things properly.

'Get a stretcher at once!' he called to the guards.' At the double. What is your name? Your name, girl —'

'Julia Engelmann.'

51

'Height?'

'Five feet and an inch.' The continental equivalent.

'Eyes?' He looked at me. 'Your eye colour — it's got to be on your pass. . . . green.'

'No, grey.'

'Don't argue, they are green. Hair brown. Special marks: dirty.' He grinned. 'They'll have to scrub you first in hospital.' My heart lurched violently. I'm going to get out! Please God, don't let him change his mind, please help me. I've *got* to get out. Just set me free and I'll never ask anything of you again. Please!

The guards put me on a stretcher, my rucksack next to me. They waited at the main camp gate for transport. I closed my eyes and stopped breathing. A lorry drew up. The guards produced my pass, opened the gate and put me on a lorry. They jumped off as it started to move.

When I dared to open my eyes we were rolling through lovely green country. The camp had disappeared in a cloud of dust. The trees struck me most of all. There had been none in the camp so that the guards could observe us better. How vast and friendly the land was. Cows were grazing in the fields, beautiful brown and white animals with heavy udders. Cosy little houses with smoke coming out of the chimneys. Women with large aprons feeding the chickens. I thought I'd never seen anything as marvellous.

The driver made straight for the hospital in the nearest town some sixty miles away. Bath, bed, dinner. Perfect heaven. A doctor came to see me in my little cubicle where I lay isolated from the other patients. You never know. . . . coming out of that camp.

'I can't find much wrong with you,' he said after a while. 'It says "fever" on your pass.' He had a good strong face, compassionate and intelligent. *And* his hands looked great. A long, beautifully shaped thumb.

I decided to risk it. 'I had to get out of the camp,' I said softly, watching his face. 'The Germans will take it over tomorrow. I could not wait for that —'

He clenched his fists. It appeared that he was not too happy with this piece of information. He put his stethoscope away and sat down by the bed.

'Aha' he said. 'You could not wait. I dare say you have your reasons. What now?' First things first.

'I have no money. I must get to Toulouse; it's not occupied yet and I have friends there. Please, could you. . . . help me? I shall return every penny —'

He took a few notes from his wallet. 'It's a gift,' he said forcefully. 'My pleasure.' He had difficulty keeping his voice down. 'Get dressed and clear out while you can, and' — he winked — 'look after yourself. You've done all right so far.' He left.

Later a nurse came with my clothes and a food parcel. 'The doctor said you must put on weight.' Bless him.

* * *

I travelled mostly on small buses, by far the safest way if one wants to avoid the path of an invading army. I never labelled myself as a fugitive at the time. But that was my status, my achievement. I *was* free to run. The news reports were bad and became worse daily. People said it was all propaganda and it could not be true. I knew otherwise. Every word was true. The fear of the Swastika sat deep inside and burned me up. The French were uneasy and hated the invaders. I feared — fear was behind all my thoughts and actions. It was a good pathfinder.

I got steadily nearer to Toulouse where I hoped to find my friends from Paris Walter and Boszi. They were Hungarians and in no immediate danger. Hungary was not at war.

Then, only a few miles from Toulouse, I ran into trouble. A troup of German soldiers approached when I stood on a cross country road waiting for a bus. They were questioning civilians on their way. I jumped into the nearest ditch, pressing my face into the ground. I cried out and lifted my head from the bed of nettles where I had fallen.

'Keep your head down, damn you!' I heard a man's harsh voice next to me. 'If you make one move I'll stick a knife into you.' Terrified I kept my face on the nettles. The soldiers were marching past, their steps getting lost in the distance.

'It's all right now,' the same voice said gently. 'They've gone. And I have not got a knife. But I thought it would keep you quiet. I'm Pierre — who are you?' He doubled up with laughter. 'You look like a cactus in full bloom.'

I took out my pocket mirror and groaned. My face was covered in a million red lumps.

'If you don't scratch the stings will go. Here, just let me hold your hands if you are tempted. I won't let you. What's

53

your name?'

'I won't tell you. Look what you've done to me.'

We scrambled out of the ditch like two chained convicts and stood by the bus stop, my hands held firmly in his.

'You don't look quite so ugly any more,' Pierre said a little later. 'Where are you going? Should you be about by yourself?'

'Ha!' I barked contemptuously. 'That's a good question.' I certainly was not going to enlighten him — you never know. Although he was a decent looking chap, quite young, but with deep furrows between nose and mouth. He looked strained and tense. Now why did *he* want to hide?

'What do you do?' I asked. 'I mean your work.'

He hesitated for a fraction of a second, his dark brows meeting in a frown. 'I'm a surveyor'.

'Just what do you survey?' I asked, not really expecting an answer.

'Railways,' he said briefly.

Blows them up, I thought immediately. A resistance chap. The secret French organisation had just started working. That's the way my mind went: for or against. If a man jumps into a ditch —

We travelled on together, careful to choose our hotel. Neither could afford to register, it seemed. He said to me in the middle of the night that he liked me — very much. But he still wanted me to know —

'I don't want to know,' I said quickly. We all have somebody somewhere. . . .' I started sobbing, losing control, crying out for Sebastian in the dark, hoping against hope, willing him to hear me, crying on Pierre's shoulder who stroked my hair and said all would be well in the end.

*   *   *

We said goodbye the next morning. I sat in a country bus which would take me to the outskirts of Toulouse. All of a sudden I got the oddest feeling of elation. There was nothing outside which could account for it. Rain was beating down on the fields, almost drowning the flat scenery. Inside were mostly local people looking disgruntled and wet. The future looked uncertain, to say the least.

But it suddenly dawned on me that I could do — and *had* done — exactly as I pleased, even under stress, even under

54

entirely hostile circumstances; that nothing short of physical pain or illness would break me. I had enough sense to
know that. A will o' the wisp was jumping about inside of
me. No, that's too poetical a word. It was more like a demented frog: I can do what I like. I shall do what I want, even
if the earth splits under me. Pure tremendous elation! I
needed a mental rope to cling to, and that was it: a feeling of
irresistible strength. Although the earth was not splitting at
the moment, it carried me like a mother.

Toulouse: filled to bursting point with refugees from the
Germans. They were camping in parks, streets, staircases,
by the river. So were the fleas. And the bugs, cockroaches,
outsize rats, mice, stray dogs and giant whining mosquitos.
They all had a great time with nowhere for people to wash,
bits of food lying around everywhere and no sanitation to
speak of. And still more people arrived daily from the occupied zone. But soon everyone was wading as cheerfully
through filth and decomposing food as through a flower
dotted field.

Everybody seemed to congregate on the main square for a
café crème in the afternoon. That's where I located Walter
and Boszi pretty soon, sitting on one of the crowded terraces,
drinking and bickering as usual. Some astrological charts
were spread out in front of them. Incongruous but somehow
encouraging. At least we could look up to the Heavens.

'You've made it then,' Boszi said. 'I knew you would. Bad
pennies. . . .' She put her head on one side. 'You can live
with us, we're privileged, we've got a room.' She then proceeded to explain her charts. They showed an early debacle
of Germany and the end of Hitler's government, because
Saturn was just. . . .

'I do not want to hear this rubbish any more, you stupid
stupid woman. It doesn't mean anything at all!' Walter
pulled her long black hair forcefully. She turned round furiously and slapped his face. He had insulted her deepest
beliefs. Her husband said calmly that she had gone round
the bend, that there could not possibly be a connection
between the remote stars and our own lives.

'Walter, listen to me: I know there is a purpose behind
events, a connection between everything.'

'If you believe that. . . .' His eyes narrowed with contempt.
He lifted his chin, sticking his fair beard out like a weapon.
'What proof except your own credulous mind!'

'I can prove it. When you were born —'

'That was a most unfortunate day, I don't want to hear any more about it. Throw your charts away, I can tell you the future without them: we'll all end up in the camps.'

'We won't. My horoscope says so.'

'It does? Well, then — what do you make of *that*?' He showed us the latest regulations for foreign refugees issued by the police of Toulouse: either you could prove that you had means to live without working or you would be interned without further ado.

'How can they possibly find out who is and who is not French in this madhouse?' Boszi said defiantly, but her dark eyes were wide with fear. Walter shrugged. They only have to ask for your papers; they only have to look at you or hear you speak. It won't take them long. We joked about the charts but were scared stiff. Enough money to live without working? For how long? Walter's scientific brain went into action. He did research in Chemistry. Badly underpaid. I was selling newspapers since this morning.

Other friends and acquaintances joined our table, almost mute with tension. Walter was still thinking, his head in his hands. Then he looked up.

'How much money have you got — each of you?' Murmurs of 'far too little' and 'hardly worth while counting'.

'Never mind — put it in front of you, now!' It amounted to quite a bit. In fact it would have kept one of us alive for some time.

'Pity,' Boszi said, 'I wish it all belonged to me.'

'But it could so easily — don't you see?' Walter went on with suppressed excitement: 'Don't you understand what I'm trying to say? It *will* belong to you, at least when you show it to the gentlemen at the Police Station. They won't take down the numbers of our notes, they are not looking for bankrobbers.' Then, triumphantly: 'We are going to show them the same money over and over again. They won't know the difference. One note looks very much like another. We'll get an official stamp in our papers and won't be bothered any more. A rich Jew is better than a poor one. Strange logic — but who are we to argue? It's up to each of you to make a proper living — or an improper one.' He winked at me: 'Did you get funny offers this morning?' No, I hadn't. Maybe I looked too disreputable.

We walked from the square to my friends' room. Lucky to

56

have a home, even if there was nothing in it. Four walls and the bare floorboards. A gloomy little bulb hanging from the ceiling. Blankets, two cases, a thermos flask and two cups. Home. We talked for a bit. Boszi combed her dark hair.

We were in no way prepared for Walter's sudden outburst. I've never witnessed anybody banging his head against the wall. Walter was doing it now. Repeatedly and with great hollow sounding thumps. One moment he was sitting cross-legged on the floor, the next he was beating his head against the wall like a caged animal.

'I'm not giving in, I'm not giving in — the bastards, the bastards!' He suddenly crumpled up, beating the floor with his fists. 'Beasts, beasts! I have not *done* anything. Why *us*, why? I haven't harmed anybody ever. Have I murdered, looted, burnt? What is my *crime*? Where did I go wrong, tell me, what did I do wrong?'

Boszi rocked him like a child and murmured: 'They lost the last war, they will lose this one too, you'll see.' She stroked his shoulders. 'You've found a way for us, darling. We shall do exactly what you said. . . . you can't go to pieces now. We need you — I need you.' Walter looked at her, tears rolling down his cheeks. Boszi stood up, arms outstretched. Like a winged statue, almost mythical, her dark hair streaming down her back. 'We shall still be there when they are dead and buried. I know —'

Walter gazed at her silently, his mouth open, eyes suddenly trusting like a child's: 'Some of us will,' he said, 'I believe that. . . .'

*　　*　　*

The crumpled banknotes were passing from hand to hand and it worked like a charm. None of us went into camps. Grotesque! A brainwave from a clever man and here we were in a village at the foot of the Pyrenees as if we were on holiday. Ah, but maybe it isn't all that odd, maybe there is some sinister logic in it. Brain — reason — intelligence. It triumphs over brute force. Right. Now we are here, we must adapt ourselves to our surroundings. It took a lot of adapting and even more goodwill from our new neighbours. Because the peasants and the farmers were none too keen on us.

What were we doing here anyway? Right in the middle of

their meadows, pigs, cows, streams, sheep, chickens and flowers. I'd never seen so many different flowers in my life. Like a botanical garden. Shrubs and bushes everywhere. And snowy mountain peaks in the distance. That was the second time (the first was in the camp) that those peaks loomed up on the horizon. There would be a third contact yet, strange, personal, intimate, almost human.

We had a hard time convincing the villagers that we had much more to fear from the Germans than they had. They eventually understood. I was to spend two years there and by then they were used to us, even worrying about our safety. We did little jobs for them. Gardening, teaching their children, helping on the farms. One man became a gravedigger. And why not? It's important, I would say vital if it did not sound odd.

One freezing winter morning I found a large bag with woollies in front of my door. Anonymous. It said in big clumsy letters: Your raincoat is too thin. I felt absurdly grateful. Warmth, protection and compassion. All in the woolly bundle.

At the time I lived with a chap called Martin, who had also used Walter's miraculous money device to keep out of the camps. I need company, an echo, day and night. I would speak to my shadow if I were on a desert island. My friend Anja was deeply shocked when I said: rather a one-eyed dwarf than alone. Where was my sense of values, she asked. My pride and independence? I wondered. . . .

But I *was* fond of Martin, very fond. Even though he interfered with Sebastian's inviolable domain, for he taught the piano to local children and it hurt each time I heard him play. Fortunately he could not be likened to my friend. He had a superficial gift — none of Sebastian's passion and genius. He was absolutely nowhere compared with him. Good. He also looked tougher, earthier, almost stocky. Not at all out of place in the village. Tanned, with nice twinkling grey eyes. I could not imagine him ill, ever. He planted things, dug the gardens, milked the cows. He fitted in perfectly. Maybe too well — there was none of the remoteness and mystery which seems to me the height of attraction. So it was no betrayal.

Anja's husband was his brother. She herself was tall, righteous feet firmly on the ground, short hair blowing in the wind. She was constantly disapproving of me and therefore stimulating and excellent company.

As the Vichy Government did not allow us to leave the village we were mostly pacing up and down the main street on sunny days. Animals and farmers were jostling along. The doors of their small houses were open, their bead curtains swinging in the wind. Anja was hammering away at me as usual: 'I cannot understand why you look so unruffled. And why do you keep on painting your eyes?' (Strange, how this harmless adornment of my narrow little peepers seemed to upset people.) 'It's also the expression on your face. As if nothing had happened. As if none of the horrors around us were your concern.'

'That might turn out to be an advantage. Ultimately. I don't think that a few compassionate creases would change the course of history. But perhaps I don't choose to wear my nightmares on my sleeve.' Actually I *had* frequent nightmares. Waking up in a cold sweat and throwing myself into Martin's arms as if I were drowning.

I said: 'What good would it do if I cried from morning to night?'

'Don't be so flippant. What do you propose to do about our desperate situation? How can it go on?'

Hm — that question was justified. We were stuck in this village for good — to all intents and purposes. And lucky to be here, by the grace of the authorities of the Haute Garonne and Walter's resourcefulness. He and Boszi were in the same village.

The police kept an eye on us, but only at the beginning. They were quite decent; anyway there was nowhere for us to run to at the moment. This little Southern Siberia seemed as good a place as any. There was even a village cinema down the road, where I saw the comedy *Ma Soeur, Masseuse* six times. But that was as far as our freedom went.

I still had not answered Anja's question. What could one 'do about it'? I looked at her, at the high mountains in the distance and said: 'Eventually we will *have* to do something. Get out. . . . leave this little paradise.'

'You see what I mean. Flippant and selfish to the core.'

'You hypocrite! Can you suggest anything else? You can't even post a letter without the whole neighbourhood knowing about it. We can't move an inch without the police interfering. What would I do then — if I were not selfish? Go out and organise an attack on the German infantry?'

Anja was silent. I heard cowbells tinkling. The sun was shooting its last dark red rays at the hills. We turned back at the end of the road according to regulations, stopping by the little stream flowing through the village. We leant over the railings on the bridge and gazed into the water. How quiet and untroubled — I hesitate to say peaceful. But it was, charming, remote and peaceful. If only we could stay here.

'Anja, why don't you say something? Are you afraid? What will you do if matters get worse? What is *anybody* doing for that matter? Come on, tell me, who's interested in our fate? Who? Any offers? Any country invite us in? Well, did they? Or perhaps help us out of this one? My sweet, nobody — do you hear? — nobody cares. What are you hoping for? A heavenly intervention? Soon we've got to get out of here, if you like living. If you like it enough. . . .'

'But when?'

'Quite soon, I think. Before the Germans come and get us.'

'You always assume the worst.'

'The worst always happens. Didn't you know?'

*   *   *

We went on to Monsieur Lafranche's bistro where the men played cards. Every day and most of the night. The bistro was their office, their 'calling', their stabilizer.

They clocked in every day at three; nobody was ever late. They plunged into the game and were lost to the world. Mr. Greenstein dragged himself to the bistro even when sick and trembling, with a temperature of a hundred and three. He'd rather have died with the cards in his hands than missed the game.

Sometimes the owner of the bistro joined them. Monsieur Lafranche unstrapped his wooden leg, sat down and hollered for his beer. His girlfriend, anaemic, blonde and submissive like a dog, kept up a constant supply. His wife had died two months before and he had not stopped celebrating. She had been a formidable nagger.

There was also Celine, the raven haired daughter, bulging out in all directions and disappearing now and then into her bedroom with one of the guests. She was soon to leave the village to work in one of the brothels of the famous rue du Canal in Toulouse. More variety there, she said. She was the only one able to calm Monsieur Lafranche if he flew into one of his drunken rages.

I loved seeing him hurl the crockery at the wall. What a liberating experience! Glass flying, beer splashing about, Lafranche stamping and cursing, his face on fire. He was in a paroxysm of fury — his blood must have been at boiling point. Celine had a way with him. Or perhaps he with her — so nasty people said. She helped him behind the counter, put a wet flannel on his forehead and said he was a good man and always right. Then he calmed down quickly and joined the card players.

Martin and I lived just above the bistro. Our room looked out on a disused railway. (The symbolism glaring from those empty tracks was ghastly.) We loved to hear the glasses clanking and crashing, the murmur of the customers' voices and Monsieur Lafranche bellowing. One was part of a community, not lost, not ostracised. The bistro smelled of wood, wine, beer and cowdung — what a pleasant, homely mixture. Reassuring somehow.

Our men played cards like other people go to church. With absolute concentration, dedication and utter seriousness. As if life depended on it. It did to a certain degree. While their minds were on the cards they could not worry themselves sick over the state of the world and their own fate in particular. No doctor could have devised a better therapy.

They broke off their game at six, went for a stroll round the village and sat down to dinner at seven. An excellent routine. The women kept homes of a sort. As much as you can do in one or two rooms. They cooked, washed, cleaned and mended the tattered clothes over and over again. But nobody was complaining too much — it could have been so much worse.

After dinner we often managed to tune in to the Free French service of the BBC.

On that particular evening we did not listen. We were gazing at the moon, just rising over the hills, pale and silvery, round as a plate. The birds had gone to sleep. So had the cows and sheep. It was perfectly still and quiet, except for the chirping of the crickets. At this moment Martin's friend Hans burst into the room.

'We've just heard, they said on the radio, they're coming, the Germans are coming, we've got to leave at once. Quick, get ready, I don't know where they got it from, but it's true. I

61

don't. . . . don't. . . .' He became incoherent, mumbling and stumbling over his words. We understood that there had been an announcement that all Jewish foreigners were to be deported from the still unoccupied zone. Although soldiers were swarming about everywhere, the zone had not been officially declared occupied. Stunned silence for a minute. We did not doubt the truth of the message. After a moment we packed our bags, throwing in anything that came to hand.

One hour later there was not a single refugee left in the village. We dispersed in all directions with remarkable speed. On foot, by bus, by railway from the nearest town. Thank God it was dark. But no thanks to God at all that He made us run like rabbits. We made our way to Toulouse where Martin had friends. They took us in, fed us and found us a place to sleep — there weren't many such people about. I was just about to thank God again for finding us a place of refuge, but stopped myself from that humble gesture.

He really did not look after us that well, all things considered. Maybe He had forgotten about His people. His people! The ferocious irony was driven home to me forcefully. Or maybe so many claimed His services at this time that he could not attend to them all. Don't blaspheme, I told myself, there's always a way out. If you don't want to die in a camp you just keep out of the way long enough and far enough.

Suddenly there was good news. The American Consul in Marseilles would issue visas for German refugees, visas for the promised land, which was at this particular time the United States of America.

Ah — you see! There's help, there's goodwill and humanity. True friendship for those in need. Be ashamed of your blasphemy.

New York! That was a long way off and far enough from the turmoil. Except that we never made it. We had crept out of Toulouse and reached Marseilles only to find that the consul, in his wisdom, had decided that we needed a recommendation, a certificate of good conduct, from our home town: Berlin, the Capital of Nazi Germany.

It could not possibly be true. But it was. There must have been a misunderstanding — it was unthinkable. My mind was reeling. I mean, the man must have been in the picture, for God's sake! The Nazis searching through their files and delivering good behaviour certificates to Marseilles? So that we could get out of their clutches? Can you believe it? This

62

man, this woman, has never stolen anything, not set fire to the town hall, not attacked a policeman, is of good sound character, always helped old ladies across the road. . . .

'But this rule is applied equally to everyone,' we were told politely at the Consulate. There's the rub, you see. We are not everyone; I wish we were. I wish I were blandly and uniformly everyone. Untroubled, smooth and sober — everyone. In a catastrophic situation it's the worst possible mistake to be someone.

Whereas we had been outcasts up to then, we now became outlaws. We could not go back to the village until we knew that the Germans had swept through it. We were definitely not supposed to run around in Marseilles without permission. We were supposed to sit still, waiting for fate to overtake us, like the Pompeians.

Nevertheless we decided to stay in the city by hook or by crook. Crook was the word. Honest people, who would not have picked up a penny in the street, changed into expert forgers almost overnight. There were police raids every day. They were not particularly looking for us, but for everybody who stayed in the city unlawfully — agents, criminals, fugitives of any kind. The right kind of identity paper was essential and so naturally a flourishing trade in this commodity sprang up. Official documents were filled in by unauthorized people, faked papers were filled in by officials (sometimes because they were against the Germans; sometimes *for* a lot of money), or, most preposterous of all, documents were filled in by ourselves with beautifully looped French handwriting.

Those papers changed hands a dozen times, were bought and resold with profit. There were new names, new birthdates, new professions, new religions of course: a veritable stock exchange of personalia. The new papers were casually tucked into books or newspapers just in case you lacked the courage to use them at the crucial moment, for you had to throw your real papers away first. Two sets would have been most suspicious in a raid!

The edges of reality became somewhat blurred. You might be born in Vienna, in Bucharest, or even be a native of Alsace Lorraine, to explain away your foreign accent. You were Roman Catholic, Greek Orthodox, Moslem, Protestant, Buddhist. But never Jewish. The fanciful new particulars had to be learnt by heart as if you were an amnesiac.

I was drifting through the narrow streets by the old harbour with my false papers under my arm. What a stink! But what an atmosphere, what tremendously voluminous girls sprawling on the streets and out of windows, leaning over the sills to advertise their ware. Cats gorging themselves on fish, sailors gorging themselves on women. The colours, the cries and the movements, the deep blue sky and hot sun, hundreds of boats swaying on the water. It all looked incredibly good. And here was I creeping about with those false papers, undecided whether to use them in an emergency or own up to my status.

Make up your mind, girl; decide who you want to be! Finally I hid the real papers in my shoes and put the new ones in my handbag.

'Hey, skinny, where are you off to?' A sailor touched my shoulder, a nice fairhaired boy with a faraway sea-look in his eyes.

'If I knew that,' I said softly. My pale, wintry smile wasn't very alluring, I think.

'You were dragging your feet,' the sailor said perceptively. Heavens, yes. I was dragging them. I really heard the chains clanking. My whole body felt sluggish, and I was limping along like an old, old woman, grey and leaden inside, partly from hunger, partly from hopelesness.

I carried on my way, shuffling through the narrow streets, which were bursting with life, as if I was in a funeral procession. The sailor was swallowed up in one of the dark doorways. I plodded on towards the harbour.

Something soft and furry was rubbing against my leg. A black alley cat. Skinny little thing. It kept following me, mewing softly. I could see its ribs under the black fur. Green eyes, nicely turned up at the edges.

'I can't give you anything,' I said to the cat. 'I haven't anything to give. Don't the big cats let you get at the fish? You know, I don't eat all that much either. In fact I haven't had anything since yesterday. Do you hear me? I'm hungry. At least you can stay here as long as you like. Much better off than I am. I can't even do that. Now go away — why do you follow me around like that, cat?'

The cat clung to me like a shadow. It must have liked my plaintive voice, full of self pity and hopelessness. I crouched down on the pavement, picked up the cat and carried it with me, I don't know why. It nestled in my arms, mewed gently and put its head on my hand. That did something to me, that warm living touch, those green insolent eyes looking into mine. What are you trying to tell me? Are you saying that you are doing better than I? That I give up too easily? That I'm a dead loss? What's your world like? Worse than mine? You must be joking.

The cat's eyes sparkled, her head rubbing against my skin: you're young, healthy, you've got a man, you are still free. It didn't exactly say use your loaf, sister, but the cattish equivalent. Slink away, it said, fly away, run away, go into the deepest cellar, climb the highest — My dear, sweet God, yes! Yes! The highest mountain. The snowy peak near the village loomed up in my mind. *That's* what I must do. Climb up and up and out — out of this trap. As they say: the hand most willing to help is at the end of your own arm. Very dramatic, but true.

I met Martin by the harbour. We sat down amongst the sailors in a little bar and plotted our escape there and then.

*   *   *

When the immediate danger had passed, we and most of the other refugees returned to the village. The German army had not yet occupied it. But we were advised by well informed people (Frenchmen and other refugees) to leave again pretty soon. This time there would be no return. We would have to go up the mountains and down in to Spain on the other side. But you couldn't wander around in those wild regions without a guide.

Monsieur Lafranche said he knew the very person. He was reliable, experienced and brave. Not expensive. He could vouch for him, as he had got countless people across. (Amazing what went on right under your very eyes.) The man would get us across too, Monsieur Lafranche would see to it. I silently apologized for all the unflattering adjectives I had used against the French population.

Martin approached the man and they came to an agreement on the day, the manner of payment and the starting point. I implored Anja and her husband Joseph to go with us.

'Where to? Into a Spanish jail?' Joseph asked. 'You must be mad. I know for a fact that people without visas are clapped into prison right away. Or did you intend to approach the Spanish Government? You can't be serious.'

'But I am — entirely.' As proof I showed him Martin's rucksack and mine, half packed already. I am proud to relate that even the immediate danger to my life did not prevent me wrapping my make-up in a waterproof bag.

'You'll never make it. It's winter now and there will be snow on those mountains. How will you find your way downhill, once the guide has left you at the frontier? You'll freeze to death! No, thank you!' Joseph could not be convinced.

I felt desperate, gripped Anja's shoulders and shook her. 'You've *got* to go! It's suicide to stay. You have no choice, can't you grasp that fact? Rather go to a Spanish jail than to a German camp!' I shuddered. 'People do get out of jail — but the camps. . . .' I looked at Anja's closed, hostile face and started shouting, tears streaming down my face. 'You'll die, Anja, you'll all die — every one of you. Don't you *want* to see? You know they'll get you, you know what will happen. Anything's better than being caught like a rat in a trap. You cannot just sit here and wait.'

Anja turned away from me, Joseph shrugged his shoulders. They did not even change their mind when they saw German troops marching through the village. Only a small group of advance troops, but it was enough for me. God in heaven! Those boots, banners and insignias. Dread.

Our guide confirmed that he had taken many people across. Hundreds, he said. This was his private contribution to the war effort.

Anja tried again to stop us leaving: 'The man does not look honest. Those shifty eyes. You will end up dead in a ditch while he makes off with the money. Who's going to find out? He'll say that he got you safely across the frontier. Who would check up and how? And who is going to care anyway? The French police? I've heard such terrible things. Don't, don't do it!'

It occurred to me that crossing the mountains was like survival after death: you'd only *know* if you got to 'the other side'.

But it certainly was the lesser evil. There was *hope* — that was all that mattered. It would be foolish to deny that it was a tremendous risk. But, as ordinary patterns of behaviour had broken down, I thought that perhaps unorthodox means could be reassuring.

I got hold of the guide in the bistro downstairs and ordered two large cognacs. That's how they did it in films.

'Monsieur Orlac,' I said, feeling like a seasoned spy catcher, 'have you taken many people across the mountains?'

'Yes, miss,' he said, lifting his small brown eyes from the drink, 'and I'll take you and anybody else who wants to go too.'

'Is it a long walk?'

'It is that — but you'll make it. Everybody has.' Ah, that's what he *says*, but did they? Or were they left lying in a ravine? I had to make sure, to nail him down somehow.

I ordered more drinks, feeling very crafty, very much in command. The more I drank, the better I felt. He couldn't fool *me*. I looked him straight in the eye: 'Monsieur — are you a crook? You won't leave us lying in a ravine, will you? Are you an honest man? Can you swear by Almighty God you'll get us safely across?' It was utterly preposterous. But it worked. The man had been softened up by the drinks for otherwise he would have punched me on the nose, he looked that outraged.

'I only kill Boches,' he said thickly. 'I would not harm *you*, I want to help!' He looked hurt. He banged on the table and this time he ordered the drinks himself.

'I'm a decent chap,' he said mumbling into his glass, 'I help good people, people who run away from the Boches. You can trust me, I give you my word — my solemn word.' Then the mist cleared for a moment and he said distinctly: '*Je ne triche pas*'. I don't play tricks. God is my witness. I believed him. He looked so sincere, so utterly honest, with just the right mixture of confusion and hurt, that he would have to be an actor of staggering talent if he was pretending now.

We settled everything, shaking hands over the empty glasses to seal the bargain. He would take three people across the mountains. The third was Benjamin, the friend from Paris days.

A few days after I had first arrived in the village, Benjamin had emerged from the local bus which arrived every lunchtime in the village square. I could hardly believe my eyes. He had come to stay — like us. My mood soared immediately. Benjamin would not be here, if he had thought it unsuitable. He was commonsense personified, tremendously intuitive and intelligent. What a comfort! In the end he had been the only one who could be persuaded to join Martin and myself in the escape. We could not have wished for a better companion — civilized, composed and courageous. Nobody else joined us, a thing I could not understand then and can't now. Perhaps most people live on the 'it can't happen to me' track. I always felt it will happen and certainly to me.

When I'm in trouble I pray; it's a childhood reflex. Most beneficial. When I'm happy I also pray to keep things moving. It *has* occurred to me that there might be nobody at the receiving end. I dismiss that. Somebody's *got* to listen. I never stop asking, demanding and bargaining as if in an oriental bazaar. I'll do this, but please give me that. Or, more urgently, I'll give this up but let me keep the other. I frequently threw my life into the balance: if you let me see Sebastian again, I'll die on the spot. Most of my demands were refused. I went on regardless, listening for an answer, waiting for a sign. None ever came.

I also threw my dice (taken from a Christmas cracker back in Paris). A double number meant yes. Another combination: try again. Another: also meant yes, but I was at liberty to do the opposite. Cunning. I had forged my own private line to fate.

On this occasion the dice gave me a clear yes. Trust the man and set out in the morning. Urgent. We heard years later that the Nazis occupied the village shortly after our departure.

*　　*　　*

Would we have cancelled the arrangement if we would have known what was involved, what kind of effort was in store? As it was, we just imagined a long tiring climb. There is a helpful mechanism which transforms great physical danger into great mental adventure. It was certainly at work then.

Without any interference from the local police the three of us got on a bus. I happened to be sitting next to the Mayor, who was travelling to the next village. He was a fierce looking man with shrewd dark eyes. He glanced at our bulging rucksacks and sleeping bags, saying evenly: 'You know that you are not allowed out of the village. Last time when you all disappeared I turned a blind eye. Now, I suppose, as it's getting near Christmas, you want to do some shopping. That will be all right as long as you are back by tonight. Let's say I haven't seen you.'

'Yes,' we said, 'just a bit of shopping. We'll be back without fail.' When he left the bus, he murmured under his breath 'Good luck' and was gone. A friend — a good omen.

The bus started winding its way up the hills on that sunny winter morning. We felt and behaved as if we were playing truant. It's a good way of dealing with a situation of stress. We did not say to ourselves: we have started running. Rather: I wonder what it will be like. We were relaxed and cheerful; therefore nobody suspected us. Lawbreakers don't smile — usually.

Big milk churns rattled at the back of the bus. By and by the farmers left, nodding to us. We were soon the only passengers.

The guide said: 'We'll have a good night's rest in the next village. After that. . . .' He coughed in embarrassment. 'A girl should not really be made to. . . .' He did not finish his sentence and I dismissed any grim interpretation at once.

Our identity papers were stowed away in a tin filled up with baked beans. It seemed a very original hiding place. We had it all planned: if we were stopped at the frontier we would say that we were Canadians on our way home. If we managed to get to Madrid we would present ourselves to the British Consulate, the men offering to join the Allied forces. The more we thought about it, the funnier it seemed.

'Imagine!' Martin exclaimed almost choking with mirth, 'Imagine the Consul asking for our papers and us groping among the baked beans! Just a moment, sir, they're right at the bottom. We had to hide them of course, oh, here they are, a bit soggy, but quite all right, the genuine product.' It does not seem all that hilarious now, but then we giggled ourselves to sleep.

The guide had received half his fee in advance and would get the remainder at the frontier. He did not say much during the first part of the climb. We were still in the foothills. It was pleasant walking among the evergreen shrubs and plants along a small river. It was not very cold. If only the rucksacks were lighter. They contained drinks, sandwiches, books, clothes; and in mine, the waterproof bag with my make-up and a pair of high-heeled shoes which I would not have left behind for the world.

Odd things were happening in my mind: part of a continuous process which only became apparent during the climb. It had started much earlier, of course; perhaps on that fatal day by the lake when I saw Sebastian for the last time. My thoughts before that had been flat, superficial, easily brushed off. My thinking itself was shallow, skin deep. If more substantial thoughts intruded, they evaporated immediately; I was not able to 'handle' them.

The very words I had used — to others and within my own mind — had been frivolous, glib, almost impersonal. Then events began to give me a hammering. I was not crushed, though — quite the opposite. It was as if a box, which acted as a receiving station, was prised open more and more; previously it had only accepted feeble signals, but now in the mountains it began to work almost at full strength. My body gave all it had to give; my mind unfolded; my thoughts became deeper, rounder, as it were, filled with new meaning, more away, more conscious, more probing. I can say without embarrassment that I felt myself live.

If the men had similar experiences it was not apparent. They were fully occupied negotiating the slopes which became steeper, more and more difficult to climb. Martin wore two suits one on top of the other, as he thought it would get very cold higher up. He looked like a teddy bear trundling along in front of me. Benjamin was behind me. We walked in a single file, the guide out in front. He turned round now and then to make sure that we were following.

We stopped after three hours' steady walking to sit down by the river. We had sandwiches, lemonade, some chocolate but no coffee. Each thought the other would take a thermos.

The guide got up without saying a word, removed two large stones from under a tree and brought out two earthenware flasks. They contained black coffee, sweet, strong and piping hot.

'I have a brother living nearby,' he said. I imagined his brother, a sort of leprechaun, creeping out at dawn to hide the two flasks. The coffee was like a shot in the arm.

'Will it be very long?' I asked.

'Yes.' He did not add anything more.

After a while he said, 'We'd better get a move on. The Germans are patrolling a stretch of the road we have to cross.'

'Oh,' I said, having forgotten the immediate danger in the effort of climbing, 'what will we do if we meet them?'

The guide put a hand into the pocket of his anorak and produced a gun. It lay flat on his palm. I looked at it as if it was a rattlesnake. There had been no guns figuring in *my* life.

'Did you ever use it?'

'I had to. Once or twice.'

I shivered. No more questions from me. I was afraid of the answers.

We walked in silence for some time, keeping up a steady pace, and crossed the dangerous road in perfect safety. The beat of our steps made us feel easier, the imminent feeling of threat passed.

'Where is the frontier?' Martin asked some hours later. 'We oughtn't to be very far.' The guide pointed straight ahead. There it stood, a towering wall of red solid rock, gigantic, its top lost in the clouds.

'Not over *that*?' I groaned.

He nodded without speaking. He wanted to conserve all his energy for the climb.

I thought dumbly that anything but a mountain goat would collapse half way up. As we came nearer to the rock we could distinguish ridges, steps, even a small path. Another four hours climbing. We sat down on the ground once more.

'Let me see that gun again,' I asked. 'I'd like to hold it.' He gave it to me. It was steely grey, heavy, well oiled and well worn. I closed my hand over it expecting it to be cold. But it was warm as it had been kept close to the man's body.

'We shall eat now, before the real climb, you need proper nourishment.'

'But we've eaten all we had,' Benjamin was upset. 'We did not know how long it would take, we thought....' His voice trailed off. He wearily sat down on a tree trunk. The guide pushed away some leaves and loose earth and produced another container: hot soup with meat and potatoes. We began to think that he belonged to a different species altogether. Or perhaps another brother lived nearby. Unlikely though — we were high up now and could see around for miles. No human habitation in sight.

We looked back over the ground already covered, then again at the mountain looming in front of us. We certainly could not turn back. So we had to go forward. The real climb was just beginning. The idea that I or the boys would

71

not be able to make it never crossed my mind.

As we climbed slowly and painfully higher and higher the air became thinner. I felt lightheaded, almost dreamy. I saw myself, my little sisters and my parents climbing up a mountain in Bavaria. We had done that many times when I was small, going up to the high mountains in the holidays, wearing hobnailed boots and carrying rucksacks just like the one I was carrying now, only not so heavy. We used to find Edelweiss and Gentian. I felt the soft furry leaves of the Edelweiss, saw the deep blue of the Gentian. . . . my family, so very far away, a world out of reach. Maybe we'll find the flowers here too. Why not? I'll pick them and keep them and later on I'll press them between the pages of a book. To remind me.

Articulate thought stopped more or less then. I felt the hard granite under my feet, I was aware of the weight on my back and the leather straps cutting into my shoulders. The effort of climbing became so great, so charged with concentration and willpower, so much above and beyond the ordinary range of feelings, that there did not seem much room for thinking. I saw Martin's rucksack bouncing up and down in front of me and heard Benjamin's heavy shuffling steps behind me.

I was so bound and conditioned by the effort that I would not have welcomed an interruption, not even an end to it. The hidden clips of my willpower held me in an iron grip and commanded me to go on as long as necessary.

I frowned with annoyance as I heard Benjamin gasp behind me: 'I've got to stop — I can't breathe.' I turned round and saw him clutching his throat as he flopped to the ground.

'It's the height.' His voice was rasping. 'I can't stand thin air.' We all sat down. There was little pity in our hearts.

'Five minutes,' the guide said to Martin and me in a low voice. 'We can be seen from below at this spot, we can rest later on.' Then, more urgently: 'He's *got* to get up, you must make him.' I looked at Benjamin's grey exhausted face. Did I look like that too? How could we make him go on if he found it hard to breathe?

'Do you want to leave him?' the guide asked.

'Leave him — what do you mean?'

'We could leave him here for a while. When he's got his strength back he'll catch up with us. We must reach the frontier before dark. There is no path on the last bit. If we don't press on now we'll never make it.'

'Julia?' Martin put his hand under my chin, tilting up my face. He really had no need to ask whether I would want to follow the guide's practical but monstrous suggestion.

'Of course not, it's out of the question. Let's think — he's got to make an effort. I'll *force* him!' I felt no compassion just an immense rage. An obstacle at the decisive moment. I would not let him be in the way, I'd *make* him walk. But I'd stick a gun in his ribs before I would leave him here, lying helpless on the ground. I drew my breath in: there *was* a gun.

'Jacques,' I whispered to the guide, 'let me have your gun. Just put the catch on, I'm not used to it.' He handed it to me without a word. I put it down next to my rucksack and got out my brandy flask, pouring a few drops of morphine into it. I shook the mixture like a cocktail and approached Benjamin. He was lying slumped on the rocks and had turned his face to the ground so that we should not witness the agony he was going through. I held the flask against his lips and hissed:

'Drink it — all of it, now!' He was so weak that he could hardly swallow. I made him drink it all.

'Better,' he murmured drowsily, 'much better.'

'Now get up,' I said close to his ear, 'get up at once!'

The two others looked on without interfering. Benjamin lay still. I picked up the gun and pointed it straight at him, trembling like a leaf. 'Look at me. Look *up*!'

'What's that you are holding?' he said thickly. I was surprised he could formulate a sentence after the weird mixture I had given him.

'Not nice,' he said, grinning. 'No nice girl would hold a thing like that. . . . it's dangerous. . . .'

'I'll save you even if I have to shoot,' I said grandly if not very logically.

'Never believed you, and never — shall,' he said smilingly, stretched out and went to sleep. I poked him with the gun, quite hard. There I stood, poised for the great dramatic moment and he was asleep. I would have so liked to say, 'Now walk or I'll shoot!'

'Water!' Martin shouted. 'We've got to get water!' That was easy. We were now at the source of the little brook which we had followed from the beginning. Jacques and

Martin went to fill the flasks. I looked at Benjamin's peaceful, relaxed face. He slept like a baby, not a care in the world. I cursed him, I shouted, I tore at his hair. No reaction. Then I emptied one of the flasks with ice cold water right over his head. He sat up.

'I slept,' he said in utter surprise, shaking the water out of his hair, 'I actually went to sleep.' He breathed deeply, looking at me. 'What did you put in that drink? I feel so much better — I think I'll be all right now.'

'If you don't get a move on,' Martin shouted in exasperation, 'we will never make it. It will be your fault, yours alone! I hold you responsible!' They were squabbling, wasting precious time. Jacques pocketed the gun and simply started climbing without glancing back. Everybody followed. This time Martin was walking at the back.

It had become bitterly cold. The sun started to sink. I felt a fleeting regret that I could not appreciate the unearthly beauty of the mountains lit up pink and golden under the rays of the setting sun. But there was not time.

The rucksack became so heavy that I thought I might abandon it altogether. Just when I pleaded silently, no more, please no more, the guide retraced his steps and lifted the burden off my back.

'You are only a girl,' he said almost tenderly, putting the straps over his shoulders.

We climbed and climbed. The path had ended long ago. As soon as we had managed to get over one rocky face another appeared in front of us. There was no end to it. I wish now that I could have felt that each step on this monstrous staircase was a step towards freedom. I did not feel anything. I was no longer aware why we were climbing and I never gave a thought about what was going to happen once the climb was over. I put one foot in front of the other. That was all. Put your foot here, that's a safe spot, now the next step and the next. A bit higher, and higher, and up and up for an eternity.

Jacques stopped, pointing ahead to a giant wall: 'That will be the last.'

I do not know how we did it. It was not willpower that drove us up that last bit. We went on like a bullet that's been fired. It cannot stop in mid air. The three of us, involuntary hero each, had acquired a certain way of functioning under stress. There was no other way to behave. It would have been a greater effort to change our course of behaviour.

It was dusk when Jacques dropped my rucksack and sat down.

'We are there. This is the frontier.' He pointed to a heap of smooth black stones. 'You can't see the real frontier of course, but I know it's right here. You must each pick a stone like this from the mountain and add it to the pile. They all did. Everyone who came here with me. It brings luck — you'll need it.' The black oblong stones lay all around us on the mountainside. What a pathetic little monument. We each added our stone, thinking the symbolic gesture very adequate.

Benjamin looked much better despite the height. Martin was all right too. I wished for a moment that he'd ask me how I felt. He did not even look at me. No room for niceties. Yet I *was* a girl, the hardship was greater for me. As I became more relaxed I started to resent his unconcern.

Jacques pointed across to the Spanish side of the mountain. 'You will keep on walking straight down the slope. You must reach shelter before the sun sets altogether or you'll be lost.' He looked at the sky. 'You'd better hurry; it looks bad. It might start snowing and then where will you be. . . . you will see a little brook, very much like the one we were following on this side. Keep close to it and you will come upon a hut on the other side. First you must cross the bridge. It's an old barn, the door is open and there is plenty` of straw. You won't feel the cold once you are inside. There are a couple of old blankets and some food under the stairs. Hurry now — the sun's nearly gone!'

We gave him the rest of the money and shook hands. Then we said that we could not have wished for a better man and we would never forget him. He patted the men on the back, smiled at me, saying, 'Bet you feel sorry you couldn't use that gun,' and made ready to go. We promised to look him up in the village when the war was over. He waved, turned back towards France and melted quickly away in the dusk. We were on our own.

We started to descend on the Spanish side. It wasn't half as bad as the French one — quite a gentle slope, easy to walk on. We pretended not to notice that it had begun to snow and that it was almost completely dark. We were striding out quickly, singing and whistling, partly from sheer relief that we had made it, partly to cover a growing uneasiness

75

because we could not see the brook. Martin produced a torch, lighting up a narrow circle around us. The country had nearly flattened out, but still no brook. Panic was just about kept at bay, for we had to go on walking. We finally found the stream, but not the bridge. Did the guide say upstream or downstream? Was it a large bridge or just a few stones for stepping across the water? It seemed more reasonable to walk downstream away from the mountains. The snow was falling thick and fast as we followed the narrow bends of the river.

I kept pace with the men — outwardly. But now I began to crumble inside. We had been on our feet since yesterday morning at five o'clock. And it had not been a stroll either. If only I could lie down and sleep for five minutes.

'There's the barn, over there. Don't you see?' Martin shouted. 'It must be the barn!' It was not, it was a large boulder. Bulky shapes of huts and barns loomed up all over the place, dwindling as we came closer, vanishing like mirages in the desert.

We never found the bridge or the barn and carried on walking out of sheer desperation. After stumbling on for a few miles we slumped down by the brook, defeated. The torch was still on, but flickered constantly. I looked at Martin and Benjamin lying against their rucksacks, grim-faced, pale and helpless, ghostlike under the rising moon. The snow had stopped.

I gritted my teeth. We must not give up now after this superhuman effort. I felt really mad, offended by the passivity of my friends, deeply outraged. Ah! *Ça ne se passera pas comme ça!* They were men, supposed to run the affairs of this world, not to be beaten by a miserable bridge! I worked myself into a truly magnificent inner rage, summoning the original female spirit in a flood of tears and sobs.

'*Do* something, you fools! Anything! Do you want us to die of pneumonia? It'll start snowing again any minute now. You're useless, utterly useless! How absurd you look sitting there. Why don't you think? Think, you stupid apes!'

The situation was truly dangerous — impossible to deny that. I *still* had a great time: having got going, my accusations became more fantastic. It was all *their* fault, why didn't they listen properly to the guide, why did we have to cross that beastly mountain at all, the war was their fault too, women would not have started it in the first place. And if this was how they coped in an emergency, one could not be surprised at the general mess they had led the world into. . . . When I had hurled every word in the book at them I put my head on my arms and closed my eyes. I had done my bit.

A faint crackling sound made me open my eyes. A small fire was dancing at my feet, made from twigs and leaves. No pneumonia — saved. The snow began to melt round our little camp. I dried my tears and warmed my icy hands at the fire. We kept watch over it all night, nourishing it steadily. As there was nothing to eat we drank water from the brook. Back to the dawn of mankind: earth, fire, water. We slept a little, drank more water, slept again. What time could it be? We had forgotten to wind up our watches.

It should have been morning — the sun should rise. Maybe the laws of the Universe had changed and it was never going to rise again. I scanned the horizon for the first signs of the sun. Nothing. Martin slept deeply, curled up by the fire. Benjamin put my head on his lap.

'Go to sleep, Julia,' he said softly. 'You must sleep.'

'Will the sun ever rise?' I asked hazily.

'It will, it will. But first you must sleep, sleep. . . .'

His voice was far away. It did not seem cold any more. I could smell the smoke from the fire.

*　　*　　*

I woke up, the rays of the rising sun on my eyes. The two men were asleep; the fire had gone out. Three soldiers in grey uniform with black lacquered hats stood in front of us: Spanish guards on duty near the frontier. I blinked, trying to adjust my mind. The sleeping men were blissfully unaware of the soldiers. Didn't they sense in their sleep that we were no longer alone? What does one do in such a situation? Run away? Out of the question. How could we explain what we were doing here at the foot of the mountain in the middle of December? Camping? Lost our way? Had strayed over the frontier by mistake? A likely story. I shook Martin awake. He sat bold upright, said something preposterous in Spanish like 'Good Morning' and that he had a good sleep. The soldiers looked at each, murmuring 'loca' — he's round the bend.

Benjamin woke up too, staring at the three soldiers in confusion. Martin collected his wits, said he was glad somebody had turned up at all (all in quite good Spanish, picked up from a *book* in the village), and asked what was going to happen now. I tried to make out their conversation, still stunned by the soldiers' presence, but not really afraid. They were country lads, fresh faced, expressionless and completely ignorant of our situation or their part in it. They only knew that they had to take everybody crossing the frontier to the nearest town. And put them into prison. Unless of course we could pay our way, in which case we could sleep in a hotel. Those were their orders. A little money bought us freedom once more — at least for the moment.

Martin waved some notes about, grinned, and said how reasonable it all was and we would not give them any trouble at all. Both my friends looked like bandits with their stubbly beards, dirty, bits of sand and grass sticking to them, unkempt, unwashed and wholly romantic. They immediately became identified with every outlaw I'd ever watched on the screen, crafty, tough and getting the better of the police.

The six of us got going along the little stream. One soldier in front, two at the back. The sun was shining, the sky was blue, the air seemed milder than in France. Other little groups joined us: refugees with their own soldier guards. They had crossed the mountains at a different point. Soon we were about fifty people marching along the valley. Somebody started singing. It seemed quite natural. The whole scene was so unreal, so fantastic and picturesque, that fear had no place in it.

When life is at its strongest, its most powerful and stirring, it seems most remote from reality. I could never make that out, but it happened again and again. Perhaps we are so used to it dawdling along gently that when it picks up and swamps us we no longer recognise it. It's outsize, we say, it can't be true. Maybe we are asleep most of the time and only truly wake when things grip us by the scruff of the neck. Who knows.

After a few hours walking we arrived at the town. Some went to prison, others to hotels. Some refugees were offered money by the more fortunate but refused out of pride.

We slept like logs. Had breakfast and a shower. Then we were picked up by the soldiers again and put under guard on a train to the interior. We shared a compartment with men

78

prisoners with shaven heads and grey faces. They wore striped prison suits, white and grey. It struck me that the stripes were of the same colour as their skin. I offered one of them a cigarette. He asked me to light it for him as his hands were chained together. I tried hard to keep from trembling but I shook so much that I had to light three matches in succession. It's unlucky, I thought, they said so in the last war. The train started moving and I wondered whether they were going to chain us too.

Again it strikes me how hard it is to reproduce on the blank page the constant cold shiver, to convey the beginning of a deep dread, of an alarm so profound, a constant obscene shudder of fear and terror. *What* are they going to do to us?

The scene was going against the natural order, I felt. For the first time I was in the presence of something unspeakable. There — one cannot 'speak of it' properly. I can scream, cry, shout, freeze. But not just simply speak. One outwardly accepts of course, for there is nothing else to do. I could not tear the chains away from the prisoners' bodies. I could not protest aloud. But my mind, alternately frozen and feverish, underwent the most dramatic change. It was forcibly opened up. You see, you see, said the mind, it's happening all the time, not just in books, not just in newspapers, but now it's happening to you. You witness it. You thought you were immune, admit it, even two hours ago, before you boarded the train you thought: they'll never catch me, they don't *mean* me. And now it's changed. Now you know it's you they want. They wanted you all the time and now they've got you.

A long time ago Benjamin said that when you think you've reached rock bottom, it's only starting. The bottom is going to drop out and you keep falling. Something will hit you and you'll go on falling. I did not know then what he was talking about.

The train stopped, the prisoners got out, waving at us with their chained hands. My very blood thickened. I found it hard to breathe.

*　　*　　*

We too left the train a few stops later. We stood around on the station of a small town, apprehensive and shivering.

Suddenly the guards separated the men from the women and whipped them off the platform before we realized what was happening. The women were led through the streets where people avoided looking at us. They turned their faces away as if we had a contagious disease, or as if the mere sight of us might harm them in some way. Nobody spoke.

It felt like walking on quicksand, sinking deeper with every step but not daring to stop. In complete disbelief we went through an iron gate, up a staircase, through a thick wooden door, heard a key turn in the lock and collapsed on the stone floor of the town's municipal prison. For good, I felt. No amount of money would get us out of this.

'Inside' was everything the books said: cold, dirty, the food pure muck, the drinks rotten. And yet. And yet. It was not the end. After the first minutes of terror I knew it with absolute certainty. Maybe it was the reception the Spanish girls gave us. We were five refugee women, sitting on the floor, hardly daring to look around.

'Here are our visitors. Come on girls, let's see your faces. My goodness — just look at them — what's wrong with you? Don't you like it here? Choosey, eh? But we'll make you so comfy you won't ever want to leave. Heard of Spanish hospitality? Well, you're going to get a taste of it,' or words to that effect. A fat motherly looking woman opened a straw basket: homemade cakes and a bottle of wine. In a prison — wine? Did they not inspect the baskets? And where did they come from?

They were sent by the prisoners' families, who were expected to provide food, money, knitting wool, anything the girls might want. It kept the prison costs at their lowest. The fat woman was called Juanita and was a convicted murderess. Five times over. We thought the girls were joking or our Spanish wasn't up to much. But they were not joking. In fact, they were quite proud of that fat little monster who had killed her entire family, to get hold of an inheritance. Five people — just for money. You could not improve on that.

I kept looking at her face: maybe I could discern traces of her warped mind, hideous distortions of her features. But her skin was smooth with two charming dimples, her face round and cheerful like a doll's, completely untroubled. Fair hair wound twice round her head in thick plaits. The picture of homeliness. Just goes to show. Her family

80

probably adored her to the last breath. She was a calm, placid person — we never saw her bad tempered. How odd to leave her together with the minor offenders. Maybe she was a sort of showpiece for the remainder of her life, which would be spent precisely in the place where she was. She did a lot of knitting for the girls, especially for Lola.

Lola was a stunner. Paint a picture in your mind of the typical Spanish beauty: dark hair, flashing eyes, white teeth, marvellous curved body. That was Lola. She had pinched a coat from her workplace for an outing with her boy. She meant to put it back but forgot.

I asked her quite timidly where we were going to sleep. There were no mattresses for the newcomers.

'I know for a fact,' she said in a throaty voice, 'that you will have enough mattresses tonight.'

'Who told you?'

'One of the warders, the one who let you in. Five men are going to be shot in an hour. You'll get their mattresses. You are not going to faint, are you? They don't usually shoot women — unless they are "political" of course. You are not, are you?'

I said I was not sure. I had no papers, no entry visa, no passport.

'That's nothing,' Lola said. 'Did you do anything against the government — any of you?'

No, I said, we didn't. None of us.

'Well then, you'll be all right, you'll see.'

Later at night the heavy wooden door was opened and five mattresses were pushed through. I looked at them as if expecting to find the blood splattered corpses on top. But they were harmless enough. Quite clean and large. Lola had pointed out that the warders were good natured and would not let us sleep on the floor.

Lola was eighteen. She said she had difficulty in reading or writing, but her words were sophistication itself: 'Stop thinking,' she advised. 'It's never done anybody any good in here. Just sleep and forget.' I did. We all did — slept soundly and dreamlessly on those mattresses.

We picked up basic Spanish quickly. It's not difficult if you know French. Juanita said it was no use moping for the past — especially as there was not much of a future for somebody like herself. And there was so much to enjoy inside. She winked at Lola whose mattress and blankets she shared.

In fact, the two of them enjoyed themselves so loudly at night that Lisl, a thin, spinsterish refugee girl, was disgusted.

'Shut up you bitches, I want to sleep!' she shouted at them one night.

'With whom darling?' Juanitá called back, 'I'm booked for tonight. But there's Ines, all by herself, poor kid. Give her a good time, go on then. No need to worry, sweet — she can't make you a baby. . . .' Juanita and Lola were a regular couple. But most of the girls changed partners frequently, unable to settle down.

I marvelled at the speed with which our minds adjusted. Mine in particular. I was young, nothing hurt me, I wasn't sick a single day and, after all, I was safe here to a certain extent. The girls did not know of anybody having been sent back to France or being extradited to the Germans. And — perhaps most important of all — we only saw the warders at mealtimes and were never made to work.

Once I climbed on to the windowsill to look out into the courtyard. It was bleak, grey, surrounded by prison buildings with iron bars on the windows. The guards outside caught sight of my head and waved their guns about. I was down in a flash. At night they would patrol in the yard hour after hour, shouting *'Alerta Una, Alerta Dos, Alerta Tres'* every ten minutes to keep awake. Not a very enviable profession.

The only time we had contact with the prison personnel was in the morning at assembly. We had to sing a hymn to General Franco, the head of the state. At the end we shouted 'Franco' three times, gave the fascist salute and were led back to our large cell. Neither the hymn nor the salute made me feel particularly bad. It just showed me how empty any kind of gesture was, if you did not let it get at you.

One evening the Spanish girls put all the mattresses together and asked us to sit down on them. Lola said they were just in the mood and they wanted to entertain us. Guests must be treated nicely, and they just knew we would love it. They were better than professionals: they clapped, danced, sang, twirled, stamped, leapt about and finally bowed. Sheer magic. I swear I could see red flouncy skirts swirling, I could hear castanets and guitars, I could see the grey walls melting and feel the world welcoming us once more. We cried because it was so beautiful. Or perhaps we felt that if this could be done, here in this damp horrible place, all was not lost. Life would assert itself again.

Only Johanna, a young Austrian girl, was not caught up in this incredible scene. She objected strongly: 'You are stupid, you are pretending. I will have no part in this carnival.'

Ines, the lonely girl, came up to her, still flushed and excited from the dance and put her arms around her, trying to kiss her cheek.

'You filthy little slut!' Johanna cried out. 'Take your hands off me, do you hear! You dirty little whore — get away from me, I won't have any of that. Get away or I'll call the guards!'

We roared with laughter. What a fitting end to the performance.

The food baskets continued to arrive regularly. Most prisoners had families or friends providing generously: knitting wool, embroidery with silkthreads in all colours, cosmetics, soap, brushes and food of course. Never a book, sometimes pencils and paper for writing. Newspapers were not allowed.

The days passed. It became still colder. A small brazier was burning all day but did not seem to produce much warmth. I stopped looking into my little handmirror for I could no longer bear the sight of my face: grey, a little sunken and beginning to acquire that shut-away prison look. That was my true face, those were my true feelings showing on it. I was not aware of despair on the surface. But it was all working away underneath and the skin, the barometer of the mind, signalled that I was close to hopelessness.

Then one day, one amazing day, Lola found a note in her basket addressed to me.

'Julia darling,' it said, 'the news is good, very good. All will be well. We shall meet soon. I love you. Martin.' Like a bombshell. I could not believe my eyes — how on earth did that note get into Lola's basket? Martin had slipped his watch to one of the warders and he had arranged it. I believed the message instantly. I just knew it was true or Martin would not have sent it.

'The least you could do,' said Lola, 'is to let us all share in your little love letter. After all it's come in my basket. Go on, tell us all —' I read it aloud still numb with amazement.

'Is he a good lover? Too quick? Too slow? Just what does

83

he do? How many had you had? Or is he the first one?'

I bowed my head as Sebastian's image floated up. It tore at me for a brief moment, then ducked away again. No, I said, he was not the first one and looked right into Lola's dark eyes. I didn't have to spell it out — she shut up immediately and briefly stroked my hair.

A few days later one of the warders entered the cell at noon.

'The five foreign girls will leave in an hour. Get ready. That's all.' An invisible wall rose immediately between us and the Spanish girls. We kissed, embraced, promised to send money once we were in Madrid. Still more money when we were united with our families. We would never forget any of them, nor the food they shared with us or the songs they sang.

'They all say that,' said Juanita, 'but no one ever does anything.'

I will, I promised myself, I will. Here is the place to say that I did not keep my promise. Nor did the others. But that's no excuse. Was it just selfishness? Fear of being associated with the girls in prison? Desire to forget as fast as possible? Meanness? Or that I had hardly any money at my disposal? All of that — *all* of that. My fine soul was at its shabbiest, its most disreputable. I feel abject shame thinking about it now. Why, oh why did I not send at least a token? Too much trouble to go to the *Correos* and post a letter with a few pesetas? How mean can you get. I despise the word 'sin' usually — it's pretty meaningless. But I will use it now if I use it at all. I committed the sin of negligence, of avarice, of ungenerosity. And I don't feel any better for saying so. I often wonder whether they have forgiven me —.

The guards let us out and we thought we were truly free. Johanna, Lisl and myself went into the nearest eating place and stuffed ourselves for an hour with every food available. We had lived on scraps for so long. We then went straight to the men's prison as we'd been told that they could have visitors at certain hours. Johanna and Lisl said at the prison gate that they were Canadians. They could easily be: tall, solidly built, blue eyed and blond haired. One of them was Jewish, the other was not and kept very quiet about the reasons which made her scale the mountains in mid-winter.

The prison governor asked what my nationality was.

'English,' I said. He laughed and said I was the smallest

Englishwoman he'd ever seen and was I sure. I looked offended, said I would not lie to a kind man like him and he could ask my Consul if he had any doubts. I just lost my papers in the snow. I got a pass like the others entitling me to twenty minutes conversation with Martin and Benjamin.

We entered a large room with two rows of wire netting separating the prisoners from their visitors. There was a gap of ten feet between the wires. We started yelling at each other across the wires all at once. Martin looked pale and morose, Benjamin seemed all right. What can you say at the top of your voice with thirty people screaming at each other — and in English at that. Not much beyond, how are you, I'm fine, and you'll be out in no time.

'I'll leave my address with the British Consul in Madrid,' I shouted. 'Look after yourselves!' Not a very appropriate remark under the circumstances.

A tall, fairhaired man stood next to my two friends. He had no visitors. He was older than most of the others and wore a crumpled grey tweed jacket, his shirt open at the neck. There was a dark blue signet ring on the third finger of his left hand and he was gripping the wire netting.

Whenever I thought later of Martin and Benjamin the tall fair man popped up in my mind's eye. He looked so composed and unruffled, an invisible circle of diffidence and privacy about him, creating his own mental climate despite the prison and the noise and the shouting. Were his eyes grey or blue? Light in any case. I could see him smiling, probably at my schoolbook English. I knew he understood us, I also knew that he looked at me with particular attention. Now why would that be? Maybe he liked girls with dirty hair, tattered clothes and a fanatical look in their eyes, as if holding on with their last ounce of strength to a big funfair dipper.

The guards who had let us into the men's prison insisted on coming with us to the station. We would find our own way easily, we said. It was only a small town. But they would not hear of it. It was their duty to see us safely into the train to Madrid.

They actually got into the train with us. I was bitterly disappointed. Would we be really free once we got off in Madrid? Or were they taking us somewhere else? Stony silence. The beautiful sunlit scenery looked sinister and menacing. I remembered the chained prisoners and felt cold. The most unpleasant possibilities crossed my mind. Another prison. A camp. A trial because we had entered the country illegally. A long sentence. We might be sent back to France or worse — to Germany. God — no!

The train arrived in Madrid at midnight. Once more we went through dark streets under guard, our steps echoing on the pavement. There was nobody about. The street lamps shone on our pale drawn faces. Two guards in front, two at the back, guns pointing. And we were only five women.

At last we went down a narrow staircase into a large, faintly-lit basement. We all sat down, except Lisl. She lay in a dead faint at the bottom of the stairs. She must have been the only one to see the inscription over the entrance of the building: Seguridad.

This means nothing more sinister than 'security'. But it had often been likened to a Gestapo headquarters. That's where the political prisoners were brought in. It had the most frightening reputation: nobody ever got out in one piece.

No daylight. A single electric bulb on the ceiling. The filth and the stink — people must have been sick all over the place. Women everywhere — on mattresses, on the floor, some leaning against the wall still as statues. No talking, no sound, nobody moved.

Why didn't they speak to each other? Why this deadly silence? Were they forbidden to communicate? With us, perhaps — but they could talk to each other.

I could bear the silence no longer, I thought I would go crazy if I did not speak. I turned to my neighbour, a Spanish girl, who had her arm round another woman.

'What is happening?' I whispered. 'Why doesn't anybody speak?' The girl looked at me for a while without answering. She shook her head silently, then pulled the blouse from her friend's back. I looked at it and fell into a pit. I shivered. My heart started to race. I could not breathe properly. My whole body refused to function.

I looked again at the girl's back and saw deep bloody streaks all over. I stared, not thinking any further. Not connecting. I refused to acknowledge that I had come face to face with what I feared and loathed most in the world. We had been running half across Europe because we knew it was happening elsewhere and it might happen to us. But now that I saw it in front of my eyes I failed to comprehend.

It took me some time to understand that the woman had not fallen, was not ill, was not hurt by accident. That thing, which I refuse to name, had been done to her deliberately and methodically, to her and many others in that place.

Her friend covered her up again and started stroking her head with soft slow movements, as if to obliterate the cruel marks on her body. I never saw her face.

Neither I nor any of the others who had come with me talked at all during the time we spent in the basement. There was an ever present monstrous dread. Words did not belong there. We got food once a day. At first I was too dazed to move, sitting in the same position for many hours. Later I stretched myself out on a mattress next to Lisl; I was writing furiously.

Why did I write down there? What made me suddenly grip a pencil? Maybe I needed to make a gesture of private assertion to show that I had some willpower left, that I was not completely crushed, that I would not submit.

I found the pages later, crumpled and almost illegible. I had written a story about a little house in the middle of a forest. A child's fairy-tale in a blue exercise book with lined paper.

*　　*　　*

After forty-eight hours underground a prison officer entered the basement and called us five girls. He led us out into the street without any further ado. A bus was waiting there which brought us to one of the finest hotels in Madrid. We got rooms with a shower and a telephone by the bed.

What had happened? Who accomplished that switch from deepest horror to ultimate comfort? Had they locked us up by mistake?

By then the war in North Africa had begun to go well for the Allies. Maybe the Spanish thought they had backed the wrong side. We all made extensive enquiries but never found out just why and by whom we were released.

All I remember is that I entered my hotel room in a daze, too confused to think clearly. I put my rucksack on the floor, washed my face and hands and started to comb my hair quite mechanically, looking into the mirror above the washstand. Not me, I thought, that's not my face. I looked anaesthetized, apathetic. Numb and soulless like a sleepwalker. Bloodless lips. I vaguely felt that I must not hide this face, that I should not cover it up or disguise it. Let everybody see.

I went slowly down into the dining room, expecting people to look like myself. I was shocked to see a crowd of about fifty or so eating, drinking, laughing and shouting. Smooth faces and clean dresses and shirts. I remained standing at the door and looked helplessly from one table to the other. What should I do? I stood still as if I had forgotten how to move properly. I still had that stricken feeling from the prison basement, as if my soul had been killed inside my body.

Maybe I had gone insane and was imagining the whole scene. Or I had become delirious with fever. Men and women were calling from one table to the other. Great bursts of laughter, I was shaking my head: why are they all so happy?

A woman came up to me and said softly:

'You've just arrived, haven't you? You've come out of. . . . that place. I can tell. Come and sit down. Have some wine. What's your name.?'

'Julia. I'm so hungry.'

There were tears in the woman's eyes. 'The bastards,' she said and gave me a glass of wine. She held it to my lips and made me drink. Red wine with a heavy sweet taste. I gulped it down in one go.

'Slowly,' said the woman, 'take it easy. Eat in between.' She put a plate with food in front of me. 'Eat — eat — you must.' I started eating, thawing out as if I'd been frozen over. I began to focus on my surroundings properly.

'Who are all those people and why are they so noisy?'

'It only seems noisy. They just make the most of it.'

'The most of what?'

'The most of their freedom. They've nearly all been in some dreadful place or other — they want to forget. How else can they go on?'

'I don't want to go on. It does not seem worth it.'

'You don't mean it, Julia, you would not be eating if you did. I see you're smiling! My name's Kate.'

'Kate? What else? Sorry, I shouldn't have asked.'

'Right. You shouldn't. Anyway, I've had so many different names I hardly recall my own. I'm English.'

'Me too. . . . Sorry. Of course not. I'm from Berlin.'

'Passport?'

I shook my head. 'Bad luck, kid. As you obviously can't turn to the German Consulate for help, you've got to find somewhere else. Usually everybody goes to their own consulate, if they are in trouble. That's part of their duty. Too bad. But not as grim as you think. Haven't you been wondering who's paying the bill here at the hotel? The Quakers are. They're quite marvellous. Have you any money at all?'

'No. It's all gone.' It only occurred to me now that I really had no money at all. Strange, how quickly one gets out of the habit of counting the pennies. The last time I handled money was in the hotel near the Spanish frontier. The meal outside the prison was paid by Johanna, who seemed to have unlimited funds.

I opened my little red purse to show Kate that I was speaking the truth. The purse was empty: and it did not upset me at all.

'Ask the Quakers,' Kate said. 'There's their man over there by the counter. 'Tell him who you are and he'll help. Just the truth — for a change.' Kate kept filling my glass. She asked me whether I was married, or was there a man around?

'Two friends,' I said. 'I wonder where they will be.'

'In Miranda de Ebro,' Kate said. 'That's where they send the men. It's a camp.'

'Oh my God.'

'It's quite bad — but they'll survive, you'll see.'

'I must know. . . .'

'Go to the British Consulate and find out. The British have assumed responsibility for most men in the camps. They know everything. They are looking after the men, I'm sure.'

I drank more wine. None of it is true, I thought, those ghostlike people with their hidden wounds behaving as if they hadn't a care in the world, talking and laughing. Like myself. 'They're drinking so much wine,' I said, indicating the merrymakers. 'Why don't they cut their throats?'

You don't see the ones who did,' Kate said next to me. 'No good cutting your throat. It won't help anybody. Don't give in. In the end you'll be the stronger.'

'Says the wine. *I* say so. . . . I say —' My head fell on to the table.

I woke up in my bed. Kate was sitting next to me. A good looking woman with hazel eyes, a red mouth and plenty of

89

dark hair curling round her ears. Forty-five or so.

'You put me to bed,' I said, stroking the cover. 'Like a mother. . . .'

She smiled. 'Not for long though. I'm leaving tomorrow.' A short wave of her hand cut off all further questions. 'Isn't this Mariella's room they've put you in?'

'I've no idea. I did not know there was somebody else. . . .'

'I think you'd better find out.'

'Does it matter? Who is Mariella?'

'She's a tart. By profession.'

'But here, at the hotel? I mean she can't just —'

'Oh yes. She can and she does. It's obviously needed. But I think she'll prefer to be on her own. Perhaps they can put you somewhere else, although it's pretty crowded at the moment. Right, I may see you tonight. I've got to pack now. You look all right — are you?'

'Yes. I believe I am.' I did not see Kate again. I've often wondered about her. A courier? A spy? Private trouble? And all those other people — had they crossed the mountains like us? When and why? How long had they been in Madrid? Did they have to leave France or did they do some kind of job — military? What had they come for? There was only a comparatively small percentage of Jewish men and women.

Most people spoke French. Some spoke Dutch or Polish. There were British and Americans, and one person from Luxembourg. Nobody spoke German. That was reserved for the uniformed Germans I saw everywhere in the town. As Spain was Germany's ally and they were working closely together it must have seemed quite natural to the Spaniards. It was not natural to me. I avoided looking at them too closely for fear of catching some unspeakable disease. Like leprosy.

After a few days of readjustment I began to wonder what to do next. Locate the men; find my own family. I visited the Red Cross and heard later that my family had left Germany shortly before the war. I already knew that from friends who had seen them off at the time. But were they in England or in America or even in China — some refugees had even gone there. One friend said they were in the States; another said Canada. I would find them sooner or later.

Every day I went to the British Consulate, hoping to hear from Martin and Benjamin. The days passed and I got nervous. The war went on and on. What was going to happen in Spain? The Quakers might not be there for long. At long last there was a letter in Benjamin's handwriting. He was well, Martin not quite so well: there was a pain in Martin's chest, but nothing the sun would not cure. Would I send my address and as much food as I could. Nothing about conditions in the camp. That was bad and could mean only one thing — their letters were censored. If things are good you don't need a censor.

I must send a food parcel right away. But where was the money to come from? I had barely enough for a stamp. I could not, as the German saying goes, 'cut it out of my ribs'. I told people that I needed money for a parcel to Miranda and they opened their wallets. Can you believe it? Pesetas galore. I bought sausages, fruit, cheese, that delicious Spanish marzipan, nuts and raisins. Martin and Benjamin would not go hungry.

I'd been given a room next to Mariella's with surprising speed. Maybe she was paying a percentage of her earnings to the hotel. One night there was such a noise next door that I banged furiously on the wall connecting our two rooms. In French, English and Spanish I said I couldn't sleep. My door flew open and a girl appeared in her slip, brown hair down to her shoulders. A marvellously corsetted figure, clean scrubbed face, high heeled slippers and a cloud of perfume.

'You are disturbing me!' she shouted furiously. 'You scare my customers — can't you be quiet?'

'I want to sleep. . . .'

'So do they — with me.' She suddenly giggled. 'Why don't you come and join the party?'

I blinked: 'Thanks — but I've got a man in the camp. It wouldn't be right.'

She looked at me closely. 'You are not — a virgin?'

'No — it's a long time. You must be Mariella?' I was curious and wanted to know more about her. 'Why do you carry on like that?'

'I don't carry on, I work.'

'But why — there must be easier ways.'

'Not for me. I earn a lot, you know.' She was proud of her earning power and had as many as ten men a night. I don't know how her body could have withstood the onslaught. She must have been an athlete in this particular field of human endeavour. Did she like it? No, she was completely frigid, she said cheerfully. But that was a great advantage in her line of business. She never got attached to anybody. No complications, no trouble. Her boyfriend did not mind. She was fond of him and had followed him across the mountains when he left; there had been some unpleasant business with the Germans. She would marry him soon and set up as a hairdresser. Anywhere in the world — she was not fussy. If only that war would end!

That was the one thought on everybody's mind. And especially on mine. I had begun to feel a bit peculiar in the mornings and went to see a doctor. 'Yes,' he said almost immediately. 'Three months, maybe four. Can't you remember?'

'No, I can't. I thought it might be the effort of climbing over the mountains, or the shock in the prison or different food in a new country.' It wasn't. It was a baby. 'I can't have it. My friend is — not available.'

The doctor said there was nothing he could do about it. I was a healthy girl — and anyway it was out of the question. Far too risky for him or anybody else. No use looking around. Get hold of your friend, the doctor advised. And marry him. I left his consulting room and flopped down in the nearest cafe.

I wrote to Martin and said jokingly that the food parcels would become less opulent as I needed to eat a lot just now. Then I told him. I posted it and felt a bit better. But not much.

The answer to my letter came from Benjamin. Martin was ill. Too ill to write? Then I remembered how he looked when we talked through the prison wire. Pale and morose. So very unlike the strong healthy boy he used to be. But I attributed that to the prison atmosphere and the bad food, never to illness.

It appeared that there had been a hunger strike in the camp, a nightmarish experience. Some people died. Some fell ill, like Martin. Some — as transpired later — were damaged for life. But they had to convince the Spanish authorities that they were unjustly held and should be released without delay. They achieved their aim — eventually. But it was too late for Martin. Benjamin's letters were carefully worded, but I got more and more panicky. Could Martin not just scribble his name under a letter, just give me a sign of some sort? He was weak, Benjamin wrote and he did not want to worry him unnecessarily. It was essential for me, I wrote back — I've got to know.

Another letter came a week later: 'Martin died peacefully this morning. "Tell Julia —" were his last words. I'm doing it now, although I can hardly see the paper for tears. I don't know what else to say. I shall be out soon and will contact you immediately. Please hold on till then — B.'

How can one hold on? I went to pieces and just sat on my bed and cried. Friends came to see me and left again, saying, we can't help if you don't respond. Mariella brought fruit and cheese. Lisl brought some wine. I did not touch anything. Neither could I stop crying.

Later I screamed at the empty walls that Martin was well out of it and he wasn't missing anything. However the world improved in the future didn't matter, for it took no notice of us now. I was alone in a foreign land, no money, no proper care, the baby due in a few months and nowhere to live. No hotel would take the two of us.

'I'll be a foreigner all my life,' I howled at the walls. 'An alien: do you know what that means? Foreign posters on the walls, the street signs wrong, I can't say what I mean; I grope around for the right words. I'm cut off from the source, I'm stifled, I can't relax on unfamiliar ground where I'm forced to function. Oh my God, help me, help me. . . .' Self pity swamped me. Rightly so. If no one pities me, I must do it for myself.

'Is there nobody to understand?' The tears were flowing once more. 'Somebody take care of me, please! My strength is running out. Where will I go? I want to sit down in a place where I'm at home. At *home*, where the colours are my colours, the shapes my shapes, where I know the trees, where people's music is my music and their words, oh their words are mine, the ones I always knew, the ones which come without effort, my place, my *place* where I belong, where everybody is *like* me, has grown up like me.' I stopped dead and thought savagely: where people *like me* are herded into camps and murdered. You mad stupid woman! You've got out! Every new day is a victory — despite the loss.

Your 'music' indeed. Nazi songs? Your shapes. The swastika? What are you crying for? German snow falling on a German Christmas tree? Berlin? Your picture books? Soon the bombs will drop and the whole bloody mess will be buried under a heap of rubble. Go down and eat. Feed the

93

baby.

I felt hungry and thirsty and the baby kicked me. I wished the food had been less oily.

*　　*　　*

I could not locate my family, but the Red Cross would keep on trying. As they had got out of Germany it would only be a matter of time. They would be found eventually. The more voluminous I got, the better I felt, physically and mentally. Marvellous what a woman's body can do in such a situation. Some solution would present itself, it had to.

When I'd been in Madrid for a couple of months, Mariella and two friends came to collect me one afternoon to go to a bullfight. Can't do that, I thought. Martin. . . . And the baby might not like it, all that shouting and the heat: it was spring by now and the sun was beating down on the Madrid pavement, making it steam like an oven. Bullfights are unethical, so much cruelty and blood. Rather start knitting. No — rather be foolish one last time and go to the bullfight. You know you want to see it — just one.

We sat on the cheap sunny side in the middle of a roaring crowd, drinking wine from a bottle. It was like being in the centre of a hurricane: the movement and the noise, the cries drowned by the blaring music, blood spilt on the sand, the dying horses and the madly excited crowd, black bulls charging ferociously, looking like giant porcupines with banderillas quivering madly in their hide.

I was sick afterwards but felt a lot easier. Maybe that is the purpose of the bullfights: a general purge of the mind and the emotions. A momentary abating of confusion present at all times, even if it's not voiced. Mariella guided me out of the surging crowd carefully. A mother by proxy.

Then one afternoon I literally bumped into Alan, the tall fair man I had seen next to my friends in the prison.

'I thought I was seeing things,' he said. I was as round as a barrel. We had drinks under the trees opposite the Prado.

'He doesn't look too bad,' I thought. 'Makes a nice change from all those black-haired, dark-eyed Spaniards.' I liked *his* eyes. They were blue and very bright, with a hint of goodness and calm. How does goodness look in someone's eyes? I know it when I see it. It was there then. No high voltage, no heart stopping arrows as shot out from Sebastian's eyes, no charging of batteries. But I felt happy, easy and at rest in Alan's company. I appreciated his typically English way of making simple statements, which prove to be far bigger traps than any questions.

'I expected you to look unhappy,' he said.

I had not yet acquired the invaluable knack of retorting 'did you?' or 'really?' therefore sending the ball back into your partner's field without having properly played yourself. I nodded and said: 'So did I.' I wondered whether he would go on being crafty or slip discreetly into safer waters.

He did neither but asked: 'When is the baby due?'

'In two months,' I said uneasily. 'I hope I'll be more comfortable by then. Somehow, more peaceful.'

Alan ordered some coffee and then made the fatal gesture, fatal in the true sense of the word, a gesture of fate. He ordered some cake from a passing waiter, who had the most marvellous concoctions on his tray. I was so grateful I could have cried. Insane of course, to fall for a man because he buys you a piece of cake. But it is plain to see what tipped the balance at that second: he looked *after* me, he spoiled me, he protected me. Why not the coffee or the drinks? Ordering those was an ordinary polite gesture. The cake was an emotional statement. That is a perfectly valid thing to say. The cake stood for all sorts of good things: safety, consolation, lost childhood pleasures, homeliness, protection.

That small piece of pastry touched me so deeply that I stammered: 'Thank you for that l-lovely cake. It's the best thing anybody ever. ...' A tear dropped on to a cream-covered strawberry. That tear got *him*, because he understood everything as if I had spelt it out. He felt the whole complex of my being. He *knew* why I was crying over my cake. If only I could stay with him, all would be well. On the other hand, looking as I did —

We met every day at the same place at his suggestion. He knew what he was doing. Same place, same hour, same table. Continuity. I learnt very little besides his name, Alan Percival, and the fact that he had escaped from a German prison camp. He had been captured after parachuting from his burning plane.

In civilian life he was an architect, lecturing occasionally at universities, but mostly designing houses. Very simple, he said, clean modern lines, uncluttered, lots of space and air.

What about me? I was only too glad to tell him — there was so much. But I kept Sebastian under lock and key once more. It was wiser and less painful.

Alan nodded, smiled at me and said to my surprise that he believed almost everything I said. Then, one afternoon, he asked out of the blue: 'Could you marry a man for his passport?'

'Definitely. But you might not like me when I'm back to normal, and. . . . and —'

He did not let me down and said promptly: 'What shall we call it?' We had a lovely time thinking of a name. I liked 'Juanita' but he thought that would be asking for trouble. 'Martine' he suggested tactfully. I dismissed that.

'Let's marry in London,' I said. 'It sounds so utterly out of reach and romantic. London.'

Alan said that would suit him fine, that's where his house was and where his family had a flat, although they usually lived in the South West. His family! They would be mine. We would have this big house and a garden with a thick hedge, a lilypond with a small curving bridge. The baby could be out in the open all day. And he would convert his attic into a nursery — he made a little drawing on the tablecloth, knocking a wall down here, building an extension there. He loved it all.

'You need a visa, of course. Did you think of that?'

I hadn't and he said he would apply for one immediately.

He rang me next evening from his hotel. He had to leave for England that very night. Official orders. They needed every single pilot.

I sat by the phone with his English address scribbled on a piece of paper, my hand clutching the receiver.

'If you have not joined me in a fortnight,' he said, 'I'll make a raid on Madrid. I am starting all the arrangements for your visa right now. You go and collect it tomorrow morning. Have you got that?' He sounded breathless.

'I've written it down,' I said flatly.

'Now don't be stupid!' He sounded cross.

'I know,' I said, 'there's a war on.'

'I swear by Almighty God,' that incredible man said over the phone, 'that we shall be married before your baby arrives.'

'I hope the Germans hear you, I hope their fighter pilots do.' I was crying shamelessly by now. 'I hope the whole bloody world gets blown to pieces!'

'That's my girl,' Alan laughed, 'so tenderhearted. I love you, darling. You'll make it, you won't leave me standing alone in the Church — eh — did you want to marry in a synagogue?'

'They won't have you, you heathen,' I said tenderly.

'Anywhere you choose.'

'Goodbye,' I said. I didn't move until Mariella came and rescued me. We went to the bar of the hotel and drank Manzanilla. It tastes lovely and knocks you out in no time at all.

'It's not good for the baby,' I heard Mariella's voice saying before I passed out. 'Stop it at once!'

My visa was ready for me the next morning. Mariella, Lisl and Benjamin saw me off at the Railway Station. I crossed the Spanish border at La Linea where I looked for the last time at General Franco's portrait. I entered Gibraltar as if it were the Garden of Eden.

*　　*　　*

They had the most beautiful gardens at Gibraltar, full of Bougainvillaea spilling down the hill, shrubs and flowers everywhere and a view right across the deep blue sea to rend your heart. A wide sweeping bay on one side, Spanish Morocco outlined in the hazy distance.

But the deep blue sea was full of mines and criss crossed with nets to catch any marauding submarines; nobody was allowed near the cliff which was fortified to the hilt. The place was crammed with soldiers. No women, except nurses, cleaning staff and, at night, the Spanish dancers from La Linea to entertain the forces.

I tried to get on a boat to England. They took one look at me and said they were sorry, but not after seven months. They understood my position; it was just too bad, but those were the regulations. After a week I ran out of cash and got a little frantic.

'Let me get on a plane then,' I pleaded a week later. 'I know they fly over almost every day.' I was politely told that the few seats available were reserved for high ranking officers. There was nothing they could do about it. I blew my top, sobbed and screamed that I held them responsible if something happened to the baby.

They asked me, still more politely, whether I had gone off

my nut. Yes, I said, suddenly calm, smiling through my tears, I had indeed. I could not pay for the fare even if they put me on board at once. I apologised, sighed and turned to go.

'Just a moment — have you any money at all?'

'No — not much.'

'You will go for your meals to the local hospital, it's just up the hill — till we find you a seat.'

'On a plane?'

'Yes. On a plane. You'll have to pay for your ticket when you have arrived safely. I understand your future husband is waiting.'

I should have sent a prayer to heaven and shut up. I could not. 'What about all those generals?'

'You could sit out on the wing — light as a bird.' The man grinned, said, take care, and slightly waved his hand either to say goodbye or to imitate the flight of a bird. What a lot of good people one meets.

Three days later I got a seat. They did not like babies being born in a fortified area like Gibraltar. At least not in nineteen-forty-three.

For the last time I was walking through the streets crowded with men in uniform. They greeted me cheerfully as I pushed my ungainly body past the shops and eased myself into a wicker armchair outside one of the many cafes in the main street. London, I thought, looking out into the shimmering heat — cool green hedges, Alan, the new family, the baby. Safety and a home. I can stop running. None of the soldiers at the neighbouring tables made jokes about my 'condition' or absence of a wedding ring. They only asked when the baby was due and looked a little wistful, a little sad. Their wives and sweethearts were out of reach and this sight of bulging life in their midst and within the formidable armoury of Gibraltar must have struck them as incongruous.

Suddenly all heads tilted back. A single German plane appeared over the town, silverslim in the brilliant blue sky. The air shook as a thousand guns went into action. The plane disappeared in a flash. The soldiers laughed and said that the pilot must have been mad.

Not at all, said an officer from the next table, he had come to take aerial photographs. We talked for a while.

'Joining your husband?'

'I'm going to London.'

'Which ship will you be on?'

'I'm flying. They wouldn't have me on a boat. It might be too slow — for me.'

He whistled. 'You got a seat on a plane?'

'Tomorrow morning, all being well.'

'*Some* string pulling! Your husband?' He looked at me attentively, chewing the ends of his brown moustache.

Why didn't I just nod and let it go at that? I disliked the probing look in his narrow blue eyes. 'I'm not married.' Aggressively continental, as I realised later. But why look for a fight? Still later I understood that I had to pick a fight — fights — until the moment the accumulated poison had disappeared. Watch any chemistry experiment at school and you will know what I mean.

'Ah,' the officer said, somewhat put out. 'I'm sorry.'

'What about?'

'Sorry that — I mean, sorry I asked.' He paused, then said, his head a little to one side: 'You are not English.'

I said that was very perceptive of him.

His intense curiosity showed in the way he abruptly turned his chair round to face me and leant forward. 'May I ask where you come from?'

'You may.' I grinned.

'Well?'

'Well what?' I ordered another coffee.

'Where *do* you come from?' I could say that I was French or Hungarian or Spanish, as my skin was deep brown from all that sunbathing in the gardens on the Rock. I could *not* say Germany and leave it at that. Such a wild statement would have to be qualified, especially here, explained, elucidated, drawing in its wake the entire story of my life. I could have said 'Kasze', 'Klimtsche' or 'Plitzovia', looking impenetrable and defying him to show his ignorance in geographical matters.

I know many things you don't, mate, I thought, feeling superior, and what's more I dislike you. But I'm not going to show it; I'm going to be womanly and clever. No good upsetting myself. I breathed calmly a couple of times, uttered a few 'tz, tz', drank some coffee and pronounced a little sadly: 'You know, people can't always say what they want to say.' A small, precise gesture cutting off any further enquiries: 'There is a war on.'

99

He drew himself up: 'Forgive me for asking. You are perfectly right.' He almost saluted when he left. Small triumph — but Madame Renault would have been proud of me.

* * *

I left early next morning as scheduled. Everybody on board that plane seemed to have a walrus moustache and an awful number of pips on their khaki uniforms. The plane was small, had a very noisy engine and boarded-up windows. Very disappointing — this was my first flight. I so wanted to watch the take-off and the soaring up into the sky. I extracted a little pocket mirror from my handbag and was about to insert it between the wood and the outside glass.

'Young lady,' said a deep voice next to me, 'it's all done without mirrors.'

I did not understand the pun, but the firm pressure on my arm reminded me with a shock that we were on top of Gibraltar's most secret fortifications and that I was not exactly the best person to watch them.

'Will the Germans fire at us?' I asked the red pips next to me.

'They might have a try', he said, sounding genuinely amused, as if he was playing some sort of game.

The flight passed without incident. . . .

As I slowly descended the steps from the plane, conscious of the fact that for the first time in years I was going to be on friendly territory, a woman in uniform met me without a smile or a helping hand. She asked my name, said I was expected and would I follow her. I want to ring my fiance, I said, and what was the quickest way to London. She said I could ring but not go to London just yet.

'Alan, I'm here, I have arrived just now, I'm in England!'

'Where — whereabouts, tell me! I'll come and collect you!' Alan's voice was dead right, happy, eager.

'I don't know. But I can find out.'

The woman grabbed the receiver and said: 'We will send your' — significant little pause — 'good lady off to London presently. There are some formalities first.'

I heard Alan's clipped voice at the other end: 'But I must see her now — she is in no condition — I'll come and get her.'

'No need to upset yourself, Sir,', the woman's lips curved

downward, her chin dropping. 'I'll put her on the train myself. We will advise you of her arrival.' She put the phone down quite roughly, propelled me into the building next to the airport without a word. She carried my rucksack and raincoat (a man's — one of the soldiers had given it to me for luck. 'It always rains in England.') It was a dazzling hot day. I was almost disappointed as I had been looking forward to grey skies and cool dripping leaves after all that heat.

The woman motioned me to a large room, opened the door and disappeared. Three men sat behind a table, two in uniform, one in a black suit. I was given a chair and a glass of water. I was puzzled about the function of these three persons and it was a long time before I grasped that they were interrogating me to find out whether I was the genuine article.

When it finally dawned on me I started giggling uncontrollably, drank some water too quickly, coughed madly and blurted out: 'You surely can't have thought that I was trying to 'infiltrate'.' I was very proud of my vocabulary.

There was the tiniest smile on the face of the man in black. 'Convince us,' he said.

I patted my tummy. 'In this condition? And I did say I'm from Berlin.' I shook my head. 'What more do you want to know?' I spread out my hands helplessly, palms upward. 'If you don't win that war, if *we* don't win it. . . .'

The questions came thick and fast for almost two hours. Where did I learn English? What school, what street? When did I leave Germany, where did my parents go and why did I not go with them? How did I manage to keep out of the camps after I had escaped from the first one? What happened in Toulouse? Whom did I know? Then all about our little village by the mountains. All about Martin, the camp in Miranda, his death, the hotel in Madrid, the people I knew there. Then Gibraltar? Who helped me? Then back to the crossing of the Pyrenees — when did we leave, where did we start, did we meet anybody, the name of the guide, his looks and behaviour, how much money did he get from us and where exactly did we cross over into Spain? What precisely did the Spanish guards say when they found us?

'Right,' said the man in black, 'what was the place called where you crossed the frontier?' I said I could not answer that as it had no proper name, but I could describe it — and find it — with my eyes closed.

'Do it then,' the man said urgently. 'We need to know.' *They* need to know? What for? I bit my left forefinger in utter surprise when in a flash I understood. I had presented them with a new escape route from enemy territory.

'We want every detail, every single one. Even if you think it's unimportant. Try to remember.

I leant against the back of the chair, closed my eyes and held my fingers to my head to help me concentrate. I was not interrupted once. No questions, no comments. I believe I forgot where and why I was talking. I relived the whole trip as intensely as the actual experience: the way we set off, the coffee flasks under the bushes, the fast little river we went along, Benjamin's collapse and the gun in my hand, the terraces of sheer rock looming up one after the other, the pathetic little heap of black stones at the frontier and the desperate search for somewhere to sleep at night.

'We did not find the hut, so I sat down and cried,' I said finally, sobbing now as I did then, tears running down my cheek.

'It's over,' one of the men said gently. 'You are among friends.'

I wept and wept and could not stop. 'It's the relief.' I took a deep breath. 'The sheer relief.'

The man in black picked up the phone and told Alan I would arrive that night in London. He smiled and said I had a helpful memory. Was it always that good? No, it wasn't — only for things that touched my emotions. They stuck forever.

PART TWO

Upper Deck

Riding in the train which bore me through the green countryside I wondered about my country, my new house and, of course, the man himself. Alan stood on the platform anxiously scanning the windows of the incoming train. In a blue uniform. I felt a little ashamed for I could not recall his face properly. I kissed him shyly and he said he hoped I would do better in future. Never known a man who put me at ease so swiftly.

'Don't get a shock,' he said, 'but my family is waiting for you at home. You'll find them quite acceptable.'

See what I mean. Tact personified.

His parents were just as tactful and civilized, plying me with food and drinks, saying they were one up on everybody else, receiving a German girl in wartime. We know everything, Mr. Percival declared, our son has briefed us, we know it all backwards.

Alan's father wore a beard, but otherwise looked just like his son with his fine long face and slightly curved nose. He came from a long line of architects, building everything from 'cowsheds to cathedrals'. He patted me on the back, smiled Alan's lovely warm smile and took to me — and I to him — in the first minute.

Alan's mother neither smiled at me nor did she pat me on the back. I could hear the icicles crackling the moment she set eyes on me. I was sure a cold front had been forming ever since she heard about me. *My* mother would have been more welcoming, I thought. Ah — I was touched to the quick.

Maybe the lady objected to my family background. Don't! I said to myself, all she would feel was pity. She would not and could not object to anything. What rubbish! But was it?

I have noticed a curious distortion in the human mind: when a group of people is persecuted *as* a group, the others feel so uneasy that they either turn away or think there must be a reason for it. They all do it, every one of them. Them? You just hitched your life to one of them.

'Always speak out, Julia,' our family doctor used to say, 'never swallow things up. They give you a bad complexion and ulcers.' So I always spoke up, kept the ulcers at bay and did not get any nasty lines running across my face.

Therefore, disregarding a rule I had just learned (don't be personal — it may offend people), I said, 'You must have been very alarmed when Alan told you about me.' The cold front was definitely drifting towards me, I could feel the draught, but persisted nevertheless: 'My nationality, my family, my religion, and Alan's first meeting me. . . . which was not exactly brought about by a formal introduction.' (I saw myself standing in the men's prison, yelling across the wire at Martin and Benjamin.) 'All that separates people belongs to the Dark Ages, wouldn't you agree?'

'There are certain natural barriers of upbringing and background.'

'Yes,' I said sorrowfully,' there are barriers, but they are man-made, wouldn't you say? And we, the informed part of the public, are and always have been the first to overcome them. The higher you go in the social scale, the more flexibility there is.'

Those superior remarks, coming from a woman half her age, must have grated nastily on Mrs Percival's nerves. 'You seem to have given it a lot of thought,' she said tartly.

'I so want us to understand each other.'

Mrs Percival's features relaxed noticeably. 'I think I have underestimated you. You've got. . . .'

'My head screwed on?'

'That too — but I meant that you see more than most young people.'

'I'm not so young,' I said bitterly. 'I've had no time to be young. I've gone through more in those years than most people do in a lifetime.'

'Granted,' Alan's mother said, 'and you won't let us forget it for a single minute.'

I laughed aloud and said she was marvellous.

A truce was declared. The Percivals soon went back to Cornwall and I started to make myself at home in the new house. I really settled down despite the turmoil in the outer world; I concentrated wholly on my physical state. Alan and I talked incessantly. One might have thought that the new language would inhibit me. Not a bit: I turned the words round with joy, gradually discovering their full meaning, playing with them, trying them out like a new exotic dish.

They say that you have as many lives as you have languages. French was added to my own language out of sheer necessity, so was basic Spanish. But English — I *wanted* to know it. I read greedily: books, papers, magazines, letters. I listened to every word on the radio, I went to plays and films obsessively. Like a deep sea diver I discovered amazing treasures under the surface. All those *words*, so many more than in my own language. They yielded an amazing crop of new meanings — I was constantly discovering expressions I never dreamt existed. I knew I would never get to the bottom of it and that was most likely what fascinated me.

I got a good crop of words from Alan's friends, mostly architects, marvellously articulate on just how they were going to tidy up the world after the war, and a few scientists whom he knew from his Cambridge days. The scientists were an amazing lot. All engaged on some war work only mentioned in whispers. They too were going to 'tidy up' later. But there was something else — they seemed to be on most intimate terms with 'mother' nature. Despite war, despite the inhuman suffering going on all around, they had a very private, very personal relationship with that nebulous mother. 'She knows what she's doing,' they said; or 'she's got a few tricks up her sleeve'; or, most perplexing, '*we* can ask the questions but we can't expect her to present us with answers on a platter — it's up to us to find the key'. Nobody mentioned a deity but their talk implied nevertheless some sort of plan, some ulterior pattern and immense beauty. It was most interesting — no, much more than that. I felt that they were dealing with essentials, that everything else was only 'overlaid', that here was a different reality from the one I knew.

I said as much to Melissa Sterling, one of the few women in Alan's circle. She was an actress. Well-known and continuously working. Her appearance must have helped. She looked like a glamorous fox, red hair and a pointed little nose, shrewd sparkling eyes, glossy from head to toe and a mind to match. It did not take us two minutes to size each other up: we were opposites in the emotional field.

'I envy those men, especially the scientists,' I said. 'They've found a track to the heart of the matter.'

'So will you, only yours lies in a different direction.'

'Where then? My education was cut somewhat short.'

'So you can concentrate on what you've got.'

'And what's that?'

'Your emotions. They can be used to enormous advantage.'

'What do you mean?'

She cupped her chin and pursed her lips, now looking like a thoughtful fox. 'You can use them like those men do their telescopes and their machines. They'll get you wherever you want to go. You heard what your scientists said — there's a key somewhere to open the door. There's always only one key, didn't you know?'

I didn't. Neither had I ever met a woman like her. What a formidable intelligence. And I wasn't aware that I'd been trying to open any particular door. I laughed out aloud: 'The doors I've been trying to open were made of solid wood!'

'I'd like to hear more about that,' she said.

'Gladly. But remember — you asked for it.'

After that we met regularly. It was a most wonderful addition to my life.

* * *

The baby was due any time now. I was walking up and down in the garden, standing on the tiny bridge, admiring the lilies in the pond. Suddenly I started to cry. There was no reason at all; nothing was *wrong*. I was still crying.

I remembered Cecile, a girl from Paris with a lovely soprano voice who also studied with Madame Renault. She led quite a hectic life and wished she could have found relief in tears now and then. But she was unable to make them flow and stocked up so much tension that she found it impossible to cope. Then she met a man who suggested a 'weekly cry' — guaranteed or her money back. She used to go to this man's house, sit and howl for an hour, paid her money — a considerable sum — and came out fresh as a morning breeze. She did a nightly stint in a cabaret in Montmartre and immediately put her 'tear money' by when she got paid. It worked to perfection.

I thought of all my friends in Paris, of Madame Renault, of Joc and Martin, and my tears flowed once more. I must have shed so many by now — enough to keep the Mississippi amply supplied. The balance had to be redressed somehow and tears seemed the best way to do it. All that running and cunning, that huffing and puffing — what fanatical energy had gone into it. What a pity I had not more to show for it. Just me and my baby. Maybe that *is* quite a lot.

I looked ugly. I saw my face mirrored in the pond — ugh! Swollen and bloated. I wondered what Sebastian would think of me now — don't, don't! Stop this at once. Have seven children and forget the past. Create new life all the time. A really fine idea as I was still looking round frantically for a baby's nurse, impossible to find of course because of the war. I gazed at my face once more. It was tanned, dark brown, quite smooth despite its puffed-out air. The hunted look of an alley cat was gone, so was the hysterical depth in the eyes. I looked quite smug. Maybe it was the cod liver oil which I swallowed by the mouthful; it made my skin so smooth. Look at the Eskimos — not a wrinkle among them. What was that? That pain. There it was again. Not yet, not yet, it couldn't be — but it was.

I yelled for my mother-in-law who had come down from Cornwall for the birth of the baby. 'Mrs Percival.' I was screaming in a trance. I heard my voice ringing in my ears, shouting madly, not being able to move. Then I no longer formed words and just yelled, feeling unbearable pressure. I lay, supine by the lilypond, roaring. The clouds were sailing by above my head and the leaves waved in the summer-breeze. Birds were singing and the bees went on humming. Cries and moans emerged from my body and the baby weighed a thousand tons. Steps were rapidly approaching as I passed out. . . .

'Wake up, darling, wake up!' Alan's face was hanging over me, smiling like an angel. 'You've got a son! How do you feel?' I patted my flat tummy, touched my matted hair, said 'fine' and tried to sit up, could not, tried again and fell back on the pillow.

'Does it hurt?'

'No.' Amazing, nothing hurt, everything back to normal.

A nurse came in, propped two pillows up at the back, made me sit up and put the baby in my arms. I put my head next to it, touched its hand; the tiny fingers immediately

109

closed round my thumb. I felt a shiver between my shoulder blades and was promptly swamped by a giant wave of mother love. I went under and said, baby, baby, holding the warm body against mine. The nurse nodded: everything according to plan. The bond was established, nature had asserted herself. The self-concerned heart had melted and was henceforth to direct its owner to jump out of bed during the night at frequent intervals, to develop ears finer than a police dog, to wonder whether the baby 'knew' how to wake up in the morning, to invent the silliest names for that unique creature and to feel 'fulfilled' although flat and empty now.

'We still haven't got a name,' said Alan.

'John,' I proposed looking into Alan's eyes, 'just John. It's so English. Alan — do your parents know? I mean did you tell them?'

'Not really. I did not want to disappoint them. I want them to think it's mine.'

'It's easier, you mean?' It upset me, although it should not really matter. 'Well, you've lied, my sweet. I wonder why?'

'Don't get excited,' the nurse intervened. 'The milk might dry up.'

'Milk?' I was quite overcome. The baby sucked like a devil. It hurt. But I swear this was all I wanted and I would not have changed places with any creature on earth. I was hooked.

*   *   *

Our house was outside London and not on the path of the flying bombs. I followed the battles with intense, personal interest, although the past receded, became blurred, did not bother me so much. For once everybody else had a stake in present events. I adapted my days to the baby's rhythm, kept house, worked in the garden.

'I ought to help in some way,' I said uneasily to Alan. 'Everybody is working — after all it's *my* war.'

'You keep up the morale of one pilot — that's essential.'

'Is that enough?'

Alan nodded. 'Do what you have to do. I ought to get ready. . . .'

'Look after yourself!' I called out when he was walking away from the house. My heart stopped. That's what I had said to Martin when I left him at the men's prison and he became ill and died. Died. I ran after Alan and flung myself into his arms, murmuring, I'm so afraid, so afraid.

'Nothing will happen to me — I know. But I *didn't* know that you cared.' He was entirely serious.

'Why do you put up with everything?'

'I have no choice,' he said briefly.

I stood at the gate watching him drive off. I fell back into my old helpless habits and prayed: protect him.

I pushed the baby's pram up and down the garden path, saw him smile in his sleep and gradually lost my fear. I stood by the pond, gently rocked the pram and looked at the autumn flowers. Some were golden yellow, some white, some pink, some orange. A single flower stood a little apart from the others, smaller and tougher with deep green leaves and a tiny white head. I tried to pluck it, but it clung stubbornly to the soil. You're right, I sighed, it's cruel to uproot you. You stick to your plot. What a cheap thought, what a cheap feeling, look at all you've got. All?

*　　*　　*

The war was over.

One of the people I most wanted to see was Benjamin. He had successfully applied his considerable intelligence to the task of getting himself out of Spain and into England, then joined the Army where they made use of his writing ability and his linguistic talents (for digging trenches, in the Pioneer Corps).

Now demobbed, he intended to live in London and write as many books as fast as he could to make up for lost time. He came to see me, looking at my new surroundings without much comment. He liked the blacktiled kitchen and settled down there to consume an inordinate amount of coffee. He was the only man I knew who could drink twelve cups in a row and feel he had only just started. A freak of nature. He said it stimulated him mildly and never prevented him sleeping. He looked well, although I still objected to his moustache. It cramped his style.

'What about your family?' he asked.

'I found them quite a while ago. They've settled in America and I'm going to visit them pretty soon now. They must see John. They're quite happy over there and they don't intend to return to the Fatherland ever. Neither do I.'

'Not even as a visitor?'

'Not in a million years.'

'But they are not the same people any more.'

'Just how would you make sure of that?'

'One can't. But aren't you curious?'

'No. I don't want to know — yet.'

'What do you do with yourself apart from adoring the baby?'

'I plant things, trees, lettuces, tomatoes, strawberries, the lot. I love it.'

'Do you love Alan?' Benjamin's large brown eyes were fixed on mine.

'At certain times,' I leered, 'very much indeed.'

'Sebastian — what about *that*?'

'I can't get rid of him, he just stays there and can't be dislodged.'

'Like a cancer,' Benjamin proposed equably.

'Just a growth. But it's not deadly as you see. It's bearable. I forget at times. Maybe it's healing.' We looked at each other, then at the swallows swooping over our heads. 'Benjamin, why do we talk in English? It's ridiculous — two Germans.'

'Are we?'

'Why of course we are. Or were.'

'You still go around hating. You ought to stop.'

'Yes, I know. I *have* to a certain extent. Nothing personal in it. Just a nasty feeling. I don't want to go back and speculate about their past. What they did and what they let happen. How could it happen — how?'

Benjamin shook his head. 'I don't understand either. A general madness. Shared by millions.'

'Group hate belongs in the clinical world, says Willem van den Fluchten.'

'Who's he?'

'A Dutchman with a lot of commonsense.' I pointed to the swallows, enjoying themselves in the sky. 'No problems there — I wish I could be living like that.'

'You might one day, who knows? For the moment you've got to steer your double-decker.'

'Tell me about that.'

'The pain underneath and the longing on top.'

'Typical Benjamin — so basic. And how do you know I'm

longing?'

'It's in your eyes. It always *has* been.'

'What is it I so want?'

'That's what you've got to find out. As I said your double-decker needs a driver. Or you'll jump off the track. I can see it all — at least in your case. As long as the world was moving along nicely, in its usual track, there was no need to dive below the surface. But now the surface has been shattered. You've had a look into the depth. You need a new way of functioning — you can't be content with patterns. *You* must drive to the source.' He paused. 'You remember that day in Paris, when —'

We were off. Wallowing. Our hotel rooms, the river, Teufel the dog, the cafes, the light, the air, the years gone by, the people lost, the names forgotten and the faces remembered. Benjamin made me talk about Berlin and said, romantically, that it was no good weeping inside and having a '*kalte Schnauze*' outside, a 'cold snout', literally.

'You can't get the paving stones out of your system,' he smiled.

'Paving stones?' Then it hit me. I saw myself on roller-skates, a small girl with pigtails flying. Gliding over those very stones, feeling the edge of the hard grey squares in my whole body, little ripples shaking me, a buzzing in my ears racing along like a demon, flashes of grey and silver under my feet, the sweetness of speed intoxicating me. Paving stones. . . .

'I do remember,' I said slowly, looking away.

'Face it, Julia, it's gone and won't come back. And it's not only the place — the years are gone too.'

'Is it that important?'

Benjamin nodded, his mouth set.

'He is more important.' I pointed to John, playing at the other end of the garden.

'But he is feeling the paving stones too.'

'Nonsense. Author's jargon.'

'If it makes it easier for you.'

*   *   *

John was growing up. Except for an occasional illness he was a constant source of joy. The paving stones did not seem to have caught up with him. The Percival parents had not

113

been told and now never would be. John's skin was as light as Alan's, his eyes were blue. The hair a bit darker, but then so was mine. He grew up straight and slim and unemotional. He was intelligent, but not outstandingly so. Good at sports. Self-contained, very discreet, very English. Sometimes I looked at him in awe, as he fitted so perfectly into his surroundings. Alan adored him and (I secretly believe) had made himself forget all about Martin.

Alan was determined to teach him how to read before he went to school. There had been a major row.

'Let him play and have his freedom as long as possible,' I had argued at the time.

'He's not going to prison. English schools are not *like* that!'

'That's right. Everything's fine in this lovely country.'

'You were happy enough when you came.'

'You bloody man.'

'I don't like that kind of expression and you know it.'

'You don't like *me*. Why don't you admit it? You've made a mistake, you wish —'

'I don't wish for anything but what I've got. I wanted you the first time I saw you.'

'Aha! And what would you have done if Martin had not died?'

'I don't know. I really don't.'

'Why don't you let me bring up John the way I like, I'm his mother!' I said nastily.

'I'm sorry about that,' Alan said calmly. 'He is such a beautiful child.'

'You are sorry, you are sorry,' I mimicked him. 'What a delicate way of putting things. Why don't you say what you mean? You loathe and hate the idea that he isn't yours, don't you? Don't you?'

He did not answer, just looked long suffering. It infuriated me.

'You brush everything under the carpet, just like the rest of you fellows born in England.' (I pronounced it the German way.) '*Eng*-land, the *narrow* land, that's exactly how you are, narrow, dry, dessicated. No pep in you — controlled to the last. Ha! You've got no feelings left at all, you've kept them under for too long, you are so bloody civilized. . . .'

'I told you not to use that word.'

'You *told* me?' I unleashed a stream of swearwords of unparalleled viciousness. I really felt proud of my vocabulary. Alan turned white with fury (contrary to most continentals who turn red) and started hitting my face. I couldn't believe it. Alan *hitting* me? I was so utterly taken aback that I did not even try to protect myself and my nose started bleeding. (Slightly but dramatically.) Little red drops soiled a smart yellow silk cushion and the white fluffy bedroom carpet. Alan stopped dead. I must have a knack of bringing out the worst in people. I'd done so ever since I was about thirteen and was turning into a real devil.

'You provoked me — you provoked me beyond endurance with your foul language.'

'Good.'

'I hate you, I really do.'

'I always knew it even though you wouldn't admit it.'

'I admit nothing and I believe nothing you say. But I take this back: I don't hate you — at all.'

God — he looked fantastic. Still white, but his eyes blazing. Guilty as hell, but in love, in *love*.

He lifted me on to the bed: 'I think you do it on purpose. You upset me so and then I have to touch you, I can't help myself, I must, I must. . . .' He kissed me from the roots of my hair all the way down.

'That makes it easy,' I sighed, 'each time I want you I'll be mean, really mean —'

'How often?' he murmured his lips in my hair.

'All the time. All the time non stop.'

Sometime after this row Alan looked at me and said I was far too thin.

'I got the impression you were rather fond of thin women.'

My husband smiled his innocent, hesitant, uncertain Alan-smile, not just showing his teeth and lifting the corners of his mouth, but letting the smile surface to the skin like a light. Definitely beautiful. 'Too thin, I said.'

'What do you want me to do about it? I've seen every doctor in the book. There's nothing wrong with me, except — well you know what they said: no more babies for the time being. There's nothing wrong with me. Stop fussing.' I used to have a stomach like a camel. Could eat bark of the trees. I nearly did. Or alternatively I could eat cucumber, cream, plums, drink rivers of wine. Never the slightest trouble. But

115

now, unfortunately, the items on my food register were restricted. Most things made me ill.

At first I died with longing everytime I passed a pastry shop. A piece of cheese seemed the equivalent of paradise. I stood in front of French restaurants and read the menu like the holy Gospel.

But now I got dizzy if I smelt the cork of a bottle of Martell. I sometimes dreamt about macaroni, golden running butter, gorgeous egg yolks surrounded by their white halos and coffee — oh, the utter comfort and bliss of dark, steaming coffee. It would have been better to have stopped dreaming for a fatal connection had been established between those delights and an abysmal depression racking my mind and body, enveloping me like a boa constrictor. I wasn't imagining it, nor making it up. And I wasn't a case either. Just reasonable and observant.

Eat the forbidden food and crumble like a wet biscuit (also forbidden). My skin went dark yellow, muscles ached all over the body, my head split and my willpower vanished. It was the liver of course. I know. Some doctors admitted it. Mrs Percival said it was my nerves. She would — but it was all solid, respectable body-work. An innocent glass of milk gave me hell. A cup of tea flung me into a depression that buried me alive and a piece of white bread made me wish I'd never been born. Facts — facts. I stuck to vegetables, fruit and grills. Naturally I lost weight. But I felt fine, as long as I obeyed my body's wishes.

I was shoved in and out of countless X-ray machines. I had more barium meals than I cared to remember. I had settled down too quickly, too slowly, not at all. I couldn't come to terms with my past, or I did not look at it sufficiently: according to the mental make-up of the doctor. The emotional upset of the past cramped my digestive style or else I was making it all up because I was afraid of losing my figure. (Never gave it a thought, I swear.) I stopped consulting specialists and just suffered when people looked at me pityingly at parties.

I would have forgotten all about it, had Alan not said one day: 'I'm sure you're over all that by now and look what I've brought you!'

He unwrapped a golden brown chocolate box, said, 'It's your favourite colour, just try one and see — I'm sure you could eat a little bit, it would make such a lot of difference to your drab diet!' The devil. . . .

My body, fed on food without glory for so long, responded with an unprecedented upsurge of greed. My system might really have settled down and expurgated all past troubles; how would I know if I didn't try? I started a veritable orgy. Alan watched me like a mother seeing her child 'eat properly' after a long illness.

'After all,' he spurred me on, 'There is nothing wrong with you. They all said so. I'm sure it's a state of mind. You must simply overcome it.'

I felt like the sultan of a harem, picking the most gorgeous specimens for consumption. I knew, as never before, the intimate connection between succulent food and the thrust of bodily love. I sat on Alan's lap, alternatively kissing him and stuffing myself with the chocolates. It must have been a truly disgusting spectacle.

Time to obliterate things past (almonds). After all, you can't expect to run through half of Europe and come out smiling at the other end (marzipan). People had developed heart diseases, ulcers, eczema or had just gone plain crazy. I should count myself lucky. And what about all those who had got a buffeting similar to mine, reaching for the frying pan and cream buns, and were none the worse? I was now their equal and consumed three-quarters of the chocolates voraciously, spurred on by the secret fear that I might drop dead before I'd had enough.

I did not drop dead but I wished I had. That was thirty-six hours later. I brushed aside the usual warning signals: headache, muscle ache, abject tiredness. When my skin turned yellow I knew I was sunk. The health barometer started sinking: changeable, rain, stormy and then beyond, where there was no print left. Very apt — for words cannot describe how the world drifted out of reach, how brimstone and ashes covered every living thing, how the thought of the next minute became unbearable. Just to be there at all was as impossible as carrying a skyscraper in the palm of your hand. Movement was out of the question. Not moving equally painful.

Alan took one look at me when he came home, covered his face with his hands and said it was all his fault. He looked wildly round the room and said he was going to help, tapped his forehead, got a glass of water and made me swallow two barbiturates, whispering at least you won't notice

117

the suffering. I moaned and groaned for the next twenty minutes, then drowsiness crept over me like gossamer silk. I sank away, feeling the grip of depression lose its power, smiled feebly and murmured better, so much better and withdrew into a twenty-four hours' bottomless sleep.

Other people sleep seven or eight hours with the same dose. There are compensations.

* * *

One day I came across the little exercise book I had covered in scribbles in the Seguridad, the prison in Madrid. I re-read the odd fairy tale I had written, half insane with shock and fear. Without realising precisely what I was doing, I started to write on the same page where the fairy tale had ended, feeling vaguely that what I was writing now dipped into the same reservoir as then, that the same impulse of transformation was at work. But now the writing was strong and well defined compared with the old jittery signs crawling over the page. The regions normally kept under lock and key were opened up.

The lines were short, compact and concentrated. They automatically shaped themselves into some sort of poem. I sat down on the carpet writing hectically. A whirling mass of feelings, events and emotions spilled on to the paper unhampered by the new language. The new language? *What* language? When the earth splits, throwing out great lumps of red hot stuff, a little detail like that does not matter. Some benevolent deity had lifted the sluice gate and let the stream flow in great splashing cascades. Well, it's either red hot stuff or great splashing cascades. I assure you it was both — together. Or alternatively — I was carried off. That's all that mattered.

No drug taker was keener on his daily ration than I was on my session on the carpet. Such outpourings, such wild ravings, such spectacular breakdowns. All those tears I had spilt — oceans. The relief was divine. The word is not too strong, for I thought I had at last reached the very centre, the core of life. I had bitten into the innermost kernel and was crunching it between my teeth.

I must have bitten too hard or my teeth had fallen out. One day the writing stopped. Perhaps I needed refuelling or the opposite — rest. What now? Ring Benjamin, or Alan.

No — ring Melissa, a woman is best. My nerve ends might have been split into more jangling bits than most people's but I was blessed with the urge to communicate under any circumstances. And the communication between Melissa and myself was outstanding: we managed to keep each other at arm's length while at the same time baring our souls in no ordinary fashion.

There were men around my friend at all times, but she had never really 'landed' anywhere. At that time she lived with Gresham, stiff and starched, unworthy of her, without much human interest. My assessment was altogether wrong as was proved later.

'How are the rehearsals going?' On the phone to her dressing room at the theatre.

'You couldn't care less — I can tell.'

'I can't on the phone. . . .'

'You can and will. What's wrong?' I told her about the poems and that I felt cheated that I couldn't go on.

'Are the poems any good?'

'I don't know. Nobody has seen them.'

'It's that fellow from Berlin!'

'Poor Sebastian — Alan holds him responsible too.'

'Clever man — he's right. Your dream boy is always there, isn't he?'

'I'm not denying it. I feel all the more empty now the writing has stopped.'

'How about sitting down at the piano and yelling?'

'I've tried it, many times. It's no good. I'm croaking like a frog or whining like a mosquito. The voice is gone. And I don't *feel* like singing any more. Too much has happened.'

'Nonsense. Your training couldn't have been up to scratch — a voice doesn't just *go* if it's properly placed.'

'Melissa, I think I've lost the key to my private dungeons.'

'That's an excellent line!'

'Be serious, I'm miserable.'

'We'll meet after lunch — they're just calling me — usual place, usual time. See you.'

The usual place was one of the few continental cafes to be found in London. It had a special secluded atmosphere and you could sit there as long as you liked. Dark red walls, soft lights, comfortable leather benches surrounding six cornered tables. A black coffee for Melissa, a tomato juice for me.

'Now then,' Melissa said, looking more than ever beauti-

119

fully foxy. 'Let's have it.'

'I'm wasting my life.'

Deep rasping laughter. 'Who isn't?'

'I don't want to go on doing it.'

'Just how are you wasting it in your beautiful little house, with John and Alan around?'

'I'm shrinking, treading water, letting the sands run out.'

'Before your eggs are boiled?'

'Melissa!'

'Sorry, I couldn't resist it.'

'I'm out of things, stale, unproductive.'

'I thought Alan found you sensational.' I remained silent. 'Doesn't he any more? Why are you tapping your right knee with your left hand? Why are you so nervous? Don't tell me your marriage is going to pieces. Bad marriages bore me to bloody tears. I mean, doesn't anybody ever look before they . . . . ?'

'You're crude. Our marriage is fine. We, yes *we*, are watching John grow and he gladdens my heart every time I look at him. There is no story, but. . . . I want to break my mould — expand!'

'Pity. I always found your mould rather interesting. Some women are dead from the eyebrows up.'

'No wonder with that *apparatus* inside! Nothing but pain, discomfort and trouble. Bloody body. Any man lumbered with that contraption would take to his bed permanently.'

'Hide in despair. Weaklings. Are we ever appreciated?'

'*We* are the queens of the earth. Give me another tomato juice!'

Melissa lowered her eyes for a while (a sign that she was thinking intensely), then suddenly beamed them at me like headlamps: 'I've got a hunch — no more really. It might just do the trick. You remember Rod Rittling, our producer, the chap with the big blond mane? He goes into a huddle just before he starts working.'

'What kind of a huddle?'

'He meditates.'

'Good grief. Not one of those!' Maybe I'm prejudiced, but *no*. 'Does he go around with a begging bowl? Does he preach? Is he mild mannered and *submits*? People like that make me sick.'

'It's not *like* that. You take a gun out every time somebody

120

mentions religion. People need it, you know.'

'I don't.'

'You need something, you just said so. I know your memory's non existent, but that's why you rang this morning. I remember.' I stayed quiet. 'And Julia. . . . don't pretend too hard. I've seen strange book titles around your place lately, very odd some of them, words like "death", "meaning", "dimensions", scattered about. If that's not religion, what is? Anyway, Rod's been a bundle of nerves before and now he's calm and peaceful.'

'Like a cow in the meadow.'

'Ox.' We giggled. Wondered whether Rod's hair colour was natural and whether he had boys or girls for company or both. Girls, Melissa said quickly, smiling a bit, talented and beautiful of course. I wondered — but did not put a question.

'Look Julia, something's eating you. You don't know what it is, but it hurts.'

I nodded. Yes, it had been hurting for some time — the pointlessness, the waste, the years going by, the unresolved past, the stews to be cooked, the house to be cleaned, the curtains replaced. Who replaces my wear and tear? Who did what, anyway, and to what purpose? What exactly did I want?

'A regeneration,' I heard myself say, 'a thirst, a craving.'

'Yes. I understand. Your time has come and I'm not joking. A new approach, the "inner barbarian" wants to become civilized. I'll speak to Rod and let you know. After all, what can you lose? You can always walk out, I know it's your speciality.'

'I will if they wave prayer wheels or flags at me. I can't bear to go backwards. In time, I mean. Neither can I bear to stay on the surface. It's so sterile. I want depth and miracles and nothing I have known before. I want the New, Melissa, the Unexpected, the Unknown.'

'Take to your heels if they start preaching. Give it a try.'

Of course I would. Melissa was right. What did I have to lose? She was also right about the books at home, but I did not like to admit it. Adventure of the body can be told anywhere, boasted about and enhanced with countless details: swamps, snakes, crocodiles, glaciers, deserts. When you're starving or running or climbing, when you're killing or have the plague — *that's* adventure. But when your mind starts thrashing about, that's crazy. What do you want, people say, the moon? Yes! And the stars and the sun and the whole whirling swirling lot — no less. I want it all. The whole of life; I don't want just to nurture the little bit I've got, like a sickly plant, not just protect my tiny little corner from the rough north winds, I want to jump over the fence and expand, insubstantial, invisible and free as the wind.

My body escaped from prison: good — that was news. My mind wanted to do likewise: I was off my nut. Well, according to those books at home there were a lot of fellow travellers. Some claimed to have found a path to paradise, or even paradise itself. Some told you how to get there, others said: *I* have but i'm damned if I tell *you*. You find your own painful way — and, oh boy, was it *painful* and harsh and long and strewn with exploding hazards like a minefield. Maybe they did not want their paradise to become too crowded. But usually their hearts were full of joy and overflowing in print. There were comparatively few women amongst them, but maybe they were just being sensible. If the odds are overwhelming, turn around and run.

Each book presented a new recipe: quick stews, slow stews with oriental spices, souffles made in a minute, providing heaven on earth, heaven above or just plain heaven without a location. Amazing!

There were more spiritual outfits than I had hairs on my head, spread all over the globe from the furthest corner of Tibet to the crummiest slum in the cities. And the language! It went from the frankly poetical through the monumental to the most detailed technicalities. It became, dare I say it? — slightly repulsive. My narrow shoulders (inherited, I hasten to add, together with the smallest back and unruly hair as fine as cobwebs), those shoulders began to sag under the weight of the outpourings from the paradise seekers. But scorn as I may — I was bitten by the bug.

Did Nansen give up halfway? Did Livingstone? Did Columbus? I fancied myself as an explorer of inner space and would leave no outfit unturned, no book unread. Alan said I was covering up for something and I had better find out what it was. Could it be something nasty like my own emptiness, craving to be filled with other people's suggestions?

'You lack discrimination,' I said to him.

'And you lack commonsense.'

'Commonsense said the earth was flat.'

'I just don't like you to chase moonbeams.'

'Oh God!' I exclaimed. 'What a useless earthbound creature you are!'

Alan smiled fiendishly and said: 'Are you looking for *him* by any chance?'

'Him? Him?'

'Yes, my darling,' Alan was almost dancing about, 'yes — *him! GDO — DGO — OGD — GOD.* Just a word, but do you think he's there?'

I sank into the nearest chair with surprise: 'I don't know you like this.'

'You don't and what's more, nobody does. I *too* think, you know, my little Julia; you have no privilege of lofty ideas. I too have my private little world swirling about and I wouldn't be surprised at all if all those little worlds shot up and made' — a sly happy grin appeared on Alan's face — 'something entirely new, some atmosphere like a permanent hovering, heaving mist created by this constant begging, accusing, imploring, praying. Something palpable and real which begins to interact with those living people, all those supplications, those petitions and demands — there may be something there all right, a living thing, influencing us — and vice versa of course.'

'I feel dizzy,' I said uncomfortably.

'Good — I'm satisfied.'

He's cleverer than I. And more inventive. I'm not sure I like that.

* * *

I was sitting by the window, the curtains blowing in the breeze, the first stars appearing over the dark city at my feet. Relax — now do relax and be *content.* I couldn't — I had to think back to the past again and again. My accidental acquittal was still lying heavily on my mind. Why did *I* get away? What gave me the strength to escape? And for what? What a waste to have gone through all that turmoil and not to use it, *use* it. It was like breaking up the earth, constructing a mine and then not surfacing with the goods. Something was lying there, ready to be brought up to the daylight, I could swear to that. All I needed was the right tools.

I looked up at the sky, a perfectly round moon just rising

123

over the treetops — that heavy golden ball with a child's face smiled at me idiotically, maddeningly innocent and cold. Where was my connection to all that icy splendour? I felt a shiver running down my arms. You don't deserve your luck, you ungrateful megalomaniac, you beast. Who are you to revolt and shout 'for what?' How dare you look up at the sky and shake your fist at it (mentally speaking of course, I know better than actually to *do* it). Why are you hissing at the moon? Make me understand. . . . then, pitifully, *make* me understand. With what? With that bird's brain. . . . understand that immensity?

The first lights went on in the windows below. The moon kept on smiling, now and then obscured by a passing cloud. Unfamiliar thoughts drifted past — if you try to fathom unreachable things your brain reacts oddly. You can feel it becoming sluggish, heavy, uncomfortable; physically so. Try it out: Death. . . . Eternity. . . . End of Time. It makes me dizzy, like thinking I don't like that blue flower to be red — it's unthinkable in the true sense of the word. It throws the braincells out of gear like a badly fed computer. I'm not 'equipped' properly, I thought with surprise. My cells won't work for me, my mind doesn't know which way to jump. Lost in the jungle. Maybe somebody is going to show me the way, the way home. Home is where I want to go.

*　　*　　*

Two days later I received one of Melissa's purple envelopes with her loopy handwriting. I never ceased to be touched and flattered by her interest and understanding.

The address given was in an elegant, smart district. The house itself looked disappointingly opulent. And why not? Why should things of the spirit be kept in a humble atmosphere? I went in and was told by a secretary (how can a secretary help me to float upwards?) to bring a clean handkerchief, a fruit, and a week's wage for the 'meeting'. I wondered how much would be adequate, seeing that I did not earn a penny myself. Should I put the money in an envelope or would they think I wanted to hide the amount I was prepared to give? On the other hand it might be embarrassing to stuff a fistful of notes into the hands of a saint.

The fruit bothered me even more. Would a simple apple or a plum do? Or was I being mean in the face of the Cosmos? A pineapple is so demonstrative. I finally settled for a pear, nicely elongated, golden, with brown freckles and a little crooked stem.

I felt distinctly uncomfortable when I entered the elegant house that second time. I had been told I would be 'initiated' together with my pear and my hanky. I was given a single word, a 'Mantra' (a very ancient device, a syllable which produces special vibrations when repeated many times), and I would be checked every fortnight to make sure the word had 'taken'. The explanation was clearly 'traditional' but adapted to our modern world: give your conscious mind something to play with, then the unconscious would take over, showing its strength and wisdom and I'd be well away. It sounded feasible — if more like psychiatry than religion.

Walking on tip toes and breathing deferentially, as if she was leading me to the dentist's chair for an extraction, the secretary guided me into the inner sanctum. We went into a large room, lit only by two candles. Joss sticks were burning next to the picture of a man with a lot of beard and an angelic smile. Several people stood around in the shadowy corners speaking in subdued voices. A tall slim man in his thirties approached me without a greeting, took my offerings from me and said in a pleasant baritone voice: 'Say the same word I'm saying, use the same rhythm, just relax and let yourself be guided. Start — now!'

I'm usually allergic to commands, but I followed this one as he injected a word into me I had never heard before. I had no option but to repeat and repeat it again. Maybe he was hypnotizing me or maybe the rhythm suited me. A powerful engine whirled me around as walls, chairs and people were swinging; I was vibrating like a piano chord.

'Come back in a fortnight for a report,' somebody said when the swinging had stopped. The tall man had withdrawn into the shadows. The one who spoke now had less impact but was more approachable. I said I would be back, but what exactly did they want me to do?

'You repeat your Mantra just as you've been doing now, twice a day for twenty-five minutes.' I winced — it seemed an eternity. 'Don't tell anybody the "word" you have — it's meant for you only — and don't let your mind wander. If it does, pull yourself back and cling to the word. You need a warm quiet room, keep your back straight and the telephone off the hook. Good luck. See you again.'

Outside the room, I went to sit in a deep comfortable arm-chair to collect my wits. I started laughing, while I sank into the soft cushions. What were they going to do with all those crisp clean hankies and those mountains of fruit, which must have been piling up today and all the previous days? Was everybody sworn to secrecy? Earlier I had seen a young man with a shiny red apple and a young girl hiding a box of dates behind her back. Why all the paraphernalia? I mean, does the word become more effective because of our gifts? It puzzled me.

Ah, the word comes back, it drifts into my mind of its own accord, with a rhythm of its own as well. It sings like a melody, I can feel my throat moving. That's wrong, I know it. It should be resounding in the head only, they said so. The word was now flapping about inside me like a bird. I couldn't make it stop. It went on resounding and echoing without me. . . . so to speak. The soundwaves only ebbed away as I got up from the chair. They petered out altogether as I left the house.

At first it seemed easier to do it at home. I sat on a chair, back straight, eyes closed, hands folded in my lap, repeating the Mantra. It welled up like a source, shaped itself nicely, deepening, flattening, changing the rhythm and the frequency, moulding itself like clay. But the basic sound remained constant. The second day was not so good. All kinds of thoughts intruded and would not be silenced however much I tried. Sebastian emerged lifesize, our guide in France was walking ahead of me, carrying my rucksack, Juanita and her dimples. I enjoyed it like a Punch and Judy show. But the people did not behave like puppets — they took over completely. It was so fascinating that I said I did not feel any regret when I showed up at the Centre.

The man who was assigned to me as a sort of mentor in the spiritual maze looked at me reproachfully. 'You shouldn't have allowed the word to slip away.' His name was Mr Truelove and I'm not making it up. He was quite brisk and businesslike in a pair of striped trousers. He did not look in the least inspiring. What did I expect — a pair of wings? At least not this red, bulky face with a well groomed beard and full lipped mouth. I'd never kiss *him*, I thought, not with those lips.

'Why didn't you keep the word in place?' Mr Truelove asked a little impatiently.

'I got bored, I think. I might have felt I was shutting up the best, I was retreating from the mainstream. Also,' I leant forward confidentially, 'I've got such a terrible memory, that I'm gratified if something definite shows up. Do you know,' I almost whispered, 'that I can't even remember what happened in what century? I mix them all up. Go on ask me anything, you'll see. It's pathetic. My history teacher thought I did it on purpose. But I can't — the years just won't stay in order. Faces — yes. Words, moods — yes. But no proper sequences. I mean I can't tidy up. I was so *grateful* my memory yielded anything at all. That's why I didn't do so well, do you understand?'

'Woud you like to stop?'

'I would not. Tell me what to do.' Mr Truelove scribbled something on a pad. 'Is it about me?'

'We keep track, yes. But you can take part in a class and you might discover more about the method and the organisation.'

I *had* to say it: 'Have you run out of handkerchiefs?'

'You are not being serious. That won't do.'

'Determination?' He nodded. 'No jokes at all?' No, not here. 'Shall I try it again?' Yes, I should, right now.

'Tell me what happens, I shall do it with you.' Have a run for your money and the golden pear.... 'Don't feel guilty if your thoughts are pulling you away, be aware of the lapse and start all over again.'

Word, word, word, I drummed in my mind, repeating it with a will until the sound began to swing as on the first day.

'Any trouble?'

'Not this time.'

'Good. Why was it different now do you think?'

'Your presence maybe.' His full red lips stretched in a pleased smile. 'The unfamiliar atmosphere.' I dropped my guard. 'Is that why people build churches?'

'Perhaps. But you must build your own every time you sit down to work. See you in a fortnight.'

Build my own church. Why not a synagogue. Or a mosque. Or a railway station. Information — yes, but no fences, no hemming in. I was, of course, kidding myself as I had been given a definite word and a method to use it, even a time limit. I knew better than anybody what weight a single word could have. 'Lola' — the whole prison ward was there.

127

'Martin' — tears. The words spread and became thoughts and pictures. 'Berlin' — that was magic and conjured up frozen rivers and lakes, dense woods, grey houses and trams, faces and voices. . . . I don't seem to be able to stick to the word.

'But look,' I said to my tutor at the next meeting, 'look at all those marvellous things going on in my mind.'

'Are you telling me or am I telling you?' my red lipped Mr Truelove said. 'There are more fascinating things than your own mind.' I could not believe that. I remembered telling him last time about my shocking memory. This time I felt the urge to confess the striking metamorphosis which had taken place since I left my hometown. I am happy to say that I can set up a confessional with the most unlikely people. All I need is a warm feeling and a bumptious mood.

'Do other trainees have the same trouble? Maybe they have greater willpower. You know I'm somewhat lacking in that commodity. It's all been used up in the past — whatever there was of it.'

Mr Truelove sighed a little disapprovingly, but then settled down. 'It's the lesser evil if you get it off your chest first.'

'I was a little jellyfish to begin with,' I said, 'drifting about in the sea — a blob. Maybe somebody made the decision to knock some shape into it, no spine, no purpose, no direction. Plunge this amorphous thing into the depths and see whether it comes up again. Now I've come up again but I still have no purpose. In fact I think I'm pretty useless, Mantra or no Mantra-'

'Don't say that! How can you aspire to higher things if you can't even stick to a miserable little word in your own mind. Discipline makes the world go round, discipline! You imagine you're sitting in a cage because you can't follow your own train of thought — wrong, wrong! Hundreds of thousands are doing it all over the world, it's the road to freedom. Have you never wanted to be really free?' His eyes widening reminded me of eggs floating on a frying pan. What a nasty nature you have — a man of God! Although he said we never use 'that word', although we may mean it.

'I think I'm really not the right type for it,' I said at the next meeting. 'I can't concentrate long enough and keep drifting away.'

'Why do it at all then?'

'I wonder. Something compels me to try and try again. I

128

feel there is a curtain I must draw aside.' (Did I really say this?) 'There must be something more to life than wedding cakes and coffins!' (I did feel *this!*)

'What makes you think there is?'

'If life were just an accident,' I said, suddenly serious, 'then everything one does *in* it would be of no value whatsoever.'

Mr Truelove beamed at me. 'Yes,' he said with great emphasis. 'That's exactly it. But we must choose the right means to find out. You want to try again?' I liked him for the first time and said, yes, I would and did he do this work all day long. No, he did it only after office hours and was looking forward to it all day. That was touching. Cooped up in some little office all day, waiting for the moment of glory when he could truly be of service. Julia, your mind is warped — this man is *good*.

'I will try again with all the energy I've got and — thank you for all your help!'

I set to work as soon as I arrived home and the word started swinging up and down over my right eyelid like a butterfly. I forced it right into the centre of my mind. Then it went to the back of my head where I kept it hanging for a while, beating like a pulse. I felt my nails digging into my palm and my toes curling up. I spent more energy than a transatlantic steamer to stay on course. I sang it, breathed it, I shouted it inwardly with great force to keep my thoughts from creeping up on me. The word bobbed up like a swimmer's head over the waves. I kept it going with tremendous effort.

Effort — therein lay the fiasco. When you move about in the mental field you should not produce a cramp. Rather open up softly like a water lily. When I listened to the word like an anxious doctor with a stethoscope I almost stopped breathing with the effort. All wrong. Artificial — all that tugging and straining, that sweat and travail. Wrong, wrong!

I said as much to Alan.

'Naturally, if you slug your guts out you won't get anywhere!'

'What do you suggest?'

'I suggest you drop your morbid preoccupation and start living like everybody else. While you are so busy looking for a meaning you let the best things in life slip by.'

'And what are they?' It sounded sour, spinsterish.

'How sad that you need reminding.'

'I want perfection!'

'Listen to the woman! There is no such thing, do you understand? People have tried and failed — right through the past till this very day.'

'The past is no longer my concern.' I hoped it sounded convincing.

'You are insane, every inch of you,' he started tapping on my forehead, my shoulders, my fingers, 'every single inch is fashioned by the past. You should know that better than anybody.'

'And why do you say that?' I felt threatened immediately, I always felt threatened. I knew he emphasised my foreignness in order to explain, not to exploit. He was on his own ground, always.

'Do not upset yourself, darling, and don't get ready for a fight either. I couldn't care less whether you come from Berlin or Timbuctoo and you know it. It's just an added attraction, on the same level as your hair or your hands — you stupid girl, are you crying?'

'I'm not,' I said fighting the tears back. Then I flung my arms around him. 'You must understand,' I whispered, 'it's nothing to do with you.'

'That's what I resent. I don't want you to draw a single breath without me!' I knew this to be perfectly true. I also knew that I could commit the most hideous crimes on earth, that I could hurt him and wound him but he would never disown me — ever. He was like a father — no, a father might turn away from me. The shelter he gave me was perfect and permanent like a mother's: unconditional and absolute.

*   *   *

I continued the meditation exercises for some weeks. I felt more and more how my mind contracted instead of expanding. Instead of coming truly alive a dead weight was lodging inside. I went to see Mr Truelove once more, saying that I was beaten, but I deeply appreciated his efforts to teach me. I definitely was not the right type for the Mantra. He would not admit it and said it was right for everybody on this earth and I was just lacking in willpower.

There were no regrets on my side. I had taken an interesting stroll and was now coming back to base. Something else might present itself.

I went along the King's Road marvelling at the glamorous shop windows, the colours, the models, the inventiveness of it all. Girls and boys looking like birds of paradise paraded up and down the street, laughing and chatting. They certainly did not want Mantras — but then they did not carry a rucksack full of troubles. I dragged a great big load around with me, I was staggering under the weight even now, after all this time. I needed a stick, a third leg, to keep my balance.

Or should I have said a third eye?

* * *

I could not resign myself to the fact that part of me should remain perpetually submerged. But why not look *by* myself? Why did I have so little faith in my own powers, why did I find my own mind so *negligible?* I understood by now that a different mental process was required, not just simply 'better' thoughts. I can't invent a new mode of functioning, I reasoned, I have to be taught.

Benjamin was always ready to listen. I'd never known him to refuse a challenge. I frequently visited him and always marvelled at the simplicity of his surroundings. Nothing demonstrative, nothing done 'on purpose'. He just happened to like the basics: bed, chair, table, typewriter, a few books, clothes on a hook, running water and a little cooker. Biscuits and a coffee percolator. One big poster on the wall, a Flemish picture, maybe five hundred years old. 'Dame Nature gives her orders to Genius' it said underneath. The picture showed the corner of a walled courtyard, a beautiful young woman in a red and blue dress with a tight bodice, delicate hands and a graceful posture. A lovely serious profile. Little blackbirds flying around her. She was standing on luscious green grass. Genius, the scholar, touched his cap to her; he was sturdy and intelligent — but less than she somehow, much less. The poster was typical for Benjamin, sparse, precise, a big truth in a small space.

'You look like a bloodhound on the scent,' he said immediately I entered. That's the kind of friend to have: right to the heart of the matter.

131

'I've lost the scent,' I said. 'The Mantra's no good for me.'

'If you insist on burning matches when there is a great big fire to warm you.'

'Please, Benjamin — no riddles. I'm tired, I've walked for hours, I can't be up to the mark all the time.'

'Won't.'

'Can't. It exhausts me. I'm not used to high voltage.'

'Glad to hear you admit it.'

'What great big fire were you talking about?'

'Buddhism.'

'God Almighty!'

'You see?'

'Why not the Dancing Dervishes? Be serious!'

'I am perfectly serious. It might appeal to you. It's logic, commonsense, artistry.'

'Why don't *you* go then if they are so fantastic?'

'I do go there regularly — for courses.'

My mouth dropped open. 'You never breathed a word —'

'You might not have been interested before. Are you afraid to try?'

'It makes me feel uncomfortable. It's so — alien.'

'Say "new" instead. They won't eat you. Tell them I sent you.'

*　　*　　*

I went the same day, feeling rather curious and expectant. All those saffron robes, I had vaguely thought, joss sticks and begging bowls. But there was nothing like that in the room I was shown into. The walls were lined with books, there were writing desks, comfortable armchairs and masses of flowers. The doors were flung open and a man entered, or rather bounced in like a rubber ball.

'I'm Ted Collins,' he said, shaking hands. He was short, pink and smooth skinned, round all over. Almost bald, except for a tuft of sandy coloured hair in the middle. Astonishing green eyes, deep set and penetrating — almost frighteningly so.

'Benjamin sent me. I thought you would be wearing a different kind of garb.' I looked at his grey jumper and flannel trousers.

Mr Collins' face split into a rosy water melon grin: 'It is not important what people wear. Why have you come?'

'I wish I could tell you exactly. . . . To find out how I function perhaps. Once I know that I might discover why. . . .'

'Zen,' he said promptly. 'That's what I'm teaching.'

'But that's just another system,' I said greatly disappointed, 'wrapped up, sealed and organised.'

'So is your body. You're prejudiced.'

'The world's all wrong,' I said helplessly.

'And you are not?'

'Naturally — I'm part of it.'

'Then why not start with that part?'

'Can I come and listen? And if I feel —'

'If you feel I'm spoon-feeding you just look for another nanny.' Ted's green eyes were dancing. 'There's a meeting once a week, you don't pay and I grow my own fruit.' I had told him about my previous experience. 'My wife also sees to it that I'm never short of hankies.'

'May I ask — I don't want to be rude — but have you any children?'

'Three,' Ted almost giggled, 'two boys and a little girl. You want their ages, names, and place of birth?'

Good — excellent. Most people I met and was to meet during this kind of research — I mean "search" of course, but it sounds corny — seemed to belong to a curious species of half-men and half-women, a bit pale and watery, seedy or else over-confident. So many were childless or had some washed out female in tow. Their bodies, unable to create new life were slightly stooped, as if ashamed to be there at all among the solid and earthy. And some of those lugubrious faces would not have been out of place in an undertaker's outfit. Their mirthless, melancholic countenances were not the best shop window for their teaching.

Not so Ted Collins. He looked strong and happy and full of fun. He taught a group of eight people, five men and three women, I think. I'm not sure about the third woman: voice like a bassoon, hair cropped to an inch, an indefinable figure in a big coat. The others looked ordinary, settled, well educated; one imagined nice incomes, spacious bathrooms, gardens with flower borders, umbrella stands in the entrance hall.

Ted did not introduce me but plunged into his work right away. He was walking up and down going over the details of the last meeting (for my benefit, I felt), asking, discussing, asserting and questioning in turn. Sensitive and intelligent,

133

highly individual, as if he invented his method on the spot to suit the mood and capabilities of his pupils. How far did they notice their surroundings — and their reactions to it? And how would they notice those reactions? I was amazed: there was not a single item that could be termed 'religious'. ... as yet.

'Have you ever looked at a matchbox? What is it *like*?'

The descriptions were sketchy and incomplete. They weren't even sure of the colour.

'That's very poor! How will you be able to deal with (cough) greater things if you don't remember the small ones? You have to practise.' He placed a table in front of us and put a matchbox on it, narrow side up. I looked at it wonderingly: there was so much *to* it. The rough dark surface on both sides, the lighter streaks the matches had made on it, narrow yellow strips framing the surface. A soldier with bearskin hat and a rifle kept watch on the front cover. Printed information and a little puzzle game on the back. I counted six different colours in all and a wealth of small loops and ornaments. I must have looked at a box like this a few thousand times and never *seen* it. First I tried to blame it on my foul memory which made me almost a freak ('but you've *read* the book, *been* to see those people, *heard* them say....' Who, me? 'You are pretending.' It got so bad that in the end I did pretend.) but then I had to admit that one mostly acted one scene and thought of another. When you drink and read the paper, when your ears listen to music and your hands wash up. *And* the big things too. You never concentrate — except in the arms of a man. Shoo! Back to the matchbox.

A general discussion followed, inconclusive as all further ones proved to be. We received a strange schooling from Ted. He forced us — obliquely — to develop our powers of observation, of concentration and watchfulness by presenting us with a variety of objects: nails, pencils, cactus plants, scissors, india rubbers. We looked at them for several minutes then he took them away and we described them.

I could even now produce an almost photographic image of most materials I'd seen, light and shade, knobs and dots, spirals and screws. We became good at it and graduated to more complicated objects like books and pictures. Zen? Perhaps. I did not care greatly, as my powers of observation increased visibly. I thought it all quite easy.

One day we found a blank page on the table. There was nothing to say except that it was white, square and flat.

'Watch!' Ted's voice was clipped. 'Don't talk, just watch it.' We stared grimly at the empty page, expecting a Mene Tekel to appear any minute. Nothing happened. There were disappointed murmurs all round.

'What are we supposed to watch?' one Miss Todd asked plaintively. 'I can't see anything remarkable.'

'Look — you know how to focus your attention on an object. Now try it on yourself, on your own mind.'

I frowned — just how was I going to do that? 'Is it like writing?' I asked hopefully.

'Not a bit. You don't invent, you don't try to remember. You watch it all happening.' How confusing. Who watched whom? And was the one watching being watched as well? My head started spinning and, judging from the expressions on my co-students' faces, they were just as bewildered. But one interesting point was clear: I became sharply aware of my own and other people's movements, speech, expressions and peculiarities. Melissa would love this — I must tell her.

I went to see her at the theatre where I was sure to find her that day, as there were two performances. Her feet were up, a cup of coffee within reach and a soft pink light on, making her dressing room look quite cosy.

'I love to see you without make-up; it makes me feel so much better. You don't glow quite as much. Still, it must be enough for Gresham. How is he?'

'The bloody brute,' Melissa said coolly and without the slightest trace of emotion. She wisely kept her fuel for her performances.

'I saw him leaving just now. Does he often watch you?'

'Quite often. I think he likes me best when I'm up there. On the whole I find him quite useless. I really feel we are not suited to each other at all. I've thought of breaking it off before he does, it's far better for my morale. I can't cope with his recriminations and he can't cope with me when I'm not working. He feels I'm sponging on him — the idiot.'

'And are you?'

She smiled, showing her pointed foxy teeth: 'Not all the time. I may not be all that fond of him, but I certainly appreciate his style — he's such an outstanding driver.'

We laughed. Melissa was usually collected at the stage

135

door by Gresham in his pin-striped suit, having emerged from a vehicle which looked like a battleship. Naturally he was an outstanding driver. Nobody would like to get in the way of that colossus.

'If only Gresham wasn't so much like a cash register totting up what I pay in and what I take out. I think I need a change of atmosphere.'

'That's why I'm here. I'd like you to come along to the Zen meeting. It may not be "orthodox" Zen, but I'm sure you'd appreciate it.'

'You want to sell me to your greeneyed monster?'

'No, not Ted. But there is a new boy. Lucien. He's exactly your type, I know he is.'

'Funny, all those married wretches hard at match making.'

'It's not marriage I had in mind. I just want to make you happy.' I grinned.

'Hold it, Julia, hold it. Don't move!' I stood still, both hands open, one foot forward.' Yes, that's what I need, that attitude, that soft continental smile of yours. My next part.'

'But you are playing a French girl.'

'Makes no difference.' She waved the frontiers away. 'You all walk differently, smaller steps, flowing gestures.'

'I thought I had merged into my surroundings.'

'You haven't grown, dearest; neither have your hands come to rest. Yes, I will come to your meeting. Are you surprised? And Gresham can take a jump. He will of course ask me why I want to consort with a bunch of cranks. *I* don't think you are. It's sensible to follow a path. I might one day if I could do so without going into contortions. Tell me, have you ever been to Ted's home?'

'No. I'd hate to see him put the kettle on. See you at the meeting.'

*　　*　　*

Both Melissa and Gresham came to the next class. I am sure that man intended to be awkward. He wore his pin-striped suit, dark socks, black shoes polished to perfection. The knot of his discreetly patterned tie was small and tight, pierced by an unfashionable pin with a pearl as big as a thimble. Every item was a statement: I represent commonsense and affluence; I'll deflate you all in no time.

136

Ted came bouncing in, rubbing his hands in anticipation. He liked nothing better than a good fight. He talked for a bit, cracked a few jokes and put everybody, except Gresham, at ease. He told a funny Zen story (they nearly always are) then suddenly turned to Gresham: 'Any questions?'

'I have a few, yes,' Gresham said firmly sticking his chin out. Melissa threw up her hands, fingers spread out — there he goes, he's off, don't hold me responsible. Everybody in the group stared at him except Lucien, the newcomer. He stared at Melissa.

'What makes you think you have all the answers?' Gresham asked, controlled but aggressive.

'Only one answer,' Ted said pleasantly. 'Just as I only have one question.'

'Why is that?' Gresham's chin stuck out even further.

'If you can narrow it down to one thing,' Ted went on, weighing his words, 'and then go to town on it. . . .'

'That's nonsense,' Gresham said sharply. 'You are just playing with words.'

'I don't know about that,' Ted said amiably. 'I simply mean that *all* problems in existence have the same root. Underneath all the mess and turmoil lies the same question.' He faced Gresham squarely: 'How should I live?'

Gresham drew back as if he'd been hit. 'How should I live?' he repeated slowly as if stunned.

'Yes. That's it. How?' Ted enjoyed a moment's absolute silence then shot out his words at Gresham with great force: 'If you went about it in the right way you might discover one factor, one single mind-blinding factor, which would make absolute and irrefutable sense.'

'That's impossible!' Gresham called out. 'People would know all about it!'

'Maybe you move in the wrong circles and don't,' Ted said pointedly. 'The possibility is there.'

Thus started the match. My bet was on Ted. But whatever the outcome we were going to get our money's worth. Miss Todd and Mrs Grey, the shorthaired lady with the bassoon voice (three times married and divorced, I had found out to my great surprise), sat on the edge of their chairs. Lucien was still watching Melissa, cool and glittering like an ice cube. She never sent a single glance in Lucien's direction. That was odd — she usually did a quick mental strip in the first second.

Ted spoke again: 'We are just trying to find out what's wrong.'

'We *know* what's wrong.' Gresham had caught himself and now sounded very alert and brisk like a newly sharpened razor. 'There's misery and sickness all over the globe. Not to speak of various disasters, man-made and otherwise. What do you propose to do about that?' His tone was that of a chairman at the board meeting who had all the facts (hidden from everybody else) at his fingertips and was now 'going to show them'.

'I have no suggestion of any kind,' Ted said flatly. 'This is not the Red Cross.'

'What do you have in mind then?'

'It's *all* in the mind.'

'Fiddlesticks! Why not admit that you are unable to act or propose a solution and therefore content yourself digging in your own yard,' his voice became distinctly spiteful, 'like an analyst who's missed out on the latter part of his training.'

'I'm not in the adjustment business either, I'd like to make that quite clear. This is not a repair shop.' Gresham became a trifle less sure and started to wriggle on his seat. Ted pounced: 'To what do I owe the pleasure of your company?'

'To see what you are up to,' even less assured, 'for the experience, something unusual. I thought (and hoped!) the first pinprick would deflate you,' he concluded truthfully.

'And what did you find?'

'I'm not sure. Your approach is new to me. I thought you would dish out the whole unrealistic lot: love, goodwill, religious slogans. Why don't you?'

'Because I'm not "explaining" either, it's too tedious. I talk and you understand and follow or maybe you can't now and might later. I'm proposing some exercises which you can take up or leave alone.'

Gresham sharpened his claws: 'Is this your *profession*?' His face reddened. 'Is this how you make a living? And who pays you?' Well! Nobody had ever *dared*. . . .

'I am a lecturer by profession and I earn a few thousand pounds per annum, enough for me and my family, as much as I need. I pay a monthly voluntary contribution here like some of the others who feel like it. I am not paid for talking to you.'

'I have been unforgivably rude. I am truly sorry.'

'You asked and I answered. There is nothing to be sorry about.'

Gresham stood up and stiffly extended his arm to shake hands with our teacher. 'I know,' he said, his city voice dropping from him like a useless garment, 'that you have got something I haven't. Would you mind if I — I mean to say may I come again?' It was the first time I saw Melissa blush. Ted soon closed the session, knowing full well that nobody would be able to concentrate after this memorable scene.

Melissa did not return. Gresham joined the study group.

*　　*　　*

Alan was always kept informed about what he liked to call my 'rake's progress'. I told him about Gresham joining the class.

'Class,' he said. 'I loathe teachers — always did.'

'It's not *like* that. It really is worthwhile, won't you even come once?'

'No, thank you, I'm quite happy as I am.'

'But there's a dimension lacking, it's all so thin, so repetitive.'

'My work isn't,' Alan said briefly.

'But there are no sparks flying, no fireworks, no revelations.'

'One brick on top of the other making a house is a great revelation to me. *I* don't need more. And I often wonder whether. . . .'

'Yes? What made you stop? What were you going to say?'

'What is the second name, the family name of your friend from Berlin? You never told me.'

'Rostov,' I said, cold creeping over my arms and shoulders.

'I never see his name on the concert posters.'

I stared at Alan. I'd never get to the bottom of him. 'Why do you bring that up now? What has it got to do with my class?' My voice had a hysterical edge to it, for I still could not cope with my emotions. Time had not been doing its job — there had not been any healing process at all, it was just as bad, just as intense as ever, even if it was overlaid by events. I

139

might not continuously say to myself that I was unhappy — not in so many words, but the feeling of an immense void was present at all times. If a vacuum can bleed, then it did so now.

'I just wondered,' Alan went on, 'whether you would have felt the need for all this searching and seeking if you were with him?'

That really hit below the belt. 'I don't know, I don't know!' I gasped. 'You can't just grab a piece of someone's life and hold it up to the light in isolation.'

'That's not an answer. But then you are of course pre-disposed to all sorts of weird goings on.'

'Meaning?' We stared at each other like wrestlers. The fights that bedroom had seen, verbal and physical.

'You have not answered my question,' Alan insisted. 'If you had been with him —'

'But I'm not,' I said weakly. 'I'm with you.'

'You don't sound exactly pleased with it. Anyway, I meant you are throwing yourself at all sorts of cranks —'

'Ted Collins is not a crank. Gresham would not have joined if he were. And look at all those millions of Zen followers all over the world.'

'That's just what I meant. You go looking for some oriental clap trap only because you are deprived of your native base.'

'My native ba —' It took me a moment to understand the implication. I did not know that Alan could be that vicious. That was usually my preserve. When his words penetrated properly a red rage welled up in me. The stupid narrow-minded bastard, the little Englander.

'Deprived, you said? Poor little native got no bananas, can't eat with fork and knife, poor little savage. All alone amongst the whites, missing all her idols and statues.' I began to tremble uncontrollably. 'Any moment now she'll prepare for a human sacrifice. Can't you see her sharpening her knives? Can you? I wish I had one right now!' I clenched my fists in order not to put them round Alan's throat. He looked at me, mesmerised. I started again, but this time my voice was querulous, whining.

'I wish I could have stayed in my own country. I wish I could have married Sebastian and lived the good native life. But,' the whine grew stronger, 'through no fault of my own I'm far away from my native base, thrown to the wolves on a

140

foreign shore. You would admit that, wouldn't you — no fault of my own? I'm living in this bloody place,' I burst out suddenly, 'where the sun never shines and the rain soaks into people's lives till they huddle away in a corner and close their eyes and ears to every fresh thing.'

I inched nearer to Alan: 'Why burden yourself with such an awkward stranger? Sorry for little stray cats? Are you?' I was coming nearer still, whining and whimpering: 'Such a generous man, never once did he throw it in my face, never once did he hurt my delicate feelings, always the gentleman, the perfect watery vapid gentleman,' my voice was swelling like a balloon full of gas, 'a little dull and prosaic but perfectly fair, always fair. But not much imagination, no dreams, no drive where the more rewarding things of life are concerned. Your creative energy,' I hissed, 'is being stifled by bricks and mortar.

'No wonder you can't manage to get to the peaks, your rucksack is filled with lead and waterpipes!' I gasped: 'Drainage, my friend, drainage! That's more like you, you. . . . you pedestrian.'

Alan flung his arms around me hugging my body, trying to squeeze me into silence. My breath came in great big gulps.

'Let me go, let me go, I can't get any air — do you want to kill me?'

He released me from his grip and I collapsed on the bed. Nobody spoke. There was no more to say. The fight ended in each other's arms as it always did. The nasty words were brushed aside as if they had never been spoken. Until the next time.

*   *   *

That was at a friend's house, Billy, short for George William Travers. He was a fellow architect, not quite as modern as Alan in his work, much more ornate, less neat and pleasing. There were deep soft armchairs, velvet curtains, patterned carpets, that sort of thing. The quarrel was not actually between Alan and me, but he took Billy's part which was almost worse.

That unfortunate man said to me at the dinner table, (a bad place for me anyway, as I could not properly partake in the gorgeous food) with a total lack of imagination: 'I often

141

listened to you, Julia, and never understood why you keep going back to the past so frequently. It isn't as if you'd done anything special — you just saved your own skin.'

'Oh yes?'

'He means,' Alan explained helpfully, 'that you have not accomplished anything in particular or new.'

'Like a general,' I proposed, 'or a great actor.'

'Yes,' Billy said, 'that's what I mean.'

'Or a famous sociologist.'

'Ye-es. Neither have you invented anything.'

'I wouldn't say that.' My voice remained even, almost serene. 'I would maintain that I have shown remarkable powers of invention, I and a few hundred others. In fact, I would go even further and say that each of us invented their own particular way of living from scratch. I find that truly remarkable.'

Alan, ever conscious of the danger of sudden outbreaks, said: 'You're right, of course. But let's talk about more important things.'

'I can't really think of anything more important at the moment, Alan dear. I was going to say that I've found a way of living entirely suited to my own character in hostile circumstances. Surely that would rate as an achievement.'

'You misunderstand us' (us!) 'deliberately,' said Alan. 'All Billy meant is that you are not especially *famous* for anything in particular.'

'But I am, dearest, I am. Only perhaps not in the circles you are moving in.' My voice became warm, animated, really friendly and intimate: 'You mean it would be all the more fascinating if I could point my finger at the symphony I composed whilst running away. Or a handful of poems might have shed their glow over my humble story — rucksack on my back and pen poised at the ready? But you're both wrong, don't you see? ' I started whispering like a conspirator and the two men had to lean forward to catch my words.

'There wouldn't have *been* any story, can't you grasp that? Helping hands would have shot out all over the globe, headlines in the papers, men and women falling over themselves, eager to get a share in the glory of the famous fugitive. As it was I did the lot myself. Like a bird being stoned by nasty boys I invented the most cunning ways of flying. Yes, we *were* great inventors, every one of us.' I went on

142

almost dreamily: 'Famous ad-libbers, improvisers, very skilled operators indeed. So resourceful, such ingenious stratagems and dodges. Such foresight, such tricks and machinations. Isn't *that* famous?'

Alan and Billy had both lowered their eyes. Like swords in a duel. It acknowledged their defeat. Well — embarrassment is a kind of defeat, isn't it?

*　　*　　*

I sometimes regretted my outbursts but knew they were strictly necessary. There might be a time when all would be sunshine and light — but not yet. I had never told my story to Ted and did not propose to do so. Alan had been right as usual — damn him. I might not have cried for the moon if Sebastian had been with me. But — this thought struck me forcefully — his absence was just as potent as his presence; it propelled me into fresh waters. Therefore back to the Zen class.

Of course it was a class and of course we were 'taught'. Some things in the teaching worried me but I would not have stayed away for the world. If — so Herman Hesse says — you don't find out what you are meant to do in this life, then you are like a clock without hands. I did not fancy being an empty clockface, so I went off to listen once more to Ted. The next session was lively.

One of three women, a rabbity little creature, suddenly piped up in the discussion: 'I don't see where all our talk is leading to. We never seem to get anywhere, let alone experience Satori.'

Ted winced. So did a few others. Satori or Enlightenment was the ultimate goal of all Zen teaching and looked, to our minds, like Peace, Freedom, the switch to the Universal Powerhouse or pure and simple Bliss. But it was never mentioned in so many words. Thou shalt not speak the name. . . . we did not speak.

Now we were told there was no 'way' to it, that on the one hand you could do nothing to get there, but the 'nothing' was not altogether zero. Confusing, but riveting. One thought of all those monks in the Zen monasteries sweating away doing nothing. Amazing, not to say maddening.

I missed a few sentences from the rabbity woman and just caught: '. . . . no good concentrating because I can't really control myself.'

'Can't you?' Ted asked amiably, 'just who is doing the controlling?'

'Why — myself, of course.'

'Just you then. That's what you mean, isn't it?'

'Of course. There is nobody else.'

'If there's nobody else — who's controlling whom?' Silence. 'Who gives the orders and who obeys?' Ted insisted.

'There must be two then,' Lucien said. He was the boy who had stared so hard at Melissa. 'One who commands and one who carries out the orders.'

'Or maybe there are three — the third one decides whether to obey or not.' Ted's rosy face was split in a grin. 'We *are* getting crowded. No wonder everything is in a mess if you have to accommodate a slinging match every time you make a decision.'

'There is no fight,' Lucien said with dignity. 'I do what my conscience tells me.'

'Ooooh, I see,' Ted said gleefully, 'you've got a little man sitting there, a sort of referee. Where exactly does he sit?'

'In my mind of course.'

'He sits in *your* mind like in occupied territory?'

'He means his subconscious,' an older man said.

'Good grief!' Ted threw up his hands. Then he said coarsely: 'I'm not a headshrinker, Sir. You've come to the wrong place.'

'Show us the way to the right one,' the older man said. We were all thinking it anyway. Ted started singing:

'Show us the way to go home,' in a drunken voice and left the room.

We must have been the most frustrated bunch this side of the ocean. The godseekers were frustrated because there was no God in Zen, so were the 'love your neighbourites' as there wasn't any love yet. The people who hoped Ted would come up with a nice replacement for a deity were disappointed and the do-it-yourself eastern psychology brigade did not fare any better.

Despite all that, we felt that Ted was 'superior'. He laughed a lot, was immensely knowledgeable and shot his answers off like bullets.

'Tell us the truth, Ted,' we begged.

He stood in front of us, grinning. Walked up and down, faced us again and roared: 'You want the truth? And

144

nothing but? I'll tell you! It's gotta add up, make sense. Let's have a bookkeeper, an accountant — he'll wrap it up for you and tie it with ribbons. The truth? What *are* you talking about? Ours? Yours and mine? The chinaman's? The pussy-cats? Or all of them? Where do the trees come in and the bumblebees?'

We all thought he had a secret weapon.

* * *

'I'll take you out for dinner, Julia, unless you're having one of your soulscraper evenings.'

'Grills and salads, oh, and oysters, I can eat those.'

'And no doubt lobsters and caviar.'

'Yes, dearest, they're on my diet sheet.'

'Would you have come if Ted the Magnificent had called?'

'I don't think so.' I kissed him. 'It's time you woke up to the facts. Give me a few years and Ted's subject will be on the curriculum of every school, every university. Perhaps not just in this particular way — but as a basic. It will be unthinkable to future generations to leave the inner world unexplored.

'I thought that was done in the consulting room.'

'For sick people, dearest. Those with boundless energy will explore their own mind. Want a bet?' I smiled at Alan happily: 'There'll be the most tremendous discoveries, things you can't even dream of. I can't bear the idea that I won't be there any more when that happens! I'll get ready.' I looked into the mirror and thought my face was less spiritual than I would have wished. But it was strangely smooth and unlined, small grey eyes tilted at the corner, hair still cut in a fringe with nail scissors. The expression in the eyes had changed though — maybe the spirit was breaking through after all. Or I just could not come to grips with the sad fact that I could never — ever — eat a cream bun for the rest of my life.

* * *

Ted, as ever dressed in flannels and jumper, never one to slink about mournfully as so many spiritual giants did, entered the classroom even more energetically than usual.

145

He practically bounced off the floor and said we were going to 'attack' the Koan today.

Koan: the bulldozer which would break through the wall of our ignorance and make us see into our 'true' nature with more questions. There was, of course, the most famous of them all: what is the sound of one hand clapping? As generations before us, we sat down and started to 'think' logically. We always tried this method, even later on when we knew it was no good at all. It's almost unthinkable to break out of a pattern.

You would wriggle like a worm on a hook, or sit tight and try to force a reasonable answer until your brain got overheated, steam coming out of your ears, all the while thinking there's *got* to be an answer, there must be some way to get at it, or they would not have put the question. Well there was *no* answer, at least not one you could have called 'normal'.

The question got a hold on you, eating its way into your mind, digging about like a dog for a buried bone, throwing up a lot of muck in the process. Thinking was quite rational to begin with: There can't possibly *be* a sound, if only one hand keeps thrashing through the air. Did the hand hit something or other? Did he perhaps mean a different interpretation of the word 'sound'? Does he mean movement? Or is he perhaps mad?

Maybe I am. Isn't it an awful waste of time to imagine this lonely hand without its twin? Why can't it hit something nice and solid and produce a normal healthy noise? Or is the noise symbolic? Symbolic of what?

Another Koan was: What was your original face before you were born? This might give more scope for roaming around. I wondered what the other students were doing. I opened my eyes for a split second and took in the other faces in the class, looking as tormented as if about to enter the gates of hell. They really were suffering intensely. At this moment Ted added by way of confusing us completely: 'your original face when your mind is not dwelling on the dualism of good and evil.' Now what does he mean by that? In the biblical sense? Or like a court of law? Morally? And what could my original face be? Does he mean my parents, my grandparents, or does it go back to Neanderthal man? He can't just mean the family — or? I really am happy that my parents took the family tree when they left Germany. A

146

splendid tree too, going right back to Don Jose de Calahora (better, much better than Percival), physician to the King of Spain in the fifteenth century. There's some original face for you. He must have had a splendid black beard and smouldering eyes, beautiful ladies of the court swooning at his approach. . . . Back to the Koan.

I think Ted means just my face. My *face?* For God's sake I did not have a face before I was born, Perhaps in my parents' mind or in God's mind. Has He got a mind or is He just mind? And why should He have my face in it? I'm sure he means my special qualities and faults, my character. I began to fidget. I heard chairs creaking, so others would be fidgeting too. I listened to the moaning and groaning of the 'Koan crackers', people about to take leave of their senses — obviously. Some were breathing deeply — oxygen increases your brain power; some were ringing their hands so strongly that I could hear the squelching noise of skin rubbing against skin. There was a lot of coughing such as comes from an audience when the action slows down. Others moved their lips, producing gasps and sighs. They were working themselves into a frenzy.

That seemed to be just what Ted required: ordinary intelligence cannot cope with this kind of question. Therefore the mind in its wisdom would overthrow the logical thought process and strike at the root of its functioning, a secret chamber of the mind would then open. He said that we should not try to solve a riddle. Just blow the cobwebs away and reveal the clear untroubled mind which had always been there from the beginning.

The cobwebs in our circle were unusually thick and persistent. Except for Miss Todd, it seemed. She cleared her throat: 'This has done me a lot good. I'm now able to assess life much better.'

'Who asked you to?' Ted asked rudely.

'Isn't that what you want us to do — on the whole?'

'Go on then, assess it!' Ted said grimly.

Miss Todd lifted her chin and looked religious. She fixed her eyes on the Great Beyond and pronounced: 'Life is one continuous effort to grow — to become one with the Universe.'

'Does the universe merge into you or you into it?' Ted kept a straight face.

'We merge into each other.' It sounded indecent.

'And how do you know when that happens?'

'I feel fulfilment, a supreme satisfaction.'

'Like a slap-up dinner.'

'But I'm serious. . . .' she almost cried.

'You call *that* being serious? You churn out the same old tunes like a barrel organ. I've heard them a million times. I want *your* words, *your* thoughts, not things you've read in a book! There's no vitality, no independence. Drop everything you've ever known, violate it, jump out of it — but don't produce a feeble echo of other people, you — copytypist!' He sounded really angry and Miss Todd looked crushed. Ted charged up and down the room like an angry bull then stormed out in a flash. He left all of us hanging on a broken thread, all except Gresham. He sat, quietly smiling to himself, eyes closed, hands folded.

After Gresham had joined the group he went through the usual stages. First he told Ted what was wrong with the group, with the world, with him; then he started making furtive appearances in the library, grabbing books haphazardly. Then he became more careful in his choice, reading night and day like a maniac. He'd been bitten by the bug like the rest of us. It wasn't that he 'got Religion' — he just turned himself inside out.

Melissa said he never talked of anything else, that he refused the company of people who could not share his all-consuming interest and that he constantly urged her to join. He really was getting down to it, wrestling like a champion.

'A whole life,' he kept saying, 'and I never suspected.' He used to look like a bulldog, scowling and aggressive. He became gentler, much quieter and of finer quality. When he found Lucien smoking he said reproachfully that there was no need for external stimulants, for it was all 'in there' pointing at the books on the shelves. We began to like him more and more as one likes a child, fondly remembering our own shortcomings.

At one meeting he decided to tackle Ted about the variety of teachings available: 'Sufism, Zen, Taoism, the Cabbalah, the Christians, all those Buddhist teachings — how will I know if I'm on the right track. What happens if I'm not?'

'You get your money back,' Ted said drily.

'It's the uncertainty. I've got to be sure —'

'There is a certain wisdom in wavering. You can't go wrong while you're searching.'

'That's true, that's very true! I've never felt that before. What a thought! Could you recommend a book?'

'I'd rather the book recommended itself to you.'

'That's — extraordinary.' Gresham had entered the stage of Ted-worship and was sitting in adoration as from now. Not that Ted enjoyed this: he demolished Gresham's attitude systematically. It was fascinating to see Gresham grow up and grow out of his preconceived notions which were legion.

I imagined a long line of ancestors producing finally Gresham Ailmsford, the big money spinner, the financial wizard — only to see him join the line of the ardent Koan crackers, waiting to be blown clean out of his mind.

'But I've got to be in my right mind to function,' he complained to Ted, 'not out of it.'

'I never said you are in it now. You always imagine you get something less than you have now. It will be more, more, *more!*'

At the coffee break Gresham told us that he would have to 'do' something about it. We had all said that at one stage or other and meant it. But nobody ever went very far. We thought Gresham was the same. He would talk, discuss, read — but never act, never let his whole life be taken over by the craving to understand it. He just was not the type.

When I saw him next he was just emerging from the battleship. This was usually quite a ceremony. He fixed a burglar's device. Quite unnecessary — no burglar in his right mind would want to be seen in this outsize vehicle. He might as well have written 'stolen' on the windscreen. Then he checked all four doors, pulling each handle in turn. After that he looked critically at the wheels, measuring the distance between them and the kerb.

He would then circle round the car, shaking his head as if to say it does not look as perfect as it could, perhaps remove a bird's dropping with a frown, rub off a small offensive spot, give the headlight a quick polish with his sleeve. He could not tear himself away from the car any more than a mother could from her baby. One felt he would have liked to wrap the whole gleaming structure in a protective blanket.

He gazed apprehensively up and down the road for hell-bent drivers who might endanger his unique treasure, then peered inside, stepped back and surveyed the vehicle once more from a little distance and, finally satisfied, patted it on the top.

But today he jumped out gingerly, slammed the door and entered the house without as much as a backward look. He sat down quietly, feet crossed, hands folded, head inclined to one side. He really looked serene, a word which would not have crossed my mind before with a harsh brittle personality like his. Ted, who never missed a thing, addressed him right away.

'You are smiling. What about?'

'I feel glad — I am happy.'

'*Who* are *you*?' This dreaded uncomfortable question was shot at us many times and we were never able to answer it to Ted's satisfaction. But Gresham was not put out at all. Only a little while ago he might have given an uninteresting account of his occupation, hobbies, emotional states — the very last thing Ted wanted to know. But as he began to talk now, he seemed like somebody with invisible earphones, listening to an inner broadcast. He was the only one who had discovered that Ted wanted a blow by blow account of the actual process of living.

'I wonder,' he said his voice trailing off. He paused thoughtfully. 'I think I'm never the same two minutes running. All can be reversed instantly by a word, a sight, a smell, a gesture, a breeze from the window or a cup of coffee. A tone of voice changes me, a smile alters my whole attitude. Only one permanent feature remains, a determination, a will to push on. . . .'

'Where to?'

'Here,' Gresham said smilingly, touching his heart. The gesture did not look out of place. 'I've explored many rooms in my house, I know all the passages but not the foundations. How can I run it properly?' (Gresham being poetic? We listened in wonder.) 'I obviously am not qualified to do so by myself, and I've found out that it's a fulltime job.' His smile deepened: 'I shall go to Japan in a fortnight.'

Dead silence. We all talked at once except Ted. I saw his eyes narrowing and his lips curve downward in an involuntary slight sneer.

Gresham looked round the room like a conjurer who still has the best trick up his sleeve: 'I'm going to enter a Zen monastery.'

Nobody moved. Ted was not exactly pleased with this astonishing bit of news. I probably imagined his rosy face becoming paler. But his self-control was unfailing and he sounded just curious when he asked: 'And how will you manage that?'

'It's done, arranged like a super business deal, wholeheartedly. This is going to be the grandest business of all — living properly.' He bowed slightly in Ted's direction: 'I apologise. But two hours a week is not enough, it's got to be twenty-four hours round the clock.' We were literally stunned into silence. Gresham of all people. . . . 'I have business friends in Tokyo. They were happy to make the arrangements. I think they would be pleased if more people would come. I can't wait.'

Gresham — a monk. I wondered how Melissa would react. We in the group all had the same reaction: a most unbecoming envy.

*　　*　　*

Melissa needed moral support. She took me along to London Airport to see Gresham off.

'I did not know him at all,' she wailed. 'I'm already beginning to miss him, now that I found I never looked at him properly.'

'Neither did he, it seems.'

'But he called those people a bunch of cranks. Why this sudden urge?'

'You know what they say — cranks of today, hopes of tomorrow. As to this sudden urge, heaps of people have it. Only they don't do anything about it.'

'No man would throw his whole life into the balance.'

'That's why they get stuck and turn around like a ferret in a wheel.'

When Gresham kissed Melissa goodbye her eyes were full of tears. She would have done anything to keep him with her, although she knew she did not stand a chance. Gresham carried a small suitcase and a rolled umbrella.

'I won't need much where I'm going,' he said happily. He left the battleship to Melissa and enough money to feed it for a lifetime. The plane soared up into the clouds and I imagined him in his seat, hands folded, feet crossed, head slightly inclined to one side, smiling.

*　　*　　*

Had Ted undergone some sort of change since Gresham's departure? Had he lost something of his undisputed authority now that it was brought home to us that he did not have the last word? Or was one evening a week really a poor substitute for the real thing?

'I want to come along once more,' Melissa said. 'I must find out what Gresham was after. I've never seen such a drastic change in all my life. Or else my powers of observation are non-existent.'

But it soon became obvious that her interest was divided to say the least. She and Lucien got together almost immediately now that Gresham was gone. Lucien's gypsy looks were the exact opposite to her last friend's. A mop of black curls down to his eyebrows (he said he had a Hungarian grandfather), coloured shirts half unbuttoned, large dark eyes with monumental lashes — one could imagine him wearing golden earrings. The pair of them drove off as soon as the class was finished. They listened to Ted during the session but were mentally holding hands all through the evening. Finally they stopped coming altogether.

Ted only referred once to their absence: 'A bed is not the worst place to find yourself in. . . .' Rather the only place, I felt, where you got true glimpses of another larger life. There was no room for anything else, all was concentrated here, now at this moment, completely right and perfect. The greatest music, the most sublime art, the most beautiful scenery — all left you longing. I admired Ted for saying so but somehow his sparkle had been dimmed. Gresham's departure must have affected him deeply. And he did not underestimate the latter's remark that two hours a week was not sufficient. It was painfully obvious that this short period would not alter anybody's mental structure, unless, like Gresham, you discovered a hidden spring strong enough to propel you onwards. Lucien and Melissa's departure added to the uneasiness spreading in the group.

Most people stayed loyal to Ted. Did I? Or did I begin to resent that we were a little cowed, a little subdued in Ted's presence? Perhaps we were overwhelmed by the familiarity of the subject he was teaching. Our questions had some measure of deference in them, they were never straight, never direct, always fearing one would look a fool if one really spoke out. Nobody ever mentioned a deity nor death either, or the obscenity of the seconds ticking away. Embarrassment? Fear? Ted might say 'there's nothing there!' and the dyke might break and let the floods in.

One day I had the courage to speak out: 'Here we sit, licking our lips, manipulating our precious minds, when there are wars everywhere, people suffering agonies, distress, horror — and all we do is take our mental temperatures!'

'What do you suggest,' Ted asked, 'a crusade?'

'A peaceful cause perhaps —'

'Like Oxfam.' Laughter. 'My dearest Julia, you lounge about on your social conscience like on a comfortable settee. Why don't you get up and do something?'

'I don't feel I can, I wouldn't know where to begin, I'm so incomplete myself.'

'There — only functioning partly, that's what I'm saying. That's why you keep coming and don't plant trees in the desert. You might one day, who knows? But while you sit here you can't stick a knife into your neighbour. Ever thought of that? While your energies go inside they don't beat hell out of somebody else. Isn't that something?' Another point for Ted. But was it enough?

*　　*　　*

Melissa, usually so eloquent, sighed deeply, put her cup down, sighed again and just said ahh.

'Is he that marvellous?' I asked.

'Yes. He's perfect. To think I would never have met him but for Gresham. I'm so grateful to him. And he doesn't hold me under the microscope like some people I know.'

'But you are watched nightly by hundreds of people.'

'I get paid for it and I do it on purpose. I always feel Alan's pinning you down.'

'It flatters me — he only wants to understand.'

'Perhaps. But the moment will come when he knows it all, when he can predict your slightest movements, what then?'

'I'm not static, I'll have you know. I'm changing all the time.'

'Even your changes will be familiar to him.'

'I'll shut up then and just make love.'

'That too will pale.'

'It doesn't. It gets better —'

'Not all the time.' She grinned maliciously: 'You can't

153

change the main attraction, that will always be the same all round.'

'Melissa! No pornography in public.' I looked around our favourite cafe — almost empty at this time in the morning. 'I would be a poor specimen if I had to *try* to keep my man interested. I'm not a performing seal. I'm just pleased that I can provide him with new and interesting details. I need an echo.'

'Where does Sebastian come in?'

'He's there all the time.'

'You look idiotically romantic.'

'That's how I feel. I can't do a thing about it.'

'Maybe you can —'

'Another one of your hunches?'

'More than that. I know a truly phenomenal clairvoyant.'

'You can't be serious.'

'Never more so. Just before I landed my present part I got so nervous waiting around that I called on him. He's well known in the theatre world.'

'So are you. It's ridiculous.'

'I assure you he was astonishing. He knew the type of part I would be getting, what the reviews would be like and the kind of reaction I would have from the public. All correct. He even mentioned the one paper which tore the play to bits and my part in it. Quite amazing. Here,' she put it all down on a piece of paper, 'that's his address. Take it — I know you'll go anyway.'

Of course I went to see Mr Peters as soon as he would have me. Sebastian still governed my every action, sat lodged inside me like a second heart. Melissa said that those feelings belonged to a bygone age. But they were there all the same; my energies reaching out into the void were atomized and lost. There was nothing Mr Peters could possibly spoil.

His house stood in a cul de sac in a quiet suburb. Quite old, with roses and ivy climbing up the front. Inside the set-up was cosy. Potted flowers on the window sill, framed family pictures, a pipe in an ashtray next to a cup of tea. Mr Peters was an old man, short and stocky, rather like a garden gnome. His hands, I noticed, were firm, well shaped with a long thumb and rosy nails (good blood circulation). In that split second, before articulate thoughts come and sit in judgement, the moment he entered the door, I felt as if somebody stirred me with a giant spoon.

He started with a routine pattern — a sort of warming up exercise: money, journeys, relations. Then he reached another stage and became more specific, scoring several direct hits. I knew better than to confirm or deny (my palm reading days had taught me the value of silence), I just let him speak. I was obviously a foreigner living in England. There would have been a great amount of upheavals in my life. He just knew his contemporary history well. It would account for some of the information he 'received' but not for specific names and places.

He was just saying: 'There is a girl, redhaired, blue-eyed called Mou — Ma — Marouchka. She is dead and you regret her still. She's the only girlfriend you really miss. Please correct me if I'm wrong.' Marouchka had been my best friend at school. We were called the heavenly twins because we were never apart. She was caught when crossing the frontier into Switzerland during the war and killed herself before her captors could. It still hurt me every time I remembered her.

'She killed herself,' Mr Peters said and regretfully I thought that he was only reading my mind. Although a considerable achievement, I would have been happier if he had picked it up from somewhere else.

'You are right,' I said, 'but what about the future?'

'I'm coming to that — if you really want it.'

'It's the only thing I want: the future.'

Mr Peters did not look at me; his eyes fixed on a point on the wall just above my head and he started talking as if he was giving the commentary to a silent film.

'I see somebody looking at your poems — you've just written them. It's a man, tall and fairhaired. He seems very pleased about your writing — but you are not. Something's missing — *somebody*! That's spoiling it for you, you want him to see your writing, you think it's not worthwhile without him reading it, but you don't know where he is, you don't even know,' Mr Peters' voice was hardly audible, 'whether he is still alive. But I am telling you he is. He *is*. I can see him and you are going to meet him quite soon.'

I could not stand it any longer and said urgently: 'When, how, what's he like? I *must* know!'

'You'll meet him by accident; it's not planned at all. You will not have to do anything about it, it will happen when you expect it least. I can see lots of people around, a big crowd, coming out of a large building. You are among them

155

and so is he. But you will not enjoy meeting him.'

'Describe him, please!'

'Tall, hardly any hair, thin. A modest sad-looking man.'

'You are wrong — you *are* wrong. I don't know any such man!'

'But you will meet him and he is the one you are thinking about. I'll stake my reputation on it. I can see him clearly, tall, sad and somewhat shabby with a briefcase under his arm.'

I was almost in tears: 'That is not the same man. The one I mean is strong and clever, everybody knows him, he's brilliant, he does marvellous things, admired throughout the world. He can't and never will be modest!'

'We are talking about the same man.' Mr Peters' voice remained calm. 'You *are* going to meet him before long and you will turn away from him as if he had the plague.'

'I will turn *away* from him?'

'As surely as you are sitting in this room. You will not be able to bear his presence — as if he was stricken by the plague.'

I paid and proceeded to forget everything the clairvoyant had said as fast as I could.

*   *   *

Naturally I said nothing to Alan but I did not mention it to Melissa either. Walking away from Mr Peters' house, I had felt a quick hot stab remembering my poems. They probably *had* stopped flowing because the one they were meant for could not be reached. I was walking through the Gardens at Kensington and thought with relief of Ted and his classes. They would chase away any ghosts quickly enough. I was going to give the teaching my whole attention and energy.

When Ted appeared on the scene I thought at first he must have been gardening. He wore a short, sandcoloured apron with a strap round his neck, rectangular, made of some coarse material which looked like hessian. Then I noticed a black stick in his hand and drew my breath in sharply. Why this masquerade all of a sudden? Why wear the insignias of the Zen teachers in Japan? What did he want to demonstrate?

Perhaps he had secretly wanted to wear it ever since

Gresham left for Japan. Maybe he was wearing a mental apron too. My spirits sank instantly. If he felt the need to show that he was different from us, *more* than us, that he needed implements to restore his authority — well. The next thing would be to prop up an image and start worshipping or dancing around it. What's the difference. I might as well convert myself to Catholicism or another Ism. Would he start talking in a foreign language, to make it all appear more mysterious, more secret and attractive? He's the boss — it's his privilege, bloody hell! He would look bigger and we smaller. I was deeply upset. The great liberation was about to fly out of the window.

But wait. Maybe he was just testing us, Zen people were known to be great practical jokers. That's indeed what made Zen so attractive, this weird, outrageous sense of humour, this lack of reverence ('Burn the Buddha if you need a fire'). My goodness! He was not going to trot out the same old tune: I've got something you haven't. 'I will not serve,' James Joyce whispered in my ear. Right. I shall not bow to anybody or anything, not on *that* territory.

If Zen was to open up Life itself and receive me in its arms I was not going to be fobbed off with an apron! No, Sir!

'Why, Ted?' I asked in a sad voice.

'Do you object to this?' He touched the apron.

'I can't take it. I'm allergic to symbols.'

'It's a detail, it should not be so important for you.'

'It has not been for you — until this moment.'

'Zen comes from the East. They do wear it there.'

'I don't wear a kimono when I listen to Madame Butterfly,' I said hotly. 'I would feel I'm dressing up, playing a part. Oh Ted! Are you going to whack us over the shoulders with that thing?' I pointed to the black stick. It was used in monasteries to crack down on the shoulders of the unfortunate monks who had nodded off in the middle of meditation. It was also known to produce sudden enlightenment when applied at the strategic moment. But a monastery in Japan was one thing and Ted Collins in London SW7 quite another.

'I fail to see why you are so upset, Julia.'

'Because you are taking it all away from me, all you have given so freely. You said Zen goes right to the heart of the matter — no frills, it's practical, quick and direct. You compared it to lightning. Lightning is natural — not clad in ceremonial robes.'

'Nobody else seems to mind.'

'But *I* do — very much. We might as well shave our heads and eyebrows and have done with it. It's a step *back*, back to the idols, symbols and the sacrifice. You can't put an apron on life. Life! Isn't that what Zen is about? How to live? It all looked so clean, so pure and original. Untainted. An apron is a fragment — where is the whole, Ted? Under the apron?'

'I am not accountable to you for my actions.'

'But you *are*. We are listening to you. That makes you accountable. I thought there were no rules and regulations. . . . the art of forgetting the self. But this! This piece of shabby cloth that brings back the whole past. It reminds us each second that you are *different*, an apron carrier. You have prepared yourself, dressed up for the performance.' I almost cried with bitterness. I felt outraged.

'You must control yourself!'

'I will not. It's too important — I'm not at school . You said it's a constant road to discovery, as new as the first song on earth, as free as a bird. You kill our freedom with a black stick. Everything is reduced to a square of hessian!'

'You are upsetting the other members in the group. You must leave if you can't control yourself.'

'I don't care if I set the house on fire. It's wrong, wrong, wrong! You've turned some corner and have come up with an *object*. Teacher's wearing it, accept it! Maybe Miss Todd wants to wear an apron too. Would you let her?'

'That would be presumptuous. It would simply look wrong.'

'But it does not look right on you either. How does this help us to look into the nature of things or into our own for that matter? "I've got it and you haven't." It's petty. A disguise.' I got very worked up for it was vital to me. Were. my heavens falling in because Ted was dressing up? Shouldn't I watch my reactions? I watched them: they told me that dressing up had become part of the teaching. They also told me Ted had just created a privilege. It went against the grain.

'You said,' I started once more, well aware that nobody in the group had said a single word, 'you said Zen was open, light and transparent like water in a brook. You said it knew no boundaries, no limits, no restrictions. You've just raised a wall at your end of the field. Your apron is blotting out the light. Bury all contrasts, you said. You've created a new one: here we are, apronless, therefore incomplete, whilst you sit on the throne in a *garment*, wielding a stick! You rule over us, the herd, the flock, the followers. It opens an abyss and —' I lost my temper altogether.

'What do I call you from now on? Not Ted? No. Reverend? Venerable? Father Superior?' (Quick march of the Prussian Army goosestepping smartly through the streets of Berlin dressed up to kill.) 'You're dressed up, dressed up, *dressed* up! Do we ask for permission to speak? Will all be taken down in evidence?' I turned away from Ted, completely isolated, judging by the looks I got from the others. Ted never met my eyes once, not even when I finished: 'I am not attending a service. Why don't you speak Latin, I mean Sanskrit, or Pali, or something, so we don't understand?' I stopped for breath, my heart beating as always when my tongue ran away with me. But I did not regret a single word. I meant everything I had said.

'I shall do just that,' Ted said. 'There will be a prayer in a language, you, Julia, will not be able to follow.' (Isolate the trouble maker by calling her by her name!) 'We shall do it at each meeting and we will turn to the East while saying it. I've brought the prayer with me in print, so you can all join in.' He handed out white cardboard sheets with foreign words spreading out like a maze.

I felt cold as the others rose from their chairs and I remained seated. They stood erect, facing east, mumbling the new words on command. It sounded quite hypnotic as the voices were low and uncertain, chanting timidly according to Ted's guidance. I wanted no part in it. Ted was building a cage — the mind, free, proud and happy, had become a prisoner once more. I felt bad indeed, rejecting such sublime teaching for a trivial alteration in procedure.

No, don't let yourself be submerged: it is *not* trivial, it poisons the atmosphere. Ted's apron had cast its gloom and ashes on it. It glittered and shimmered no longer — dulled by a piece of cloth and a black stick.

I knew the teaching was not to blame. But I could not pick up the pieces in this room. Somewhere else maybe, where I would not have to bend my own nature, where I could agree from the very depth of my heart.

I calmed down, thanked Ted for all he had done and said, overdoing it in my wish to be pleasant, that he had opened a new world for me all the same.

'Just a matchbox,' he said. 'I hope you will find what you are looking for. ... if there is such a thing.'

Then, for the first time, he put his hands together in true oriental fashion, palms joined, fingertips plunging downward. I kissed him on the cheek, waved to the other members of the group and left, feeling thoroughly dismayed. They say whoever seeks shall find. I doubted this very much at that moment.

It was a colossal let-down, there was no denying it. I had plunged into Zen like into a first love, blindly and totally. But my lover turned out to be a robot, put together on an assembly line centuries long — with a tag round his neck: manufactured in Japan.

Tags are for suitcases, as the man said.

The teaching itself was sublime and eternal. The teacher, alas! was not.

* * *

'Quite an expert in walkouts,' Alan said when I told him about the class. 'It's becoming a habit, have you noticed? You walk out of the camp, out of the country, out of the group. I wonder when you are going to walk out on me.'

'I know when I'm well off.'

'I wonder. You walked out on your parents and what about that time in the Salvation Army?' He smiled — a little condescendingly, an English smile, teeth barely showing between tight lips, eyes not lighting up.

'You are lacking in charm,' I said, 'you look like a shark.'

'Why don't you go and spill your poison on more poems?'

'I might. Why don't *you* try and show a little kindness? Understanding, sweetheart, that's what I need, just a little understanding. After all, you are at home here. I'm but a sad small guest. Show a little courtesy.'

'What are you talking about? You belong here. That's where your son was born. You are settled, integrated, your troubles are over — except the ones you create anew daily.'

'Integrated?' I made it sound offensive. 'Zorba the Greek said, go looking for trouble, it's the only way to feel alive.'

'You've got all the life you need and you are no different from the rest of us. Zorba is a piece of fiction. I'm not concerned with him. But you! You still wallow in your precious past like a hippo in the mud. No wonder you can't shake off the dirt.'

'Dirt, did you say? A most unfortunate expression. Typical though — typical for your kind of person.' I was still speaking quietly, sitting in our garden, becalmed by the sunshine and the soft sweet spring air. 'Yes, Alan, the kind of person who's never known the meaning of trouble.'

'I've seen more of it than you have. In the war for instance.'

'Have you then?'

'Indeed I have. *I* have fought, which is more than can be said of. . . .'

I got up slowly, my arms dropping by my side. 'Of whom, what do you mean, dearest?'

'I mean those people running all over the place instead of making a stand.'

Although my body began to burn I still noticed Alan's uneasiness, the shrugging of his shoulders. 'Can't contradict you there — people were running. Stupid of them really. They *should* have made a stand, arms or no arms. Odd nobody thought of that. My father was such a clever lawyer, he should have pleaded with the Germans. Of course!' I tapped my hand against my forehead. '"Look," he should have said, "we are decent honest Germans just like you, why don't we come to an understanding, we'll fight alongside you and, what's more, provide you with the right mental ammunition which you are somewhat lacking. Jews are well known for having super brains." How about that? I can't think why we were not up to the mark, why we went running all over the place.'

'You know I did not mean it like that.' Alan sounded apologetic but I was past arguments. He had touched one of the last landmines and it was going to explode. 'There's no need to sneer, I have faced death a hundred times myself.' Alan was quite agitated by now, striding up and down nervously, his heels grinding the soil.

'Death — but what kind of death? There are so many. You, my friend, soared up high in the skies with a machine gun at your fingertips. You only had to press the trigger. You fought on equal terms, with equal weapons. What do you know of trouble? You say mine are over? Where have they gone — into thin air? Gone with the wind? Don't you see *anything*? My heart, my lungs, my nerves are damaged,

161

I'm still feeling it all, still running, still hiding, still stumbling down the prison steps. I'm damaged!'

'You've got to finish with your past. It's over — settle and forget!'

'I'd rather be a falling Icarus than a mole in a hole!'

'You've got to come to terms one day.'

'Help, help, the man's a fake. Whose terms? Yours? Look at him — he reasons, he argues, he holds forth, wrapped into layers of cotton wool. Protected! Back, front and sides — swathed and soothed by his country, by his family, his colleagues and *camarades*, his club, his language, his background, his surroundings —' I became incoherent it hurt so much 'his clouds, his sun, his bloody great spider city while I,' I sobbed, 'am lost forever. My ship will never come home, it's foundered on the rocks.'

I would have murdered anybody who said so but I had not felt so well in years.

*　　*　　*

Maybe I *should* be getting rid of my particular bit of universal muck and write more poems. I had written some little verses for John but then no more. That was a year ago. Nothing interesting since my outcry to Melissa resulting in the Mantra. I sat at the back of the garden, scribbling. It was lovely to peel off layer after layer. My vitality grew, the symptoms of youth established themselves: I looked forward eagerly to each new day. There was never enough time. I rang all and sundry at odd hours. I read like a maniac, clasping books to my heart, stroking and patting them, murmuring, good, good, that's what I need, sucking strength from them like an infant.

If I can explode the last mines I won't need to row with Alan, I thought, breaking a biro into half. It was like peeping through a keyhole: so that's what she's up to. What cunning and ferocity. It can't be me, I kept saying to myself, when yet another line of savagery emerged from the second biro. If only it sounded more like poetry and less like the growls of an animal. But I became sweet and reasonable, purged of frustration and bitterness for the moment. Alan crooned over my work like a proud father. He even started illustrating the poems and reading them aloud to an uncomprehending John. What a time we had. This went on — hectically — for some while until I woke up one morning and knew — this time with absolute certainty and finality that there was no more to come. I would never write another line. I copied some on the typewriter, hoping to catch fire. No good. The machine sat under its hood like a slab in the morgue.

* * *

Opposite me Melissa sat wearing a hat. It was made of blue velvet, beautifully fashioned with a wide curving rim framing her face to perfection. But I missed the foxy mane.

'Does Lucien like it? Or does he think you look too good without it?'

'I shall stop dying my hair, it's too flashy.'

'Says Lucien.'

She nodded.

'But it catches all eyes when you're on the stage.'

'I might not be on it for very much longer. I will have to sell the battleship, we need the money.'

'We?'

'I'm marrying Lucien. We need a home. Julia, I want babies, lots of them. But not just now. You know what he said?' She started to whisper in an awestruck manner: 'He said we should not — we should wait till we are married.'

'Is he a pervert? How can you possibly tie your life to somebody you don't know?'

'I know everything about him but that. It's old-fashioned to hop into bed with everyone just for the hell of it.'

'Everyone? You are only going to be his wife for the next fifty years. It's not decent. . . . the risk you are taking.'

'He's had lots of girlfriends. He wants us to be different, unique. This is really *it*. I even adore the buttons on his shirt.'

'As long as they stay buttoned, I suppose.'

'You've got a dirty mind. There is nothing coarse about it.'

'Forgive me, but I do care.'

'Will you be my best woman at the wedding?'

'Seeing that it's your first.'

She kissed me, glowing with pleasure.

* * *

Benjamin often came to the house, enjoying long chats with both of us. Alan was always slightly guarded. We were sitting on the terrace in the dark, a little fountain splashing in the pond, trees rustling overhead. I talked about Melissa, with a barely discernible trace of envy. I said there had been a drastic transformation in my friend's character and mental make-up, as she was considering leaving the theatre. 'Abdicate' was the word I used.

'What an odd word to use for a happy woman', Alan said. 'She is just beginning. It needs courage in her case. She is successful.'

'At least she knows what she wants,' I sighed. 'I do not seem to —' The clock struck from the nearby church.

'Maybe *I* know,' Benjamin said. 'You do not want to live on your knees, mentally speaking.'

'God — yes. I want to stand up.' *What* was I after? What had been set in motion so long ago and what was it I wanted to recover? What was so important that at all times I had a sense of loss, almost of bereavement. As a child 'it' was there — often. There is a place somewhere, warm and beautiful and safe. No, no! *Not* the womb, no jargon, no platitudes. I was there once, but I've lost the way. There wonders never ceased, enchantment was my daily bread, I remember, I remember. . . .

'You are very quiet, Julia,' Alan said, 'where are you?'

'Way back,' I said softly 'where it all began, when I was home, home —'

'I know a man,' Benjamin said, 'who is always home, always on his own ground. He is coming to London this week. And he is not wearing an apron.' I could see Alan smile in the dark: 'I am sure Julia can't resist any kind of revelation, even if it's been played a thousand times.' He was damned right — I couldn't.

'Let's have a drink,' Alan said, 'to toast your new enterprise.' He switched the light on and all sorts of tiny insects swarmed around it immediately.

'I'll have a fruit juice,' I said, smiling a little crookedly to indicate my deprivation, 'no alcohol for me.'

When Benjamin left, Alan pulled up his chair to sit right opposite me and said in a quarrelsome voice: 'How many friends had the privilege of — knowing you well?'

'What on earth do you want? On such a beautiful night.' (I did not like him to 'drink' he became 'a changed man' or

164

maybe that's how he really was.)

'You mean what makes me ask? Benjamin. What goes on? What *went* on all those years.'

'You're out of your mind. You can't be serious.'

'Entirely so. He's far too concerned about you and you take all he says for gospel truth. Did you or did you not?'

'With that moustache? Alan! You're mad!'

'Answer me!'

I laughed, putting my fruit juice down. Right — let's have a bit of a continental bash-up, do you the world of good, let's have a few of your unruffled feathers flying. Although you don't look like a bird at all, more like an angry snake, rearing its head, this fine, sophisticated head with the elongated back. Even his speech became like a hiss.

'Is the moustache all that's keeping you back?'

'Perhaps.'

'I find you despicable.'

'Why don't you leave me then?'

'There *are* others — you are not the only pebble on the beach.'

To sink to those depths, to be that vulgar, banal and feeble, I must really have upset him. 'I would never have thought —'

'I know where your thoughts are, don't take me for an idiot. I know you inside out. You are never with me for a single moment. I can think of any number of women who would be glad to have my company, nicer than you, more honest, more understanding. . . .'

'Oh,' I said softly 'that is not possible. More honest than I? Was it one of your little English butterflies? The blue eyed, fair-haired variety with nice long legs and no hips?'

'Yes,' he said a bit thickly, 'as a matter of fact — it was. Janet only said the other day. . . .'

'Janet, the diving board?' (He murmured, 'nasty, nasty'.) 'The wafer thin Cambridge goddess? You can have her any time, don't forget to take a nice soft cushion.' (He said 'feeble, my girl's jealous, that's why she cracks feeble jokes.') 'And what was it she said the other day? What can she possibly say of interest — a girl who's never been further from Cambridge than Royston, mentally speaking, I mean. You're welcome to her — any time. Shall I move out then? She can start understanding you right now, this minute, you stupid, stupid man. You don't know how you will be

165

missing me.'

Alan, very tall, very strong, very unpredictable closed in on me like a force of nature. 'I know I will be missing you, I can't bear it without you — not one single day.'

'Not one hour?'

'Not one minute, now or ever.'

The man spoke the truth. The final absolute truth. What a lucky woman I was. If only I could appreciate it.

*　　*　　*

I asked Alan formally and politely to come to the meeting with me. He declined and said I was to be pitied because my own mind was so empty that I needed strangers to fill it. He compared me — in the best German tradition — to a number of animals noted for the smallness of their brains or their slow functioning, their well-programmed capacity to follow the leader. It did not deter me. I was not going to miss out on such a golden opportunity.

I set out on my own one rainy afternoon, saying tearfully to myself that I must 'understand' before I die, for death might not allow for personal enquiries. Perhaps I would even find the answer to a Zen master's famous three questions: how do we think, what do we think and why do we think, which seemed to sum up everything. My goodness — the mind boggles if one comes to grips with them, or rather if they slip out of your grip as soon as you touch them. I wish I had asked Ted, while I still had the chance, but he may have brushed it aside.

There was an expectant hum in the large hall which dimmed a little as the hour for the meeting came closer. It became quieter when there were only five minutes left. Then any kind of noise stopped altogether. I had only *heard* this kind of silence once and that was on top of Mount Vesuvius but there were no people around then. The very quality of the air changed as it does before a thunderstorm. It became dense, almost palpable. One minute before the appointed time I heard soft precise steps approaching the platform and, walking as lightly as a cat, a man appeared and sat down on a solitary chair. His hair was white, the perfectly regular face was deeply lined but he did not look old, for the expression was young, eager, expectant, a little mischievous even: I wonder what we are going to get today.

He surveyed the audience for a moment, then asked politely, 'What shall we talk about?' A strange question from a lecturer. Why did he ask *us*? Had he not prepared a definite topic? People shouted all sorts of things: how can I learn to be peaceful, is there an afterlife, what do we do about war and do you levitate?

He said he did not levitate and smiled. He really looked extraordinary: large mobile eyes missing nothing, a slim-boned figure in a grey suit, self-contained, elegant and refined in the extreme; sparse, fluid movements and a definite air of happiness, adventure and curiosity, like a boy setting out to explore an unknown continent.

I found the presence of a microphone reassuring: no mystical whispers would be lost before they could reach us. The man listened to a few more questions then said: 'If it's all right with you I'd like to talk about sorrow.' It certainly was all right by me. Some of my sorrows had literally eaten holes into me. As for other people's — you could fill oceans with them.

'If you have never experienced deep agonising sorrow,' the man said, 'then life has passed you by and forgotten you.' That really hit me, it was so new. Sorrow was something to avoid at all costs, I thought, wholly negative. The man talked for a long while and it seemed to me that all life was compressed into his words, as if he, having found the one and only answer to it all, was speaking from the depth of his being, which spread out to us in the hall and to everything and everybody outside.

Everything he said rang true, for it all came from the same universal root where all questions had been resolved. The years dropped away from me as I listened like a child in a dream. The world became once more beautiful, enchanting and miraculous.

After a while the man lifted his large, luminous eyes to the clock, said, I think I'd better stop, smiled, stood up and vanished behind a red curtain. I saw the curtain swinging, heard voices in the audience and shook myself as if waking up.

I shall have more of that, I thought. But how? What organisation, what address to turn to? I must have looked like a lost soul for a girl asked me whether I was all right. No, I said, I was not, because I did not know what to do. When was the next lecture, were there courses, could I get in touch with his outfit? The girl said that was the only lecture, there were no courses and there was no outfit. But how did all those people here know? There was a mailing list, it appeared, and a number of books. I would be put on the mailing list for the next lecture. Unfortunately that would only be in a year's time, as the speaker travelled all over the globe. The girl wrote down my name, said I would be hearing in time and gave me some book titles.

I drifted out of the hall with the crowd, feeling I had been riding on a comet and was now thrown off it into black blankness.

Then suddenly I saw him, not three yards away from me, obviously by himself, a leather case under his arm, probably with his music. Dressed shabbily, his clothes hanging loose and ill-fitting about him, thrown together anyhow; stooping like an invalid, dragging his feet, a scarecrow. A thin, haggard face and no coat. Why doesn't he wear a coat, hasn't he got one or has he pawned it? Does he ever eat? Is he sick? Sebastian!

Perhaps he heard me shouting his name inwardly because his head shot round. We approached each other slowly, dividing the crowd. I had thought I would erupt like a volcano if I met him suddenly face to face, melt in the white hot heat of an explosion or go to pieces and throw myself sobbing into his arms.

As it was I went stone-cold. I believe my blood stopped flowing. He looked — hideous. Like something thrown away, left over, defeated. I can't forgive that — everything else, perhaps, the shabbiness, the big bald patch in the middle of his thinned-out grey hair, the limp way his suit hung on him, the old worn-out black shoes. But I could not take the expression in his eyes, those eyes which used to glow and shimmer, almost hypnotizing me with his brilliance, but now dead, dull and extinct, with large pouches underneath: old men's eyes with the shutters down, they do not want to know anymore, it's finished, all over, no more to come.

We were now standing face to face but I still had not said a word. He started talking about the meeting, said he liked the man but not the message and what a coincidence that I too of all people went to listen to him. Did I know of a little place for coffee nearby?

We sat at a corner table opposite each other in a dingy little tea room off the Euston Road. He talked on, his voice none too firm, nodding to himself now and then: I'm not what I used to be and I could not care less.

Only once did a spark light up in his tired eyes when he said, like an echo of worlds disappeared: 'Remember our Shakespeare quotations? And now we are both here in England. What was the one you liked so much, oh, I know: *Love is not love that alters when it alteration finds?*' It echoed back through the years with a vengeance. He smiled at me, first with his pale lips closed, then more broadly uncovering his teeth. Three were made of gold. Nobody has golden teeth over here. People had them on the continent ages ago, how quaint and old fashioned, old, *old* and washed out, that's what you are, my love, old, finished and out of circulation. How could you let yourself go like that, how could you do that to me. What's happened to you? Where is your brilliance, your sparkle, your special mark? You look mediocre and defeated. I don't think I can bear it.

'Is that your music in the case?'

'Yes. I took it with me for my next lesson.'

'Lesson?'

'Yes. That's how I manage to make a living. I have quite a number of students.' A music teacher — peddling his stuff from door to door. 'Some of them are quite talented,' he said proudly. 'One young boy will have a concert in the Wigmore Hall next month. You ought to hear him, he's quite brilliant.'

'Is he? More brilliant than you?' I felt like murder.

'Much better. I could never have done it.'

'What? Why aren't *you* giving concerts? That was what you wanted most in life, what you worked for so madly in Berlin. I imagined you playing to people all over the world — so that's why I never saw your name on the posters. I could not understand. That's why nobody in the music world knew about you. Why no concerts? Have you given up playing?'

'I do play occasionally — to friends.'

He shouldn't have said that. I imagined a small upright piano standing in a drab bed-sitter, well-thumbed music, stale cups of coffee and Sebastian playing half-heartedly to a few stragglers who could not quite manage to focus their attention on the music, hoping that he would not go on for too long. His last piece would be a Chopin Polonaise, thumping a piano out of tune with unconvincing passion.

169

His friends would clap at the end without enthusiasm, more with relief that the ordeal was over.

Oh God — I wish I could cry, I wish I could feel truly sorry that he has not made it, I wish I could feel compassion for that bundle of misery, so resigned and humble. Perhaps I'd better buy him a meal. Sebastian! You've let me down, my love, my lover. . . . no, my love no longer, you've taken it away, destroyed my purpose, my framework, my foundation! But am I not horribly unfair? One should not judge a man, any man, by his appearance.

I implored him: 'What has happened to you — please tell me!' Let him speak of horrible disasters, of misfortunes too great to endure, let him tell me how he was broken into pieces, how he fell and got up, was pushed down again and was sick. Please let him speak of terrible afflictions, calamities and tragedies so I can save something, some little scrap to cling to. Say it was not your fault, tell me of all the trials and tribulations you went through, of madness, vice and cruelty. But do not tell me that you play to your friends. . . .

'Nothing much happened,' he said, avoiding my eyes. 'I escaped to Holland and was able to continue my studies for a bit. Then my parents died and I started to give lessons for a living. I married.'

'Who is she?' I asked and it did not hurt at all.

'Worked in a library. That's how I met her — but she left me after some time.'

'With glasses?'

'Yes. She wore glasses. Funny you saying that.'

'Where is she now?'

'Back with her parents in Holland, I believe. We both left when it became too dangerous. A nice girl. . . .' It sounded totally inept.

'Children?'

'No. That's mainly why she left me. I can't have any.' He did not sound very unhappy about it. A topic like any other. In fact he spoke altogether like a man who did not much care whether he lived or died. Was he not curious about me? Did he not want to know anything? He put a few polite questions, not listening very closely to my answers. So I married an Englishman. Was he good to me? Yes, I said, very good. I had a son. That's lucky, he said stirring his coffee. Could I pass the sugar? He was allowing himself a rare treat as he wasn't supposed to have coffee at all.

170

'When did you stop thinking of me?'

'I have thought of you often,' he said mildly. 'I could imagine you with a home, children, lots of friends — but an Englishman?' He shook his head. 'Is that not creating problems?' I said I liked having problems.

'I can still see you knocking at the flatdoor that first time, you looked so furious —' He actually chuckled at the memory. There was no pain in it, no longing, no regret. 'You see,' he said stirring his coffee with obvious pleasure, 'I'm on a diet. I usually have a cup of Bengers about this time. . . .' He nodded again, a bit shakily this time, indicating that it was the normal thing to expect, we were getting on and one has to deprive oneself of life's pleasures sooner or later.

'Have you married again?'

He shook his head, pushing his lower lip forward: it had not seemed worthwhile.

'No girl, I mean woman?' I waited.

'That's all past,' he said, smiling again, showing his bloodless gums with the gold teeth. I wish I could have said that he was as cold as ice. But there was no word by which to measure his unconcern, his infinite weariness. His connection to life had been severed, he was drifting around in a sea of total indifference. Given half a chance I can strike sparks off most people but Sebastian's presence weighed on me like a mountain.

'Very naughty of me,' he said trying to introduce a jocular note. 'I really should not drink coffee at all, the doctor said so.'

Perhaps we had something in common after all: 'I'm on a diet as well,' I said bitterly. Partly because my life blood was draining away for *you*, you impossible, hopeless drip! Do you know that? My longing for you dimmed my strength, my energy, almost crippled me, and there you sit opposite me and *fade out*. Oh God! One last try: I'll make him look at me properly or do I appear as hideous to him as he does to me?. I must throw off this unbearable pressure cutting off all my impulses, I must make a last desperate effort to catch his attention, to pull him out of this state of inertia, this all-pervading listlessness. Wake him up, make him see, understand, acknowledge my presence.

'I'm a Bengers addict,' he said just then. 'It's a good drink, a bit colourless, but I've got used to it.'

171

Help! I'm going under. It took all my strength to say with some sort of conviction: 'I have written some poetry. It was quite serious but then it stopped. It made me very unhappy, I wish I could start again.' I watched him stir his coffee, unaware of my eyes, trying to peel the skin from his face to see what went on underneath, this pale face, creased and flabby, hanging above the coffee cup, where the man's interest was entirely focused. I looked at his hands which were once such marvellous musician's hands, flexible and creative. Now they were stiff and rigid, almost ugly, covered in brown spots. Little folds were etched in the bloodless skin, blue veins stood out like roads on a map. There were only a few years between us but I felt I was sitting opposite decay itself.

'Poems?' he repeated vaguely, 'that's nice, it creates an outlet, as long as one does not take it too seriously. Do you think they have biscuits here?' God Almighty! The man's dead! I do not want to sit with a corpse — I'll bury him here and now. I cannot bear it another minute.

I felt sick and desperate as I got up and started walking towards the Underground. A hearse would have been more appropriate. Sebastian said he would come with me and see me off but I turned my head away in disgust and said I was in a hurry. I turned my head away. . . . Good grief! Mr Peters — the clairvoyant. 'Oh no!' I said so loudly that people turned round in the street. 'You will turn away from him as if he had the plague.' Those were his very words. Only the plague would have been more acceptable than this pitiful condition.

The high voltage coursing through me for half a lifetime had collapsed. No longer was the atmosphere charged with unceasing hopes and regrets. All that had withered away at the moment of our encounter for which I had been longing as for the Holy Grail.

My hero was dead. Drowned in a cup of Bengers.

*   *   *

Some cunning devil had sent Sebastian across my path the very minute I had got on to something tremendous. Why did this have to happen to me? What have I *done*? Is there no justice? Insane though — to think the world a big great grocer's shop with accounts kept in the backroom.

The shock of the meeting still lodged in my system like an outsize splinter. I'd like to make a bonfire and throw the misshapen man on top like a rag doll so he'll go up in flames and generate *some* warmth in the end. Oh Sebastian, Sebastian — how could you let this happen? There will be no glorious records to survive him, played by enchanted listeners all over the world, no eternal harmonies will fill men's hearts, only my own distress will remain forever.

Should I tell Alan about it? I owe it to him. That's a lie, you can't bear keeping quiet. You know that sooner or later you will unburden yourself — better sooner, then.

We were driving back from Cambridge on a clear sunny day. Was it a good moment now? It would of course spoil the lovely sunny afternoon driving home between fields and meadows. I wondered what Alan's reaction would be. I looked at his austere, determined profile and his firm lean hands on the wheel. No brown spots on *his* skin. He looked altogether good, yes, and distinguished. I must have been completely mad not to see that here, right next to me, was what I had been so frantically longing for — the special, the princely mark. Unobtrusive and dignified, somehow commanding. A cut above the rest. It was there every day but it failed to register. I must tell him or that wretched man would continue to stand between us for ever.

'Darling —' I stopped. Coward. Get it over with. 'I wanted to say — eh — let's pull in at this lay-by.'

Alan stopped immediately and without question, much to my surprise. I had not really given him a reason.

'What did you want to say? You look most peculiar. Is anything wrong? Did something happen yesterday — you've hardly spoken to me since. Did you go to the meeting Benjamin told you about? Where were you? I tried to get you on the phone.'

'I must have been out.'

'Aren't you sure?' He looked at me frowning. My courage failed me and I started to yawn, turning my head away. He gripped the nape of my neck so strongly it hurt. 'I was talking to you.'

'Go right on talking, then. I'm too tired.'

'Why should you be tired, you don't exactly kill yourself with work.' That was a nasty thing to say considering that all my efforts in that direction had been stopped by my anxious husband. (You must rest, relax, it isn't good for you to

dash about with hardly any food inside, you are too thin anyway, wait till your diet is less strict, till you look less pale,
etc, etc.)

'You will kindly tell me where you went yesterday afternoon.'

'I went to an art gallery,' I said, obviously lying, 'to look
at all the lovely pictures.' I veered round facing him: 'I don't
like you being husbandish.'

'There is no such word.'

I snorted: 'God, you're small.' Then wheedling, going on
my favourite track, anything to distract him: 'Can't you
make allowances for little wifey, poor little stranger amidst
all those tall upright natives? Can't express herself properly,
little peasant, can't speak the language, poor unhappy waif,
but she's trying, can't say she isn't trying, but she gets all hot
and bothered in such grand company.'

'You hot and bothered? A tank, that's what you are, an
iron tank, mowing down everything in sight. You don't
need anybody's help and I won't be sidetracked.' He knew
me too well.

I tried again, this time on a different line: 'I'm just home-
sick, Alan. Only I've not got a home to be sick for. *That's* my
malady. I want soil and roots — roots most of all, mine are
dangling in the air, can't find anything to cling to. I must
retreat into myself. . . .'

'Stop this nonsense, Julia. I know there *is* something.
You must tell me — now!'

Although I was sitting down, I felt like a soldier before a
firing squad. Alan's right, get it over with. 'I went to the
meeting Benjamin recommended and met Sebastian coming out of the hall. Just bumped into him.'

Alan's hands gripped the steering wheel so hard his
knuckles stood out like rocks. 'What happened?'

'Nothing *happened*. I hardly recognised him. We went
and had coffee.'

'Where?' Barely audible.

'In a crummy little cafe nearby.' I thought the pain had
lessened, but it still hurt very much, it was still agony to talk
about it, making it worse in a way, finalising it, putting the
lid on, for I had to say it out aloud that it was *over*. This was
going to be Sebastian's funeral, no less.

Alan's hands were still on the wheel gripping it strongly.
But his face was calm. Only his deep blue eyes were full of

174

dread. All right then, the last rites are about to start.

'There was nothing left,' I began softly, 'nothing that could matter. He looked finished and he is finished.' I raised my voice: 'A failure! Do you hear? A ghastly failure! No concerts, no tours, no public appearances. He's bungled it, botched it up, never made it, a non-starter. Entertaining a bunch of other failures in bed-sitters, teaching scales to little brats. An old, old man with funny teeth and pouches under his eyes. He's messed up everything, his profession, his marriage, his looks, he can't even. . . . can't even have children. Barren like a stubblefield.' I almost sobbed remembering: 'He doesn't walk properly, dragging his feet along. He's ugly!' I screamed, 'Ugly! Crumbling under my very eyes — he's taken a back seat, given up, gone under. God, he's decaying. He can't,' I concluded savagely, 'even drop dead. He's a zombie.'

'. . . . very much alive for you.'

'No, no! He's dead, he's just died, just this very minute, I've buried him, can't you believe me?' I took a deep breath: 'He's receding, he's been exorcised, I swear it. I *know*. It's over.'

'After all those years? How can you be so sure? What if he writes to you?'

'Writes to me?' I repeated taken aback. 'Why should he? What for? And he couldn't even if he wanted to — he does not know where I live. He never asked.' I started giggling: 'He does not know my name, do you understand, my present name, *your* name! Engelmann, that's all he knows.' Suddenly feeling a boundless relief flooding me, my mental chastity belt dynamited, my soul again my own.

'Engelmann, Engelmann, half angel, half man. I'm not a man,' hardly knowing what I was saying, 'not a bit of it, does *that* look like a man?' I took my coat off and started opening my dress. 'Or that? Have you ever seen a man like *that* before?' I flung my arms around Alan and whispered, 'There can't be many about, can there?'

'You're mad — mad. I'll show you what a man is like, a real man, I'll make you forget your friend ever lived, I'll chase your bloody zombie to hell. . . .'

We sat in the car for a long time, blissfully unaware of our surroundings. Nobody passed us, no vehicles on the road. Everything was quiet. Hills and valleys, cows grazing.

Suddenly my head shot up: 'Alan!' I pointed an accusing

175

finger at the setting sun. 'It's going down, look! Over that hill, it's sinking quickly — we won't make it in time!' Alan started the car immediately, racing along the empty roads but it was too late. He said soothingly that there was plenty of time, at least another hour before it was really dark, I should just keep my eyes closed and not worry.

'Can't you drive faster, please! We won't make it, you'll see, we'll lose our way, we won't know which turn to take.' I was almost delirious, out of my mind with fright. I reasoned with myself, I fought hard, but I knew that it would be to no avail. 'Find shelter before the sun sets,' our guide had said up in the mountains in France. Before the sun sets.

Alan was driving like a demon but I was sunk, sunk against all reason, frozen with horror. The soft green hills grew to monstrous height, the sun went down while I sat motionless trying to ward off a paralysing fear: keep a grip on yourself, look around you. You are barely twenty miles from London, in a car with Alan. Safe, safe — houses, people, roads, villages — shake it off you fool, shake it off! No use. The past reached out once more, clawed at my mind and I could put up no more resistance than a swimmer in a whirlpool. I was sucked right down to the bottom where I drifted about helplessly, battered savagely by events from long ago, losing control altogether.

Alan kept talking to me in a soothing voice, but I could not hear his words, I was blind and deaf, spun into my own trembling mind. The traumatic shock of the flight over the mountains and the desperate search for shelter on the other side had been working their way downward into my system, ready to torment me again and again, as on that late afternoon, blotting out all reasoning. I would go under, suffering agonies and torments, until the very minute I could put my key into the front door.

'We are almost there, look out of the window, we are near town, there are the lights, Julia.' He turned towards me for a second. 'Come out of it, look up!'

I lifted my head with difficulty and screamed: an enormous lorry was lumbering at us like a dinosaur, headlights ablaze. I felt my limbs being torn from my body by a superhuman shock. Then nothing.

* * *

176

The smell of Dettol. Green faded curtains surrounding my bed, trolleys rattling, a light bulb on the ceiling just over my head. Alan? A nurse came running, trying to pin me down as I was about to jump out of bed. I shook her off, tottered through the ward, hardly aware of people staring at me from the other beds, the nurse at my heels shouting, Mrs Percival, Mrs Percival, you must go back to bed. I did not pay any attention, felt drawn to the other end of the hospital, kept calling for Alan in a daze until the nurse took pity on me and took me by the arm, guiding me to a small room next to the men's ward.

There was a single bed. Alan was lying with his eyes closed, very still and very pale. He hardly breathed. No! I won't let you — you've got to wake up, got to wake up. Nurse slapped my face right and left as I was about to faint: back to bed, back to bed.

I sat down by Alan's side and did not take my eyes off that pale face. The nurse left. A doctor came in urging me to leave and saying that I could not do him any good. He did not understand. I *did* him a lot of good. I did not move, willing him to open his eyes, his deep blue eyes. Just once.

'I'm not leaving,' I said to various people drifting in and out of the room. 'It would be wrong to leave, I can't, I have only just found him, don't you see? I've only just found out. This time I shall not walk out. As long as I'm looking at him he cannot leave either. I shall hold him here.'

'Nurse, his hands are cold.'

'He is not responding to treatment,' the nurse said. I sat by Alan's bed staring down at him like in a trance, never taking my eyes off his face, observing every breath, every flutter of his eyelids. People put food next to me, took it away again untouched. Lights were switched on and off. I heard music from far away, the sound of people shuffling past in their slippers, the nurses' hard heels tapping on the floor.

All my fault. Only mine. He wanted to comfort me and turned his head away from the road for a second. The lorry was grey and high as a mountain. Intensive care unit, that's what it's called. They take care of you intensively and all the time without fail. Nothing can go wrong.

'His skin is not so pale any more,' I said later to the doctor bending over Alan.

'He is responding now,' the doctor said. 'Will you go and lie down, you'll exhaust yourself.'

177

I shook my head.

'He must speak to me,' I said. 'I cannot leave before he has spoken.'

The doctor put a blanket round my shoulders. 'That may be some time yet.'

Once more I was alone with Alan. The noise of the hospital washed round me while I focused all my strength and willpower on the sunken face in the bed. All I knew was: I cannot bear another loss.

'Julia.' Barely a whisper. Alan's eyes were open. There was a hint of a smile. I knelt down by his bed and kissed his hands, murmuring: I love you I love you I love you.

'You do now,' Alan said, his voice still hardly audible. 'So thirsty.' I fed him with spoonfuls of water like a sick child. The doctor came in and clapped his hands discreetly.

'Fine — fine. But that's enough for the first time.'

'How long?'

'Two to three weeks.'

I frowned. 'Will he be all right then?'

'Very much so. But keep your distance at feeding times.'

Alan smiled with his eyes closed, drifting into sleep once more.

'When he comes out of here,' the doctor said, 'can he manage to rest? He ought to. He would best recover right away from work. Could you go somewhere in the country?'

'Of course. I'll do anything. For how long?'

'A month would be enough. Now you, Madame, go right to bed and get your strength back or you won't be able to look after him. And eat properly!'

I was able to leave the hospital after a week, too well fed to fasten my dressing gown properly, fit, strong and determined to get Alan back on his feet. Everything would be done for him, everything in my power.

Alan thought the sun would do him good, so I booked a flight to Morocco.

*　　*　　*

We sat in the lounge of our hotel in Marrakesh. I was fully aware of the fact that life at this present moment was 'good' to me.

The country was more staggering, more exotic, more fascinating and more beautiful than all the travel brochures had

led me to believe. Alan had fully recovered. He said he was
fed up with listening to my apologies and would I stop them
and go on to more interesting topics. He agreed once and for
all that he *had* turned his head away from the road because
of me, but that he should not have done so. He had seen the
truck coming one second too late (because of me) and it was
my fault that the accident happened, because of my terrible
hang-up about the past. Would I now shut up about it?

'Some women remain silent to their peril,' I said meekly,
'then they lose the habit of talking altogether because the disgust they feel for themselves is choking them.'

'You are not one of them.'

'Let's go and see the belly dancers.'

'Rather not. Their rotating navels make me dizzy. Let's
walk in the gardens.' He took my arm and we walked under
the palm trees and sweet smelling bushes as if we were the
only couple on earth. The moon was enormous and the stars
like outsize eggs, I had never seen them so large. A bird sang.
A soft wind flowed down from the snowy mountains and
made the palm leaves tremble.

'Let's go across tomorrow,' Alan pointed to the towering
Atlas range. 'The desert is just beyond that — think of it!' I
thought of it and shivered. *That* between me and home?
What if the car broke down? What if we never got back to
London and to John, whom I had left behind. The boy
would have been bored to tears. What a cheat you are, he
would have loved it. But I needed Alan for myself.

'We would need a guide,' Alan said, 'the country is very
wild, there are only a few roads. Julia? Are you cold? I can
hear your teeth chattering.'

'It's the night air,' I said heroically. 'Let's go in. And I'd
love to go with a guide. I never. . . .' My voice trailed off,
because Jacques, our guide in the Pyrenees, was as clearly
outlined in my mind as if he stood in front of me. Those
immense walls looming up one after the other — climbing,
climbing — then we lost our way because it was dark. The
guide had gone and we went astray.

For God's sake, pull yourself together, woman! Haven't
you done enough damage, we are *tourists*, tourists! Nobody
was after us, this was going to be a pleasure trip. You can't
go back to England and not have been to the desert. Ridiculous.

'Will you arrange it, Alan? It will only be for a day.'

'It won't, you know,' Alan said. 'Two nights at least. It's quite far.' I said nothing. 'Would you rather not?' He looked at me critically. 'I give you my promise that we will not travel after dark. You will be all right, I know.'

'Of course I will be. And I'd love to go, we can't possibly miss that.' My heart was beating fast, hands clenched into fists. Drop that once and for all! Reason it out. You are dragging your past around with you like a prisoner his chains. There is nothing more to be afraid of. You will kindly overcome your impulses this minute so that Alan can have what he wants. What *he* wants.

We started off across the mountains next day. Unknown to Alan I was swallowing tranquillisers by the fistful. I was not going to spoil the trip for him, after the accident which was caused by the same mad fear. Keep it under cover. Go on, be afraid, but do not show it. Swallow your pills and be quiet.

The scenery seemed all the more magical, for the slight haze caused by the pills enveloped me during the whole journey. Alan saw me smiling, a bit heavy-lidded perhaps, but he put that down to the sleeping conditions in the two small hotels where we spent the nights. The guide, a superb looking Moroccan, drove the car.

'We must go to Erfoud,' he said, 'and see the sun set over the Sahara. There is a mountain we can just reach before nightfall. It's the most famous sunset in Africa, better than anything you have ever seen, you can't imagine —' Words failed him, he just moaned in a trance and murmured paradise, paradise, and we would never forgive ourselves if we did not see *that*. I did not want to add to all the unforgivable things (to myself mainly) and agreed that we must see it at all costs.

We drove the whole day and arrived at the foot of the mountain with an hour to spare before sunset. Alan was tired. He would have to forgo the miraculous sunset, he said, but the guide could take me up to the top. Ali had been falling asleep while we were discussing, as he had been driving non stop for hours and hours. I said I'd go by myself, got a 'look' from Alan, grinned at him and said I was a big girl.

I started immediately, walking up the winding road which was leading to the peak. It turned out to be quite a climb. The road zig-zagged, steepened and narrowed down to a small path. I did not slow down, keeping a steady pace, climbing higher and higher.

It seemed to me as if I had come all the way from London just to be in time to see this sunset, to reach the top before it was too late: the most urgent thing in the world.

Up I went, my heart beating strongly, fighting every inch of the way, attacking the mountain like a personal enemy. I kicked off my sandals without slowing down, slinging them over my shoulder, walking barefoot on the burning stones. I went quicker like that.

It never occurred to me that the tremendous effort I put into the climb was completely out of proportion, that I had seen hundreds of glowing sunsets before and would most likely see many more. But the mind does not work like that. A process had been set into motion many many years ago which had to be brought to its conclusion at all costs, *now*.

I never looked up, I never consciously assessed what I was doing, I just climbed steadily. This is what you came for, don't give in, don't waste time looking at the view, just carry on. I turned another hairpin bend, climbed higher, never taking my eyes off the path, holding my sandals with one hand, the other one stretched out like a blind woman. I was suddenly hit full in the face by such a piercing light that I had to look straight up. There was nothing between me and the sun. This time I have made it, I said aloud, deeply shocked that my mind had tricked me, had pushed me up this mountain on purpose.

There was the sun, a huge orange globe in a sky of such blueness, such shimmering, shattering blueness, hard and brilliant, radiating like a huge flame. Sand and stones glowed, as a whole continent seemed to stretch away to the horizon. I stood still, taking in the sky, the earth and the sun. There was nothing else.

When the sun looked as if it was bursting with molten gold, it started going down over the desert in a splash of mauves, pinks and greens. I waited till the last spark had disappeared and all that unearthly beauty faded into the night, before I went back, almost reluctantly, not wanting to break the connection between the mountain and myself.

Very slowly I made my way to the hotel, its lights guiding me in the darkness. It was almost black by now but I was in no hurry. I feared nothing. I could have walked for miles alone, in darkness, without a path under a foreign sky.

I turned round once more: there stood the mountain, now

silvery under the rising moon. Its triangular peak was silhouetted sharply against the sky. I thought I had never set eyes on such a brilliant sight.

*   *   *

Alan sat next to the driver on the journey back to Marrakesh.

'What did you just chuck out of the window?' he asked.

'You must have eyes at the back of your head.'

'I have — I saw you in the little side mirror. What was it though?'

'Just some pills. I do not need them any more.'

'Oh? What were they for, may I ask?'

'To help me keep my temper in your presence.'

'Why not put them in a wastepaper basket? Why this dramatic gesture?'

'The land must have them. It cured me. Do you see?'

'Your whole life is littered with symbols. Where do I fit in?'

'I could tell you.' I winked at him and he said he saw that in the mirror.

'Are you sorry to go back?' Now how did he know that.

'Yes, darling, very sorry. It's so adventurous — like a couple of explorers. I wish I could go on and on.'

'You might.' It sounded mysterious. 'Perhaps not in that way but differently — if you still want to. I'm not sure though. I've got something in mind, rather good, you know, rather special.'

'I can't wait — please tell me. Is it a present?'

'Sort of — the best you've ever had from anybody. You'll see.' He would not say any more, although I tried all the tricks I knew.

'Maybe we can return one day; that climate suits me. I never felt fitter,' said Alan.

'Am I forgiven then?'

'I'll have to think about it.'

We had never been so happy before.

*   *   *

Home again. The rain was lashing against the window panes, a blustering gale force wind scattered the leaves thickly on streets and gardens. Marrakesh and its burning

182

sun might never have been.

At times it had seemed under the brilliant blue sky of Marrakesh as if the sun had not so much touched my skin as entered bodily into me like food and drink, as if the scorching rays had lodged inside me like my own veins. My hair had started to curl and wave as I lay flat on the ground, surrounded by the sun like a tent. What bliss. I had thought of Billy, (who always provoked me into violent arguments) Alan's friend since his student days. He said once that my craving for happiness was absurd and unhealthy. Nobody lived like that, it was meaningless. While the sun had been beating me almost senseless I had felt in that cloud of warmth and light that enchantment and ecstasy were the only things worth having, that everything else was puny, sad and degrading.

But all such feelings were pushed aside when I looked at Alan, my emotional strands were now finally and irrevocably concentrated on him. He was sitting next to me, hunched over his drawing board, guiding a large black felt pencil over a white sheet of paper.

'I can't work when you are breathing down my neck,' he said as my face was touching his. Immediately little currents jumped from one skin to the other. He pulled me on his lap.

'I don't want you to work,' I said.

'What do you want then?'

'You.'

'No shame, no modesty.'

'Futile,' I murmured, 'utterly futile. That's the way I am.' He carried me all the way up.

Only after a long time, when you are really sure, when you are not in a hurry, when you are not ashamed of anything, only then does love making turn into loving. People 'make' love — they also make chairs, window frames, washing powder, electric cables, lorry engines and biscuits. What a dull affair! *Affaire!* That means: to do. No emotional content, no glory. How lovely it is to be completely aware of each other, how beautiful to know the other's slightest whim. There is no fear, no apprehension, no terror of being inadequate.

'Alan, are you asleep?'

'Yes. Fast asleep. Are you very much in love with me?'

'Yes.' A little surprised: 'Yes.'

'No zombies walking about?'

183

'None whatsoever.' My head was on his shoulder. 'Has the time come for my present? I can't stop thinking about it.'

'How can I tell you if you won't stop kissing me? Be serious. I shall take you out into the country tomorrow and — give it to you. I hope I'll get some peace then and due admiration.'

'You look positively sly and cunning.'

'I *am* cunning. I kept this in reserve as a last resort. His name is Ken Harwood.'

'A man? What is he supposed to do for me?'

'He'll be the heavenly pilot you've been pining away for, if you still want one.'

'I have never stopped.'

'Right. We'll go there in the morning and God help you if *he* doesn't help you. I'll throw you into the sea.'

I looked at my smiling husband: 'I'll never ever know you.'

'That's my sinister fascination.'

'I adore you.'

'Without reservations?'

Yes, I had none. He was almost asleep when he said, *Liebling, Liebling,* rolling the l's around in this astonishing English fashion. He made it into a new word.

*   *   *

Shortly before we drove out to see Ken Harwood the incident with the bumble bee occurred. Another of your symbolic happenings, Alan said. It *was* — in fact it mirrored my state of mind to perfection.

The bumblebee had flown in from the garden through the open window and could not find its way out. It whizzed through the room making a noise like an aeroplane, banging against the walls with such force that I was amazed it did not knock itself out from the impact. After some minutes of frantic flying at great speed from wall to wall it settled behind the glass panel of the open window. My efforts to send it on its way to freedom did not succeed. There were more desperate bumpings and crashings on the walls and the furniture, continuous anguished dronings and buzzings.

'You stupid thing,' I said angrily, 'I only want to help you, don't you see? You've got no brains. Out with you, I don't want to kill you, I'm not *after* you. Can't you see the window is open? Just fly straight ahead. Don't get so frantic, you miss it every time!'

As far as the bumblebee was concerned the room only had solid walls. No windows — at least none that were open. After its strength was spent, it crawled dejectedly up and down the glass panel, the one which was away from the outside, explored the wooden frame, then settled miserably in the utmost corner where I could not reach. It tucked its legs underneath the body, lowered its head, looking like a tiny striped fur ball. I felt compelled to get it out of the room unharmed.

I climbed on to a chair, prodding it gently with a rolled newspaper, begging it to crawl on to it so I could set it free.

Stupid thing! Once more it started flying to and fro and between the walls missing the window every time. I decided to catch it and set it free, if it took me all day. I got hold of a large wooden spoon and a paper bag. When the bumblebee got tired of hitting the walls it flew back once more to sit down behind the glass.

There was the wide open window, the air streaming in fresh and sweet from the garden, and this idiotic little insect (its original instinct blotted out) went into hiding in the most remote corner, because it could not find the way out of its prison. How it could possibly fail to fly out — even by accident — was beyond me. The window was very large, taking up almost the whole length of the fourth wall.

With great cunning and patience I finally managed to trap it in the hollow of the spoon and dip it into the paper bag which I screwed up tightly at the top. As I carried it for a brief moment, I felt the bumblebee stirring violently. Its buzzing was as penetrating as a saw.

I opened the bag at the top, shaking it towards the garden. The bumblebee shot out like a missile and disappeared buzzing triumphantly, in a straight line between the trees.

*   *   *

'This is your day then, Julia, are you ready?'

'I can't wait. What's he like and why didn't you take me before?'

'Ken is a very unassuming chap but I assure you publishers are grabbing his books as quickly as he can write them.

And often before they are written. You just don't happen to have come across them.'

'Why didn't you tell me before?'

'I waited for all those Teds and Trueloves to disappear first. On purpose.'

'You are making this up.'

'Not really — I am just less dull and stupid than you think. I won't be jealous if you fall at his feet — metaphorically speaking of course. Who knows — it might just happen. Let's go.'

It was a grey day with low clouds chasing over the sky. The closer we came to the sea the more the wind hissed and roared. Sometimes our car was shaken by strong blustering gusts. We talked little as we could not make ourselves heard. Alan stopped the car on the slope of a hill and pointed downwards to the sea. There, close to the water, on a narrow promontory, stood a few houses surrounded by thick green bushes. Great powerful waves came crashing down on the beach and I could see the bushes shaking in the wind. Stones were toppling into the water when the waves withdrew. Gulls screeched, diving into the sea like bullets.

'It looks fantastic,' I said. 'I hope your friend can match the scenery.'

'He's even better.' Alan started the car again.

Ken Harwood stood in front of his house to receive us. I felt disappointed, for his appearance was — to say the least — undistinguished. What did I expect? A halo? I saw his sandy hair straggling over a pink scalp, features blurred as swept by the unceasing wind, a squat broad body, very much shorter than Alan. It would have been hard to find a more uninspiring appearance.

I had not seen his eyes then. When I did I felt as if a sizzling hot iron was dipped into cold water. A shock.

Ken's wife Marina was an altogether different proposition. I felt vaguely jealous, not because she was beautiful. She was not outstandingly so and her kind of looks would not usually arouse my envy: large blue eyes, regular features, fair hair put up in a bun on top of the head. Pale smooth skin, much lighter than mine. It was the expression on that pale face that made me envious — thoroughly content, at peace with herself.

The house was full of books, lining the walls, squatting on the floor, sitting on tables and chairs, spilling out of cupboards. No definite plan to the house, one room merging into the other, here a bed, there an armchair, lovely pale yellow curtains, flowers everywhere. The Harwoods' two boys, slender and agile, about twelve and fourteen I think, waved to us from the outside. Ken and Marina went out into the kitchen to fetch tea.

I quickly hissed at Alan: 'Why didn't you tell me he's got such an attractive wife?'

'Do you find her attractive?'

'Don't you?'

'A bit washed out — as if she'd been in the sea too long.'

'I'm happy we have not got the same taste in women.'

Ken returned without his wife and asked point blank why I had come.

'I — I'm not altogether sure. I don't know where my place is. I mean in all this.' pointing to house, garden, sea and sky. 'What is it all for?'

'*It* — it? You must spell it out, you know.'

'Life,' I said, feeling foolish in the extreme. 'Where do I come in?'

'Why are you so sure that you've been left out?' I could not answer that. I remained silent and drank my tea. Then we went and had a stroll in the garden which looked deserted and empty, the sea just visible through the bushes and a hedge. Brown crinkly autumn leaves were rustling beneath our feet.

'Winter is coming,' I said dejectedly, 'there it all goes.'

Ken said: 'All the lovely flowers and all the pretty green trees.'

'Yes!' I called out in sudden despair. 'All the lovely flowers and you and me and everybody! What have you got to say to that?'

Ken did not answer, maybe there was nothing to say. Or he had crossed me off as a bad job already. In my heart of hearts I had been prepared of course to enter an instant heavenly lift to whizz me up to better regions, where all was meaning, understanding and purpose. But if I had been expecting to soar up like a swallow I certainly got clobbered. If I had hoped that Ken would open the book of life for me I found out in the first ten minutes that I was either blind or had learnt a different language. Ken demolished my questions as fast as I could utter them. Alan hardly interfered but I knew that he was grinning inside and not missing a single word.

We kept walking round the garden then went out to the water's edge and along it, battling against the raging wind. It seemed to me that we had been walking forever when I exclaimed: 'What do you want me to say, Ken? You've got to help me, I've tried and tried!' The wind blew strands of hair across my face, I felt cold and uncomfortable, the spray from the waves soaking into my clothes. 'I've come to you as a last resort.'

'Rubbish! You have not even started. Cut all that crap about help and assistance. You've got to be where the action is. Get up and fight that idiotic notion of the great shining Samaritan — slay it, put it on its back like a turtle and don't pretend to be a gentle helpless lady. You're a warrior — would you but know it. Look, just look. You've done everything but look!'

'Where to?'

'Right where are you — don't invent! Inside — watch the echo.'

I felt furious, cold and shivering but elated. 'Damn you!' I shouted above the wind. 'I've walked around half the coasts of England with that biting wind tearing me to bits and you say I should get up and fight! Where now? What do I *do*? And don't fob me off with some nasty tales!' Two thoughts shot through my mind in quick succession. The first was the image of the imprisoned bumble bee, the second was the idea that Ken was a giant cook waiting for the stew to get ready. ('I haven't come out of several hells to cook a stew,' I had said ages ago.) My mind worked itself up into such a turmoil that I hardly noticed we had changed direction and were turning back. I was still shivering though and Alan took off his scarf and wrapped it round me.

As we entered the house I smelled the welcoming fumes of a fire and mechanically drew near it, inhaling the acrid smell. Alan stood to my left, Ken to my right, all three staring into the dancing flames. There was a sweet dangerous calm about, like in the very last minutes of a truce on the battlefield.

'Please, Ken, talk to me,' I said in a low voice.

'Why do you mistrust your own mind so much and keep turning your head around like a lost sparrow? Why don't you throw the whole beastly burden away, forget it, forget the books, the people, the famous sayings, drop everthing you've ever known and look inside. Watch and catch life on the wing, fly with it, fall down with it, but stay there on the move. Don't pin it down and kill it. You're forever trying to pull the veil aside. There *is* no veil — your eyes are misty! *You* do the living, *you* do the controlling. *You* do the damage!'

'Suppose,' I said cautiously, 'I vaguely knew what you meant and I threw it all away. What then, what do I put in its place?'

Ken slumped down on an armchair and laughed raspingly: 'Bravo! Spoken like a true miser. "I'm prepared" — in a ladylike voice — "to give up my precious hoard of feelings and aspirations which have made the world such a good place to live in, where milk and honey flows and people go about singing with joy, where all is fair and just and beautiful. So what can you offer me in return?"'

The flames were dancing and crackling. Ken got up from his chair, pacing to and fro in front of the fire, his shadow jumping behind him: 'My goodness! Tot up your cash register. Handed over to Ken, one Leonardo, one Shakespeare, one Stockhausen, two world wars and Julia Engelmann, fifty-seven wars (smaller ones), one Taj Mahal and a million tons of tears and *what* is he giving me?'

'Yes,' I said bravely, 'what are you giving me?'

'Vitality.'

I was dumbfounded. 'I thought I'd got *that*. All during the past. . . .'

'Drop that ballast!' Ken was shouting. 'And don't wear it on your lapel like a medal. You pathetic little grocer!' I was so taken aback that tears shot into my eyes. Ken pounced on me like a tiger: 'No bargaining, do you hear? What happens now, at this second, what goes on? Come on then, record it, get going, woman, don't hedge. What goes on?'

'I am crying and looking at the fire.'

'Go on, go on!'

'I am angry that you are shouting at me, my heart begins to hurt, I can feel my fists clenching.'

'Go on, go on.'

'Now I'm thinking far back, far back — to Berlin, to my parents, now to Spain, to Lola and Juanita, now to Madrid, I'm turning my mind inside out. . . .'

'Jargon, gibberish. You are not doing anything of the kind. What are you *doing*? What is happening? The truth,

189

Julia, the truth!'

'But I am remembering.'

'Damn right — you are remembering. And you are not turning anything inside out. It's useless. You are feeling and remembering. Nothing else.'

Help — help! He's getting at me, he's taking my props away, my precious thoughts of yesterday.

'. . . . like a crab,' Ken was saying, 'scuttling like an anxious crab over the sand sideways, looking for the nearest hole. You unfeeling little brute, look straight at it. It's right in front of your eyes!'

'I can't look straight, I'm so weak and wavering.'

'Weak?' Ken laughed his head off. 'You have the hide of a rhinoceros. One step further, Julia, look, just look!' I lifted my head. 'What do you see?' Leaping orange flames against a pearly sky.

'What a lovely fire. . . .'

'Terrific!' Ken exclaimed, his eyes scintillating like stars. What am I saying, they are like a whole galaxy spinning around, like the milky way. Why can't I spin like this, why must I go plodding along heavily, dully like a lumbering dinosaur — Ken is a million light years ahead of me. 'You go too fast, I can't follow.'

'But you can, you can, you just don't try, you walk around with your eyes closed and wonder why you miss it all. Come over here, nearer, nearer still, do you see the fire, do you *see* it? Properly, closer, still closer, where is the fire, where is it? Show it to me, then. Is it the wood burning, is that it? Or is it the air consumed? Make up your mind!'

'Both,' I stammered, 'it's both, it's dancing and hot and lovely.' I drew nearer still, almost against my will, as if pulled by a magnet, nearer to the crackling leaping flames, spreading my hands out wide: 'Both — both together. The wood is dying all the time and the fire eats up the air, it's alive and moving, that's all I know, all I ever want to know. . . .'

'*Julia!*' both men shouted together. My hands — I had dipped them swiftly in and out of the flames as if into a stream of water.

Can't get hold of the fire, nothing to keep in your hands, nothing to grip even if you go to the heart of it. There's nothing *there*, but it's still moving and leaping and my hands burn like hell, the skin is blackened and scorched, the

190

pain goes right through me but I don't care, I don't care, it feels good and right and I'm seeing all this splendour of mauve, red and orange. There is the wild acrid smell of the glimmering wood, the wood which was a tree and is now a log, now it goes up in flames and now it's dust and ashes and there is a new log catching the flame —

— and now I'm crying with pain and wonder how I can live without crying all the time because of what was and what is still to come and my heart contracts with love for Alan next to me and Ken pulls me away from the fire, smiling like a demon saying, no veil, you see, I told you, no veil — my hands are burning, now they are being soothed by soft creamy ointment spread over my skin which looks like shrivelled paper, it will all heal again, does not need my help at all, it knows how to heal if I'm stupid enough to damage it.

Ken puts more logs on the fire, I watch them light up and burst, losing their shape, melting away, crumbling, looking thin and transparent like whisps of cloud shaping and reshaping. My eyes, too, begin to scintillate and dance like a million stars and I know that I am travelling on the right road at last for I feel the pain of the burn and the joy for the leaping flames whirling around inside me, one as strong as the other, there and *only* there is the action, where I feel it, where it trembles and shakes and crumbles minute after minute, hour after hour.

All my past years light up and drift away, thin and transparent like the smoke from the logs, but life inside goes on burning bright, new and shimmering, better, much better than before, stronger and more joyous, reaching out further and further, out of its small tight prison, up and over the mountains, spreading its wings.

Now I am breathing deeply, and now I must cough because the smoke of the fire gets into my eyes and now I am laughing and coughing at the same time, now Ken's wife is coming in and gives me a sweet hot drink, holding it in her fine long hands to my lips, for my own hands are slippery with all that cream and who is going to worry about a bit of skin when it has at last dawned on me that to be alive, to exist, to feel anything at *all* is the incredible, immeasurable, supreme privilege.

There is no other.

191